THE CANDIDATE CONSPIRACY

The Candidate Conspiracy

A Novel

John Odam

iUniverse, Inc.
New York   Bloomington

The Candidate Conspiracy

Copyright © 2008 by John Odam

iUniverse books may be ordered through booksellers or by contacting:

iUniverse
1663 Liberty Drive
Bloomington, IN 47403
www.iuniverse.com
1-800-Authors (1-800-288-4677)

Because of the dynamic nature of the Internet, any Web addresses
or links contained in this book may have changed
since publication and may no longer be valid.

This is a work of fiction. All of the characters, names, incidents, organizations, and
dialogue in this novel are either the products of the author's imagination or are use
dfictitiously.

ISBN: 978-0-595-46873-7 (pbk)
ISBN: 978-0-595-49347-0 (cloth)
ISBN: 978-0-595-91163-9 (ebk)

Printed in the United States of America

ADVANCE PRAISE

"Odam nails it! He captures the spirit of Texas while bringing us a great international political suspense novel. It's down right scary to think something like this could really happen ... If it hasn't already." -- Ann Richards, former Governor of Texas

John Odam's novel, *The Candidate Conspiracy,* is a gripping story of sleazy politics, international conspiracy and cold-blooded murder -- a real page-turner, but not a frivolous one. It leaves knots in the pit of your stomach and a haunting question in your mind. Could this possibly happen here? It is a beautifully written book." -- Mark White, former Governor of Texas

"What a spectacular yarn! Just when you think you've imagined everything possible in politics and fiction, along comes *The Candidate Conspiracy* and drops a grenade of imagination and suspense. The plot twists like a tornado sweeping up a cast of well-drawn characters. The action is constant, suspenseful and riveting. This book has everything we love about politics: conspiracies, corruption and murder.

The problem with this book is that it is so well crafted, we are terrified the events could actually happen. So, what are we supposed to do until Odam writes the sequel? -- Mark McKinnon, former media consultant to President George W. Bush and Senator John McCain

"A fast-paced political thriller that hums with energy and intrigue. John Odam catapults the reader along a dazzling narrative of raw politcs and international suspense." -- Wayne Slater, Austin Bureau Chief, *Dallas Morning News* and co-author of *Bush's Brain*

The Candidate Conspiracy is a page-turner from a guy who knows Texas and national politics. Odam, who came within a whisker of winning the Texas Attorney General's job over a man who later went to prison, knows the ins and outs of Texas politics. He knows, as some of our citizens are given to saying, how the cow ate the cabbage, and when that dog won't hunt. His experiences as an assistant attorney general, a statewide candidate, a county party chairman qualify him to agree with longtime Texas Senator Lloyd Bentsen's observation: 'In Texas, we consider politics a contact sport.'" -- Dave McNeely, Dean of the Texas Capitol press corps and syndicated political columnist.

"Finally! A politician has written something an old political writer enjoyed reading. Furthermore, not only did John Odam keep me enthralled as he took me through murder, mayhem and political skullduggery around the world, he left me hanging like a Florida ballot chad, wanting more. No question, the initial enormous terror in Odam's bloody power convolutions is the fear he instills that such ambitious, if thankfully inept, political deviousness actually might exist. But where Odam gives angst a new and fuller definition comes when one realizes it is Mr. Nice Guy who dreamed up all this fantastic intrigue and drama. I may never trust a mild-mannered politician again. For, on the one hand, Odam's given an old political junkie a great, easy read. On the other, he's provided monumental uneasiness. You know, it just might could happen. It really maybe could." --- Jane Ely, former political columnist, *Houston Chronicle* and *Houston Post*.

Dedication

Venkatesh Kulkarni was a recognized novelist and beloved teacher in the Rice University School of Continuing Education, Houston, Texas. He died May 3, 1998, at age 52, after a yearlong battle with leukemia.

It was my good fortune to have been one of Professor Kulkarni's students. "Fourteen minutes a day," he would tell his novel writing students. "That is all it takes to write a novel. Persistence and dedication: those are the main ingredients to successful writing." His spirit was the driving force that kept me on this project, lo these many years.

Professor Kulkarni knew a great deal about dedication. Even when he was in isolation while undergoing cancer treatment at M.D. Anderson Cancer Center, he would conduct class. His students would pass their papers to him though a glass divider or door. They would read their work and he would critique it…. even to his dying day.

Professor K., this one's for you.

Acknowledgments

There is no telling how many drafts this project has been through over the past ten years or so. Much of that is due to the reading, re-reading and editing by my wife, Peggy, and our son, Matthew. Thank you both. And thanks also goes to our daughter Paige in Chicago for all of the long distance "atta boys; you can do it, Dad." Love you all and thank you ever so much. Now y'all read it in book form, but don't tell me what you find wrong!

CHAPTER 1

▼

MAVERICK COUNTY, TEXAS
SEPTEMBER 7

The Russian wiped warm blood from the nine-inch blade of his utility knife and returned it to his shoulder holster. If all Texas lawmen are this stupid, Sergei Yazkov thought, my mission will be quick and easy.

Piercing through the dark Texas night, Yazkov's flashlight revealed the sheriff's badge on his victim's uniform. The brass nametag over the shirt pocket read Deputy Raul Hinojosa. Yazkov applied pressure to the deputy's slashed carotid artery to prevent the uniform from becoming soaked in blood.

"Raul Hinojosa. Raul Hinojosa," the Russian assassin said to himself. In perfect English he tested his new name a few times, then stripped off his wetsuit and black facemask. He quickly removed Hinojosa's uniform and carried the deputy's body a hundred yards down river where the rapids were swollen from a month of heavy rain.

After he dressed in the uniform and stowed his own gear in a waterproof backpack, the Russian dumped the body in the rapidly moving river. Since the lawman's boots didn't fit, Yazkov slipped on his own black running shoes and tossed the boots into the river. He drove the patrol car north on Ranch Road 1021 toward Eagle Pass, 20 miles away.

With few vehicles on the road at such an early hour, Yazkov easily noticed a marked, light green Chevrolet Suburban, driven by a Border Patrol officer as it pulled up behind him and flashed its headlights. He slowed, allowing the Suburban to pass. As it did, the passenger lightly touched the brim of his western hat with two fingers in a friendly, fraternal salute. The Russian smirked and flashed his own headlights in acknowledgment of his unwitting escort into America.

At 12:30 a.m., Sergei came upon Enrique's, a cantina outside the Eagle Pass city limits. A Maverick County Sheriff's car and deputy would not attract attention in South Texas, but certainly would if he drove it further north. He pulled into the parking lot across the street, backed into a space on the edge of the lot and turned off his headlights. With his window rolled down, Yazkov listened to the laughter and *tejano* music pouring into the night. He watched drunken cowboys stumble from the bar with their ladies for the night. Finally, at half past one, a man about his size came out and staggered in the direction of his pickup, waving a bottle of tequila in farewell to his companions.

Yazkov waited a few minutes before easing the car onto the highway and followed the man out of town. He trailed at a safe distance as his target traveled northwest toward San Antonio. Safely away from the lights of town, Yazkov closed on his target, activating the patrol car's flashing lights.

Slowing, the cowboy veered his pickup onto the shoulder. Yazkov parked behind him, leaving on the headlights and overhead flashers. The Russian agent could see several miles in both directions and kept turning his head as he surveyed the horizon on either side.

"*Buenas noches, señor. ¿Cómo esta?*" Yazkov said in a friendly tone.

"*Bien. Gracias. Usted?*" the young man nervously replied.

"*Bien, bien. La cédula, por favor. ¿Cómo se llama?*"

"*Me llamo Roberto Salazar.*"

"You certainly seem in quite a hurry, *mi amigo.* Do you have somewhere you need to be?" Deputy Yazkov shined his flashlight into the truck cab looking carefully for anything suspicious.

"*Mi casa*. It is very late. My wife gets mad when I stay out with my friends like this. I was trying to make up some time."

"I understand. My woman, she is the same."

"*Con permiso, señor*. I promise it will not happen again."

"No, it certainly will not. You can be assured," Yazkov replied with a knowing smile.

It was almost 2 a.m. and a passing string of vehicles drowned out the rest of this reply. Headlights beamed from three yellow school buses trailed by an entourage of cars and pickups. Several of the drivers honked and yelled; no doubt relieved it was not them consuming the time and attention of the law. Seeing headlights of several more distant cars, the Russian waited for the area to clear of any possible witnesses or detractors.

Returning his attention to Salazar, Yazkov's flashlight suddenly caught the gleam of a revolver on the passenger seat, inches from the driver's right hand. He drew the Colt .45 from his holster and pointed its six-inch barrel between the cowboy's eyes, inches from his skull.

"Do not touch that weapon, *señor*. Reach across with your right hand, open the door and step out slowly."

The cowboy responded without hesitation. Keeping his light trained in the young man's eyes, Yazkov reached across with a gloved hand and picked up the gun, examining it closely.

"Hmm. Smith and Wesson .357 Magnum, six-inch barrel. Looks like a Model 28 Highway Patrolman. Pretty heavy artillery to be carrying out here, isn't it?"

"*Si, señor*. I use it mainly for target practice but also protection. Lots of drug runners and dangerous illegals swimming the big river. Better to be safe than sorry, my foreman tells me."

"I understand. Can't say as I blame you. Better let me see your license for this, just for the record."

"License? Uh, well, I, uh, left it at home. But I can get one, I mean get it and bring it into the office tomorrow. I think Sheriff Garcia would understand, boss. Okay?"

"No, it is not okay. The law is the law. Step back here and spread-eagle on the tailgate and tell me how many drinks you had back at Enrique's? You were weaving pretty badly back there."

The cowboy spread his arms and legs at the back of the truck, the patrol car's headlights lighting up the scene. "I don't know, maybe two or three cervezas with tequila shots. We were just having a good time, payday and all."

"That's no excuse. Speeding, drinking, .357 with no license. You better have been paid pretty damn well to cover these tickets. Don't move while I pat you down."

"No tickets, *por favor*. We can't afford it. Maria would kill me."

Yazkov could not help but laugh. "Don't worry, I will personally see to it that your wife doesn't do that."

By now Roberto had managed to sober up a bit. He noticed the deputy had placed the .357 in the front seat of the county patrol car and had re-holstered his own Colt. As the Russian began to pat him down, Roberto glanced between his legs and caught sight of the black running shoes.

"Say, man … those damn shoes … You ain't no deputy. And how did you know I had been at Enrique's anyway? What the hell is going on here?"

Roberto Salazar would not have heard a reply even had there been one. Sergei Yazkov instantly pulled a razor-sharp wire garrote from his special issue wristwatch, slipped it over his victim's head and down to his throat. He pulled back with all his strength, simultaneously pressing his knee into the small of Salazar's back. Blood from severed arteries splattered onto the tailgate, gleaming in the headlights' beams. The cowboy was dead before his body hit the ground.

Yazkov ran to the car and turned off all the lights. For the second time that night, he hurriedly stripped his victim of his work clothes and changed into the cowboy's Levis and western-cut shirt. This time the boots fit. He tossed the body in the back of the truck and concealed it with a canvas tarp he found in the truck bed. Sometime before daylight, he would dump the body in Zavala or Uvalde County.

After putting on latex gloves, he parked Salazar's pickup in a dense stand of mesquite and found a livestock watering hole to dispose of the patrol car. Several yards from the edge of the stock tank, he broke off a mesquite limb and cut it to fit between the front of the seat and the gas pedal. He placed the car drive and watched it gently roll into the water and sink beneath the surface.

Yazkov hurried back to the pick-up and drove back onto the highway. Taking note of a full tank of gas, he estimated it would be daybreak before he reached San Antonio, almost 200 miles to the northeast.

His night's work had created a hunger. Sergei smirked. He deserved a flavorful breakfast of huevos rancheros and tortillas for his first few hours in the United States.

CHAPTER 2

▼

HOUSTON
SEPTEMBER 9

Jennifer Spencer surveyed the crowd at the 24-hour diner and knew the other patrons would pay little attention to her sweat-stained jogging attire. Most had their heads buried in the *Houston Chronicle* or were engaged in conversation. Many of the breakfast brunch were attired in much the same fashion, although she smugly doubted they had just completed a nine-mile run through nearby Memorial Park.

The attractive young brunette settled into one of the dark green plastic chairs to wait for Suzanne Chism, campaign manager for United States Senate candidate Warren McDonald. Chism breezed in like a miniature tornado, her loose fitting white shirt slapping against well-worn jeans.

Jennifer waved to attract her attention and stood in greeting. "Good morning."

"Too early to tell if it's going to be good," came Chism's gruff response.

"Late night?"

"My nights are always late," she replied, running fingers through her ducktail-cut brown hair. "Which means my days are *never* this early." Suzanne sniffed. "Am I down wind of some sweaty Olympians?"

Jennifer laughed. "That would be most of us in here, especially me. I ran nine miles this morning."

"Well, don't sound so damn cheerful about it," the overweight woman replied. "Are you sick or somethin'? And why are those cops staring at me?" Suzanne nodded toward the counter.

"Don't be so paranoid. They aren't staring at you. This is the Saturday hangout for runners, cops, workers, loafers. Very egalitarian. Your kind of place, patio for smoking and everything." Jennifer led the woman through the crowd to the back of the restaurant.

No sooner had they settled at a table than a waitress appeared and handed out menus. "Mornin' ladies. What can I get y'all?"

"God, not another perky morning person," Suzanne muttered under her breath, reaching into her purse for cigarettes and a lighter. She eyed the shapely waitress from head to toe, pausing an extra moment to take in her bust line under the tight, light green uniform. "Black coffee for starters," Suzanne said, flicking the lighter a half dozen times. "And how're your ashtrays holdin' out?"

The waitress turned to Jennifer, pointedly ignoring the older woman's rudeness. "And for you, miss?"

Jennifer attempted to be extra polite. "Coffee too, please, and a large glass of ice water." She used a paper napkin to wipe perspiration from her face. "I watch my diet five days a week, but Saturday's my pig-out day. I'll have bacon, eggs, hash browns, and biscuits."

"Make it for two, sweetie," Suzanne told the waitress through a haze of smoke. "And say, Hon, bring me some catsup and Tabasco sauce. I like *everything* hot and spicy. And keep the coffee coming."

Suzanne lit a fresh cigarette off the stub of the old one. "Okay, Spencer, what's up? You said on the phone it was important. It damn well better be to justify my getting up at 5 a.m. and driving down from Austin."

"Don't worry, it's important. Thanks for coming on such short notice." Jennifer wriggled uncomfortably. "This is the first campaign

I've volunteered for. I understand you've managed a lot of 'em: state reps, senators, congress, state-wides, here in Texas and elsewhere."

"Yeah, been there, done that, got a T-shirt, as they say," Suzanne replied, a smile finally softening her features. "Texas, Louisiana, New Mexico, even did a lieutenant governor race in Mississippi. Man, was that an experience. Our opponent kept yellin' 'bout how the South will *rise* again and the need for the state to secede. Once handled a presidential primary up North. God, can it ever get cold in New Hampshire."

"That's why Warren's supporters are so pleased you were hired to manage his campaign," Jennifer replied. "I don't mind volunteering to raise money because you know how to get the most bang for the buck."

"I guess twenty years in the biz has taught me a little something. So tell me, … what am I doing here?"

"Well, when Warren announced, I thought he would be the only candidate to enter the primary to take on Senator Creighton in the fall. Now we have an opponent, and he's raising and spending far more money than our campaign. If I'm going to be taking so much time away from my law practice to help raise the big bucks, I'd like to know more about Warren's opposition and, more importantly, why he's raising more money than we are."

Suzanne took a sip of coffee and nodded. "I suppose those are fair questions. First, let me ask you something. Why'd you get involved as a volunteer in the first place?"

"That's pretty easy to answer. When Warren announced for the Senate in May, I really didn't know him all that well. A mutual friend introduced us at a reception back when he was running for attorney general. I was impressed with him then, even though he lost. He was and still is honest and principled. I could tell he got into both races for the right reasons—to serve the public. He …"

"Whoa. Hold your horses." Suzanne held up a warning hand. "Political rule number one: no one gets elected on honesty, public service and all that bullshit. That's for high school student council races. Pure and simple, it's name identification. You either have it or you don't. Warren definitely ain't got it. If you don't, then you buy it.

Rule number two, money is the mother's milk of politics. Always has been, always will be."

Jennifer nodded. "If I've learned anything since I started on the campaign, it's all about the money. That's why I spend half my day making those fundraising calls. But what I don't understand is why Smith got in the primary race with Warren."

"What's so hard to understand about that?" Suzanne asked.

"Because of Senator Creighton," Jennifer said. "The guy's been in Congress 15 years. He's chairman of the Agriculture Committee, which plays *real* well out in farm and ranch country. And for the big city boys and girls he's a senior member of the Finance Committee. To top all that, he's going to seek his party's nomination for President. Why for cryin' out loud, did that school teacher in Lufkin jump in the race? It makes no sense at all."

"Let me tell you something, kid. If I knew what motivates someone to seek public office, I'd be a certified mind reader and sleeping on a bed of cash." Suzanne inhaled deeply on her cigarette. "Clearly the ego has to be strong, coupled with a strong desire for fame, power, and maybe a pinch of do-gooder for good measure. Course if Andrew Smith wanted to serve the public he could remain a Lufkin high school civics teacher."

Jennifer was deep in thought. "But no more people know him than know that cook in there slinging hash browns."

Suzanne smiled. She was enjoying being the psychology/political science prof to this young, green lawyer turned politico. "I take it, sweetheart, you don't know much about this Mr. Smith."

"Not really. Warren said at the last finance committee meeting he was a school teacher and mentioned he served in the military."

McDonald's campaign manager reached into her purse and pulled out her Filofax. She flipped through the pages until she got to Andrew Smith. "Speaks fluent Spanish ... graduated from high school in the Alamo City ... enlisted in the Marines ... volunteered for Iraq ... got the Purple Heart and Silver Star for heroism in combat."

"Damn."

"There's more. Returned to Texas, graduated from West Texas State University and got a job as a football coach down in Corpus Christi, where he met his bride-to-be, Anna Maria Almendarez. Anna Maria's daddy is a rich cattle rancher in Webb and Zapata Counties in the brush country. Pretty much has a lock on South Texas and the Hispanic vote, I'd say."

"I feel sick to my stomach." Jennifer stared across the room. "Now I wonder why Warren got in the race!"

"To top it all off, Smith developed an interest in politics and was elected to the city council. Ran for state rep four years ago and almost beat the incumbent. As a result, a number of his former students and fellow teachers urged him to run again, but this time to go statewide for the big enchilada. *Voila,* here he is, ladies and gentlemen. 'Mr. Smith goes to Washington.'"

"Suzanne, with all due respect, you've ruined my entire weekend with this Politics 101 business." Jennifer sat silently while the waitress served their breakfast. "But back to that mother's milk of politics. Who and why would anyone give big bucks to Smith?" She reached for the carafe to refill her coffee.

Suzanne liberally salted her entire plate. "I've been wondering the same thing, but I sure as hell don't have time to go snoopin' round to find out. 'Course the answer to the 'who' part is pretty easy to find out. Candidates for President, V.P., and Congress are required to file reports with the Federal Election Commission. They have to list all their contributors, names, addresses, employers and contribution amounts."

"Yeah, I know that part. I make sure to always get that info on Warren's contributors. So where is all of this for Smith? Do you have it in Austin?"

"Nope, but I suppose I could download it from the FEC website."

"Isn't it important to have, though?"

"Sure, that generally falls in the category of opposition research, but we don't have enough money to hire someone to dig up the dirt, chase down rumors, get the reports, etc."

"Well, I think we need it and that's the other reason I wanted to meet with you. Smith has been traveling a hell of a lot, sending email, snail mail, and drawing bigger crowds than Warren. Surely he's raised more than we have. I think it's important we know exactly how much and where the money's coming from. Either he's reporting his contributions or he's getting them under the table."

"I suppose I could get the information. But it would take me a while. I got a few other things a little bit more pressing right now."

"Great!" Jennifer perked back up. "I'll even come to Austin and pick them up when you get them copied. If I find nothing unusual, fine, but if I do, we then decide where to go with it."

Suzanne's demeanor abruptly changed. "Wait a minute. I'll get the damn reports and you can see them, but I'm not sayin' you can go further than that."

"And just why not? I have the time, and I want to find out who is giving to him. His campaign contributions could lead to Warren's defeat and end his political career, Suzanne."

"You seem awfully interested in Warren McDonald's future, young lady." Suzanne gave her a knowing smile. She laughed when Jennifer blushed. "Rule number three, or whatever it is now: Don't go spyin' on the opposition. Believe it or not, they really don't like it. It could also gin-up bad press for our side. Plus, if you find somethin' someone doesn't want you to know, they may have more for you than just a cross look. This is high stakes poker, my dear. We're talking US Senate and possibly the presidency."

Suzanne saw Jennifer's determination. She knew such information was important to any campaign. No use hittin' folks up for money if they were already giving to Smith. She thought she had the solution: one step forward, but not two.

She put her hand on Jennifer's and gently squeezed. "Okay, I'll get the FEC reports. You can look at them and let me know what you find out. But only that. If you find something questionable, I will be the one to decide if you should go forward."

Something is better than nothing, Jennifer thought to herself. I'll go further whether Suzanne wants me to or not. She couldn't stop what she didn't know about.

"You win, coach. You call the plays, I'll run 'em. You bench me, I'll go to the sidelines." Jennifer grinned. "After all, what's the worst that could happen?"

CHAPTER 3

▼

WASHINGTON, D. C.
SEPTEMBER 10

Jake Hardesty sat alone at his breakfast in the opulent dining room of the Madison Hotel in downtown Washington, D.C. Although he lived in nearby Georgetown, Hardesty looked forward to this once-a-week indulgence. Scanning *The Washington Post*, the seasoned lobbyist's attention was drawn to the lead story in the political section: *Creighton Announces Presidential Bid. Yesterday in the Texas state Capitol rotunda, United States Senator Russell Creighton confirmed he would seek his party's nomination for President of the United States. Creighton, the first candidate to announce, acknowledged he would also run for re-election to the Senate, the position he has held for the past fifteen years …*

Jake finished his eggs Benedict and espresso while skimming the article, which explained how a unique Texas law allowed one to run simultaneously for the two high offices. It had passed in 1960 when Senator Lyndon Baines Johnson had lobbied the Texas legislature on behalf of legislation permitting him to become a dual candidate.

Although Creighton was chairman of a powerful Senate committee, others would certainly enter the primary contest to take on the sitting president, Josh Templeton, who would undoubtedly seek re-election. Creighton would most likely face no opposition in his own party primary for re-nomination to the Senate. The article concluded by indicating it was too early to speculate on who the opposing party's nominee might be.

Jake stared at the headline. "Finally," he muttered, "this just might be my ticket." He gathered his belongings, contemplating the prospects of his fellow Texan simultaneously running for president and senator. No doubt there was a way to reap enormous political and financial rewards for those helping Creighton, and Jake Hardesty intended to one of those people.

Jake paid the waiter and headed out to K Street to hail a taxi. A pipeline regulation bill was up for consideration before the House Energy and Commerce Committee, and he needed to monitor the tedious debate. Jake thought his votes were nailed down to keep the bill from getting out of committee, but House members had been known to come unhitched.

As the cabby maneuvered through the heavy mid-morning traffic from the business district, Hardesty gazed out the window and smiled as his thoughts returned to the dual candidacy of Senator Creighton. He would certainly be nominated for re-election and had a damn good shot at the presidency. And Jake had already taken the steps necessary to be an integral part of that power play.

That evening Jake settled in at an upscale Italian restaurant at the foot of Capitol Hill. It reminded him of his favorite eatery in Austin—Madame Aldamani's. He and his ex-wife, Patty Ann, had frequented Aldamani's when he lobbied the Texas legislature on behalf of independent oil producers. After his return from Vietnam, Patty Ann had put up with his frequent drinking bouts and occasional nights of infidelity, trying to salvage their marriage for the sake of their son, Will, or maybe just to nurse him through the combat flashbacks. Whatever her motivation, it had all come to an end soon after they relocated to Washington. She hated the national lobbying pressure cooker, which only exacerbated the damage wrought on their failing marriage.

As he finished his martini and studied the menu, Jake's thoughts turned to Senator J. Russell Creighton. He had to make certain the political project he had orchestrated helped to insure Creighton's

Senate re-election. What could be worse than supporting a loser, then jockeying for position to get on the right side of some freshman senator from his home state? The ups and downs of his roller coaster lobbying experience had to level off on the high side.

Senator Creighton could not afford the time and money to fight tough political battles on both the state and national levels. In addition, he needed a worry-free environment in Texas and the appearance of invincibility to the national press. If Jake's project were successful, there would be a candidate of the opposing party the senator could virtually ignore.

Jake pulled out his Blackberry and scrolled the list until he found the name of William F. York, a fellow lobbyist who also thrived on political machinations. He noticed the American Gun Owners Association and the name Rebecca Durham, vice president for legislative affairs. Like York, Rebecca had been an eager recruit to his venture. While the AGOA's political action committee was not as powerful as the National Rifle Association's, Durham had made an impact both in Washington and in a number of state capitals. Though a rash of public school killings in Littleton, Atlanta, and Fort Worth had not made her work easier, the feisty, diminutive redhead managed to combat those who wanted to control access to handguns. AGOA reportedly contributed more money and political support to Senator Creighton than any other PAC on the Hill.

Hardesty pulled out his cell phone and placed a call to York's Alexandria, Virginia, townhouse. After three rings an answering machine advised that York would be out of the city for a week but in case of an emergency, could be reached on his cellular. Jake refreshed his Blackberry and dialed York's cell. A slow Texas drawl could be faintly heard over heavy static and background noise.

"How the hell are ya, Jake ol' buddy? What's so damned important to be paging me this time of night?"

"Where the devil are you?"

"Houston Hobby, getting ready to board a Southwest flight for Harlingen, then drive down to South Padre Island. I'm entitled to a little R & R and whatever beach view they got down there. Talk fast, they're making the last boarding call."

"Forget it, Billy boy. I'll pay for the Padre flight. Senator Creighton announced his candidacy for President yesterday."

"Yeah, I saw that on the news last night. So what do you want me to do about it?"

"It's time for you to meet with Rebecca again. Make sure her field operation is proceeding satisfactorily. If it is, then it's time to put more money in our *Tejano* project."

"Can't this wait? I could sure use some sun and babe-watching for a few days." He watched the last few passengers hand over boarding passes and enter the jet way. The gate attendant pointed to the plane and his watch, then waived York to come aboard.

"Just trust me on this one, Bill. It's time to crank it up a notch or two. Tell you what, you find Durham and I'll pick up your hotel bill and air fare wherever you have to meet her."

Intrigued, Bill motioned to the gate agent to close the jetway door. "All right, you got it. And Hardesty, this scheme of yours had better work."

CHAPTER 4

▼

EAGLE PASS, TEXAS
SEPTEMBER 13

Captain Jordan Woods, Company D of the Texas Rangers, pushed his Stetson back slightly as Lieutenant Juan Falcone entered the small interrogation room in the Maverick Country courthouse. Country Sheriff Jesse Garcia pointed out locations relevant to their investigation on a large county map.

The sheriff paused in his briefing. "Hey, Juan, *como esta?* Long time no see." He walked over and shook hands with the lean law enforcement officer.

"Yes, sir. About five years ago I guess," the former Starr County sheriff replied. "Just before I joined the DPS," referring to the Texas Department of Safety, parent organization of the Rangers.

"*Siente se, por favor.*" Sheriff Garcia motioned to a chair next to the captain. "*Cafe?*"

"*Nada, gracias. Agua, por favor.*" the thirty-two-year-old officer replied, taking a seat beside his supervisor.

"*Bienvenidos,*" Captain Woods said, slapping Juan on the shoulder. "Let me bring you up to date. DPS-Austin got a call from Sheriff Garcia yesterday morning. Sheriff Bell here from Uvalde County, called in the afternoon. Two deaths, two different counties. Given the circumstances these men will describe, the colonel decided to send us down to help with their investigation."

"But why bring in the Rangers? Their two offices could coordinate and work these cases together, share information."

"There are some details about these killings that lead us to believe they're connected and not committed by locals. By now the perp is probably long gone. Sheriff Garcia, why don't you start at the top and do a quick run-through for Lieutenant Falcone. Juan, jump in any time you a have question."

Sheriff Garcia resumed his briefing, pointing to one of 20 color photographs tacked to the wall beside the county and state road maps. "My deputy, Raul Hinojosa, an outstanding 11-year *compadre*, was found here, floating in the big river a few days ago."

"Where and by whom?" Falcone took notes on a legal pad.

"Twenty miles out of Eagle Pass. Jesus Mancias, a cowboy on the Triple X Ranch south of town. The property runs to the river. Mancias was out chasing strays. He thought one might be bogged down in the flats. He spotted the body about zero eight hundred hours, stripped naked."

Captain Woods continued. "Floater tells us the vic had sunk to the bottom and come back up. Once a body begins to decompose, gas forms in the tissues causing it to gradually float to the surface. This time of year, given the air and water temp, it probably took three or four days. It's hard to say, given the current, exactly where the body went in."

Juan studied his notes and looked across the room at several photographs of the deputy's naked body. "Drowning, accident or homicide?"

"No water in the lungs. No drowning. No accident." Captain Woods's tone grew cold. "Homicide. Come over here and examine these photos. Use this magnifying glass if you need it."

The three men crossed to the wall and Garcia pointed to the throat on a frontal view.

Falcone nodded. "I see what you mean. Deep slash mark, very clean. Any defensive wounds?"

"No, that's what makes it so damn strange. The medical examiner from San Antonio says it was done from the victim's left to right, from one carotid artery to the other. No struggle. They must have been talking and then pow, it was over for Raul." The sheriff choked a bit and paused to wipe his eyes.

Sheriff Garcia cleared his throat and resumed. "Like I said, no clothing. We notified Eagle Pass PD and they sent a photographer."

"Note the body color is greenish-red," Woods interrupted. "Discoloration already spread to the chest and thighs. No longer in rigor mortis."

"Odor?" Falcone inquired.

"Yeah, it was God-awful." Sheriff Garcia replied.

"That means gas had already started to form bacteria," Woods stated, "dissolving the tissue. Sheriff Garcia, have your men check with Border Patrol for stream current and determine the flow. Let's figure where the slicing took place. Also, have your men comb the bank on our side for footprints, signs of a struggle or any other evidence."

"Doesn't sound like illegals," the lieutenant mused. "Haven't seen or heard of any lawman killings along the river. They might knock him in the head and take off cross country, but wouldn't take the time to kill, much less undress a dead man. Might be drug runners."

"I agree on no illegals, Juan, but tell him, Sheriff, about the Border Patrol and your patrol car."

"Yes, sir. When my dispatcher tried to raise Hinojosa on the radio he didn't get a response. He went on the air to DPS and Border Patrol asking them to keep a look out. One of the Border guys reported passing Raul's patrol car at 0115 hours Saturday."

"Could they ID Hinojosa?"

"No, too dark, but the driver waved."

"A drug runner would have to be a pretty cool operator to be driving a sheriff's car and waving at the *federales*," Captain Woods said. "Plus, that's not their MO. A mule would arrange for a pickup to carry him inland. Or drop off the stuff and head back into Mexico."

Falcone nodded. Having dealt with many in Starr County, the drug crossing capital of Texas, he agreed with the MO.

The Maverick County Sheriff pointed to the county map again. "This X is where Mancias found the body. Y is the approximate spot of the Border Patrol sighting."

"How 'bout the A, B, C and the D on the state map?" Falcone pointed.

"That's the second killing. About zero nine hundred hours Sunday morning, Eagle Pass police received a missing person report when Maria Salazar called to ask if her husband was in jail. Seems he had gone out to drink Saturday night and hadn't been heard from. PD gets a lot of those calls, especially after pay day, so they just logged it but did nothing more than put it on the radio to their units."

Falcone laughed and poured a cup of coffee. "Yeah, if we had responded to every worried wife's call in Rio Grande City, we would have been full-time marriage counselors. Salazar ever show up?"

"Yep, dead. He represents D on that map. Sheriff Bell, why don't you pick it from up here."

"'Bout fifteen thirty hours yesterday we got a call from one of the locals near Sabinal. The man had gone fishin' in the river about three miles west of town. He parked beneath the bridge and walked down to the water when he smelled somethin' awful. Turned out to be Maria's wayward husband, Roberto. He was lost all right, but we done found him." He let out a loud guffaw, impressed by his own humor.

"Cause of death, Sheriff Bell?" Juan kept his eyes fixed on the notepad.

"It was a killin' too. Look at this photo." He pointed to a color photograph of the second body. "Was found buck naked, just like Sheriff Garcia's deputy. No slash mark, but a nice clean slice."

The four men closely examined the photographic evidence.

"Clean as a whistle. I called the Bexar County Medical Examiner," Wade said. "This was beyond me. The medical examiner came over from San Antone and shot these photos."

"Any other wounds, cuts, abrasions?" Captain Woods inquired.

"No, just like Deputy Hinojosa, a throat wound."

Lieutenant Falcone studied both photographs. "Well, they are different. Hinojosa's appears to have been made by something like a hunting knife. But Salazar's is a very thin slice, like he ran into a clothesline, but cleaner."

Captain Woods smiled. "*Siente se*," motioning for the men to take their seats. "You're on target, Lieutenant. The ME says it appears to be a garrote as the weapon of choice on the second vic."

Lieutenant Falcone shook his head. "Wait a minute. You lost me between Y and D. Fill in the blanks, please."

"Take him through it, Sheriff Garcia, but only the high points." The senior Ranger glanced at his watch. "We gotta move on this before the trail gets any colder."

"The A on the map is Enrique's Cantina, the last place Roberto Salazar was seen alive. B is a point on the highway to Uvalde. An Eagle Pass police officer saw Hinojosa's county vehicle early Saturday morning while accompanying the high school football team back from a game in San Antonio. C is the spot where the sheriff's patrol car was found on a ranch just off that highway."

Woods turned to Falcone. "Now it's your turn, Juan. The three of us are going out to sit on the courthouse steps. I need a chew. No spit can in here. I prefer to be outta doors for that activity anyway. I'll give you thirty minutes in here. Study these materials, then give us your take on it and where you think we should go from here. I have my ideas, but want to see if we are on the same wave length."

The three lawmen left the investigator to study in silence. Juan took off his hat and gun belt and went to work. He took the magnifying glass several times to the photos, then to the two maps, adding notes when warranted.

Sheriff Wade Bell leaned the cane-bottom chair against the courthouse wall and cleaned his fingernails with a hunting knife extracted from his boot. He kept an eye on the open-air market on the courthouse square, straining to catch a glimpse of housewives and housekeepers doing their Monday morning shopping for the coming week.

"Say, Cap'n, what makes you think that kid can figure this out? He don't look all that smart to me."

"Well, that kid ain't no kid in the first place. He's about thirty-two, thirty-three years old. He just keeps himself in a little bit better shape than some of us around here." As he responded, Woods stared at Bell's belly protruding over his gun belt and the tight fit of his western cut shirt. "He runs five miles several days a week and works out on the other days at a health club in Austin. Experience he's got too. Falcone got his degree in criminal justice from Sam Houston State and worked his way through college at the prison system headquarters there. Went back to his hometown in South Texas and signed on as a deputy. When his boss, Sheriff Gonzalez, got capped by some drug dealer, Juan was appointed his successor. Then he won at the next election."

"So why ain't he still one of us?" the Uvalde county sheriff replied, refusing to be detracted in his efforts to denigrate the Ranger lieutenant.

Sheriff Garcia piped up, "Lt. Falcone told me he wanted to be a Texas Ranger since he was in high school. He even decided to take a pay cut to become a DPS trooper, knowing that would put him a step closer to his goal.

"He did extra-duty work with the Rangers, tracking that Mexican national who hopped freight trains and killed folks from Houston to the Rio Grande," Woods added. "He caught the attention of some of the higher-ups and was asked to apply. Don't worry, Wade, he's got the smarts too. He's done a hell of a job as an investigator for the past five years."

Sheriff Garcia looked through the open door as the sound of Falcone's boots resonated down the courthouse hall. The Ranger carried 165 pounds on his lean six foot one inch frame. Garcia took pride in his fellow Hispanic's sharp appearance in the specially-tailored gabardine uniform, white Stetson hat, Ranger badge, tooled leather gun belt, Sig Sauer 9 millimeter pistol and dark brown cowboy boots.

"Well, did we stump the rookie?" Sheriff Bell asked with a big grin, tobacco juice glistening at the corners of his mouth.

Captain Woods ignored him. "Okay, son, lay it down for us. What did you come up with?"

"Our perp is no illegal or drug runner," Falcone said, studying his notepad. "He is a professionally-trained killer and probably enjoys it. He crossed the river at a secluded site. Unfortunately, Deputy Hinojosa was checking the riverbank for crossers and came upon this guy as he came out of the Rio Grande.

"We don't know if Hinojosa even had time to pull his weapon. The killer, let's refer to him as the Crosser, pulled a large blade, like a bayonet or hunting knife and slashed the vocal cords. He appears to be very strong, given the width of the slash and its depth."

Captain Woods spit into the yellowing winter grass and smiled, pleased with his protégé. "Go on. Anything else?"

"Yes, sir. The lack of clothing on the vic leads me to believe the perp needed the clothing for disguise. He dumped the body in the river and headed into Eagle Pass in the patrol car. On that drive he was spotted by the Border Patrol."

Sheriff Bell's mouth fell open. "Damn, I never thought a' that."

"The Crosser staked out Enrique's. We know his size from the two victims. Raul's boots were found in the river, indicating they didn't fit the killer, so he kept his own shoes. He followed Salazar from the cantina and waited for the right place to make the second hit. He needed another change of clothes and a different vehicle. PD spotted him but thought nothing of it. The killer stopped Roberto and took him from behind with the steel wire. He then drove the patrol car into the brush and stashed the body in the back of the pickup after he took his clothes.

"Since Roberto was found in the river east of Sabinal," the lieutenant continued, "we know he had gone past Uvalde and was probably headed toward San Antonio to ditch the truck, and either went underground in the city or hightailed it." Juan paused. "I suspect the killer speaks Spanish. Based on the clothing size, I'd say he's about six foot, 170 to 190. That's the way I read it."

"Good job, Lieutenant," Sheriff Garcia said. "That's why I asked for the Rangers."

"Well, I'll be damn," was all Sheriff Bell could say.

"And that's why I asked the colonel to assign you to this case. This is your only assignment until you hear otherwise, Lt. Falcone," Woods said. "I want you to go back to Austin immediately. I have a DPS helicopter headed this way. You'll have carte blanche to travel the state. Stay in touch by radio or cell phone. We want headquarters to know where you are at all times. You'll work out of the Austin HQ and have the complete cooperation of all levels of law enforcement. It's apparent the Crosser, as you called him, doesn't intend to be stopped easily. *Comprende?*"

"*Si, comprendo.*" Juan stood at attention as he digested his new assignment.

"From Austin go down to San Antonio and check in with DPS and our Rangers. We will put out an all-points bulletin on the pickup. By the time you get to San Antone we might have at least located the truck." Captain Woods paused. "If you spot him, call for back up. The days of 'one riot, one Ranger' are over, son. The Crosser is a killer." The senior Ranger shook Lt. Falcone's hand. "I want you with us for a long time, Juan. No hot shit cowboy stuff, ya hear?"

Sheriff Bell begrudgingly shook his hand next.

"Good work, *amigo*," said Sheriff Garcia, smiling and exchanging *abrazos*. "Be careful. Our people need young men like you. *Vaya con Dios.*"

Across the street, the sound of the DPS chopper touching down on the market parking lot caught their attention. Juan held his hat and jogged toward his transportation to the state capital. Two men lay dead in the South Texas brush country. The Crosser would regret the day he swam the Rio Grande into Texas.

CHAPTER 5

▼

SAN DIEGO, CALIFORNIA
SEPTEMBER 14

The shrill beeping of the pocket pager on the night stand startled Bill York. He was stiff from the long flight from Houston to San Diego, his head pounding from first class largess. After throwing on a hotel robe and brewing a pot of coffee, York returned the call and was connected with the subject of his trip to the Del Coronado.

"Greetings, Mr. York. Welcome to sunny Southern California. Beats the hell outta D.C., don't ya think?" asked Rebecca Durham.

York rubbed his bloodshot eyes. "No question about that. Problem is too many other folks think the same thing." Coffee cup in hand, he settled on the sofa and gazed out at the crowded park and walkway overlooking the Pacific. "Listen, Rebecca, I appreciate your agreeing to meet me on such short notice."

"No problem. I've got a three o'clock meeting in La Mesa with the president of AGOA's Southern California chapter. He's interested in our Texas project. After all, a United States Senator represents the interests of all the states, California included."

York smiled to himself as he listened to the chief in-house lobbyist for the American Gun Owners Association get directly to the point. "Sounds good. How 'bout if I meet you pool-side at your hotel about six?"

"Sounds like a winner. Six it is."

Durham, an Arizona native, had made quite an impression on Capitol Hill five years earlier when she helped organize the handgun owners association. Despite calls for stiffer gun control laws following the rash of school shootings, Durham had held firm and in fact had made quantitative strides on handgun ownership.

As York returned from a coastline jog to the hotel pool for a cool down, he recalled the deranged student who brutally shot Durham's 15 year-old daughter and six of her friends in an affluent suburban high school. Durham was convinced that if the teachers had been allowed to carry handguns her child and many others would be alive today. That random act of violence had provoked her political activism and creation of AGOA. She had been very interested in his plan to help select the next chief executive officer, one who would support her legislative agenda.

After a ferry ride to Coronado Island, York spotted Rebecca by the "Del's" pool in a lounge chair. Her petite five foot-three inch frame belied the bundle of energy within, driven and dedicated to her cause. He bent to kiss her cheek as he pulled up a lounge chair. Over a round of cocktails they talked of their respective trips to the west coast.

By 7:30 the sun had set and the air cooled. A waiter escorted them into the opulent Coronado Room to a table near the window. Following dinner, Rebecca got to the point. "Okay, Billy boy, you didn't drop a bundle to come to this Garden of Eden just to eat fine food and booze it up, great as all of that may be. What's the real purpose of your trip?"

"As I mentioned on the telephone yesterday, now that Senator Creighton has announced his presidential campaign, Jake thinks it's time we increase the political field activity in Texas on the *Tejano* project." York outlined some ideas he developed on his flight from Houston.

"I suppose my people could handle that." Rebecca turned to look out at the floodlit beach and sat in silence.

"Is there something wrong?" York asked. "I thought you were totally committed to *Tejano*?"

"Oh, I am. I want Russell Creighton in the White House as much as you and Jake. I just think it's a little weird raising money and using it to promote a Senate candidate in the opposing party. Why not give it directly to Russell's Senate race, better yet, his presidential campaign?"

"That will come later, but first we back a weak opposition candidate then cut off the money once he gets his party's nomination. The candidate stumbles, Creighton ignores him and trots around the country on his presidential bid. I'll see to it that you get more money. You just have to put it to good use in our field operations."

"And tell me again why I'm the lucky one for this assignment."

"Because Jake knew you would hate to see Josh Templeton get re-elected and continue pushing his gun control agenda. And Senator Creighton espouses relaxed federal controls on gun ownership, something your AGOA members endorse," York hastened to add. "Look, Rebecca, you're one of the best grassroots lobbyists in the country. Jake figured you would know how to use the money he raises in such a way that the fall guy wouldn't know it's coming from AGOA, much less from us. After Creighton wins, we make sure to get credit for his victory, and you have an ally in the Oval Office."

The legislative affairs director for the powerful national handgun association looked pensive. "I could probably get some more of our West Texas chapters lined up for Andy Smith. That would bring out more of our people wherever he campaigns."

Bill York smiled. "You got the picture. But no AGOA signs, just good solid folks exercising their right of free speech. They wouldn't have to mention gun control. Make it look like spontaneous support for their candidate."

Bill ordered coffee and after dinner liqueurs. "With Smith's Iraq record, those gun owners and flag wavers will be easily motivated. But, again, no fingerprints."

Rebecca smiled, intrigued with the project. "We can certainly get more activity going for Smith in South Texas. That Hispanic wife of his is a better campaigner than he is. He can *habla* a little bit of the

Español, but it's a gimme with Maria. Her old man will also be a big help. He's plugged in with all the politicos and *patrones* in Laredo."

Bill reached over and patted her hand. "You got the picture, lady."

"Just one question. How 'bout your war hero, common man for uncommon times, Mr. Smith goes to Washington?" Rebecca's fingers slowly circled the rim of her glass.

"Easy. Inexperienced. A know nothing. No legislative accomplishments. Who would want to elect a freshman senator from Texas who knows nothing about the issues? After we rough him up going into the fall, he won't know up from down. Domestic, international issues? I'm telling you, he'll be in over his head. He's been to Paris, Texas, but not Paris, France. Moscow to him is just a little 'ol loggin' community south of Lufkin. Besides, he's no Jimmy Stewart."

"You missed your calling, sweetheart." Rebecca reached under the table and squeezed his thigh. "You can write a book: 'The Making of a Twofer—President and United States Senator At the Same Time.' And the best part of it is that none of the candidates will have a clue the whole damn race is being manipulated."

"Yep, kinda like it myself." Bill drained the last of his drink. "We are political geniuses. Governor Bates appoints a Senate replacement after Creighton is elected President, and then we have access to *both* offices. It will be pay back time inside the ol' Beltway, my dear."

"Only one little problem, Wonder Boy," Rebecca said. "Money. To get Smith nominated will cost a bundle. Also, don't forget Warren McDonald. He's got money sources all over the state after his AG race. And he's got some personal wealth. My sources tell me he's willing to part with it this time, both for the primary and the general election."

Bill motioned for the waiter and paid the bill. "Don't worry 'bout that part. I've given you plenty of working capital and more is on the way. All I can say is the money side is covered. I don't mean to be short, but you don't need to know. Matter of fact, you wouldn't want to know."

"But I thought ..."

"Honey, this is the big time. Call it containment. The money compartment and the political compartment. You are the key to the latter and are known only to Jake and me. The *Tejano* funding must remain confidential." His arm slid around Rebecca's tiny waist and, leaning on her slightly, steered her toward the elevators. "Trust me, sweetheart."

Rebecca smiled and looked at her companion. "And just why should I?"

"I'll tell you why ... up in my room. I'll make it very clear."

Before Rebecca could reply the elevator arrived. Bill gently guided her inside and pushed the button for his floor. When the doors closed, he pressed her against the back wall with the weight of his body as his mouth closed over hers.

CHAPTER 6

▼

FORT WORTH, TEXAS
SEPTEMBER 18

Jake Hardesty and Dan Morton settled into plush arm chairs in Morton's office on the 25th floor of a downtown bank building.

"Welcome back to Cowtown, Jake," said Morton, chairman of the board and majority shareholder of JRP Industries, a private holding company. "It's been awhile since I've seen you. What? Six weeks since I was up to monitor hearings on that damn gun safety latch bill?"

"Yes, sir, just about that," Hardesty replied. "How's the handgun business these days?"

"Not bad." Morton replied. "Looks like I might be able to pay the bills for another month or two. Before we get down to business, can I offer you a drink?"

"Sure. Bourbon on the rocks if you don't mind. I don't think you and the missus are going to starve to death anytime soon."

"I must admit, your call the other day surprised me. Something going on with that legislation you're following on the Hill?" Morton continued as he mixed their cocktails.

"Nothing much to report on that front, sir. Senator Baxley is still trying to get a subcommittee hearing on that gun safety standards bill. So far I've been able to corral enough votes to keep it from surfacing. It's a constant battle with that ol' gal, though."

"Hell, Jake, it wasn't always this damn hard taking care of business on the Hill and over at the White House."

"Yeah, I know. Attitudes have sure changed since I left Austin and went to Washington for you." Morton handed Jake his drink. "Cheers," he said as they touched glasses. "How long ago was it that I convinced you to open an office in DC? Four years?"

"No, sir. More like eight."

"How are your other legislative endeavors fairing?"

"Plenty to keep me busy, but your work always comes first, Colonel." In truth, Jake needed more clients. His reputation had declined as word circulated about his increased drinking, especially after his divorce.

"I was really sorry about your marital problems, Jake." Dan's tone was sincere. "I remember how tough it was working the Hill and keeping the home fires burning while I was at the Pentagon."

"Pentagon? I never knew you were stationed at the puzzle palace." Jake took advantage of the opening to change the subject. "When was that?"

"After I got back from my second tour in 'Nam I was assigned to the LAO, legislative affairs office. The top brass had me over on the Hill all the time. Got to know them fuckers on a first name basis. Course it was always Congressman this, Senator that. We kissed their asses to get our budget through. Back then the guys supported the troops and gave us anything we asked for."

Jake decided to let Morton saunter down memory lane before getting into the purpose of the meeting. "Where else were you stationed?"

"Fort Knox, the home of Armor," Morton proudly replied. "Then Fort Meade, home of the 11th Armored Cavalry Regiment."

"Yeah, I remember. Wasn't your unit patch something like a black stallion reared on it's hind legs on a field of red and white?"

"Yep, you got it. Good memory, solider."

"I saw a lot of 'em when I got into Saigon. Of course, most were o.d. back then," Jake said referring to the camouflage olive drab material. "I'm afraid I remember that all too well."

"Enough about me. Obviously you were in country too. Mind telling me about it?"

Jake did mind, but reluctantly decided to share a few memories to placate Morton. "I didn't take the officer route. Sergeant E-5; artilleryman. Spent 365 and a wake-up in the Green Latrine. Landed at Cam Ranh Bay and spent a few days and nights there, sitting around the NCO club, listening to a Korean band play American rock."

"But did you ever get out in the field?" Morton felt a bit superior.

"Oh yeah. Was loaded on a C-130 and flown north to Chu Lai, the Americal Division headquarters. I was assigned to Alpha Battery, 2nd Battalion, 15th Artillery of the Americal. Headquarters was at LZ Bayonet, a settlement of green plywood buildings."

"God, it must have been exciting for you."

"Exciting? I'm not sure that's how I'd describe it. Don't think I was at the same vantage point you were, Colonel. A year of fire missions, incoming, rats in the hootches, transferring from one gun to another, taking the place of buddies who were either KIA or wounded."

"Sorry to hear it. I know it was tough. The closer one was to the killing fields, the worse it got. I must confess though, it was a real rush for me. I loved nothing more than leading those armored cav troopers into combat and running up the VC body count. That was what I'd been trained to do and I did it."

Jake was amazed, both at the contrast in their war memories and in their ranks. One led a battalion into battle, the other, a cannon cocker, one rung up the ladder from an infantry grunt. "I guess I just saw too much killing up close and personal. Guys in my battery losing arms and legs, some even dying in my arms."

Jake let another mouthful of Jake Daniels cleanse the sour taste from his mouth. "I believe you were talking about the Pentagon a moment ago, Colonel. How long were you stationed there?"

"Hmm, must have been four years. Yeah, then I joined Colt and kissed the same asses for them. Five years later, Mrs. Morton and I were back in Texas, and the rest has been history."

"I must say, sir, it was a pretty ballsy move to leave Colt and start your own company, especially with the political climate back in the late sixties."

"Hell, I'm a risk taker. Always have been, always will be. After Martin Luther King's and Bobby Kennedy's assassinations, Congress about shut down the import of foreign-made handguns. It seemed an opportune time to pump out our little Saturday night specials. But I tell you what, it's getting harder and harder to turn a buck making a simple little handgun."

"Yeah, it seems the junior senator from California wants to set the domestic standards comparable to those on imports. If Senator Baxley has her way, most of the gun makers, including us, will be out of business," Jake relaxed and steered the conversation toward his agenda.

"It burns the hell out of me how she jumped on the regulation bandwagon after those school shootings a few years ago. Guns don't kill, people do, I've always said. Those fucking teenagers were insane. Just like all those jihadis, probably high on crack or something. Rifle, shotgun, pipe bomb, AR-15, you name it, if they decide to go off the deep end, higher safety standards won't stop the criminals or the terrorists. It just makes it harder for me to eke out a living."

"Colonel, you're probably wondering why I asked for this meeting."

"The thought did cross my mind. Is there anything I need to be doing? Do I need to come back to the Capitol and twist a few more arms?"

"No, not for now, but I'll keep you advised. Frankly, Colonel, Congress is not the reason I wanted to see you tonight. Now that Senator Creighton has announced his presidential bid, I think it's time we increase the funding level of Operation *Tejano?*"

"And I suppose you want to put the touch on me again. Right?"

Jake laughed. "To be blunt about it, yes, sir. I told you from the beginning, you are our only conduit for *Tejano* funding. I assume you want to be assured of carte blanche access to the White House, access to a president who really understands our position on these gun control issues and will not let the feds join in any local government lawsuits we're having to defend?" Hardesty let his statement sink in. He pulled two cigars from his jacket, passed one to Morton, then lit both.

"Hmm, very nice," Morton said as he exhaled. "Go on, what were you saying about the White House?"

"Better yet, how 'bout a cabinet position? Or maybe an ambassadorship? Mrs. Morton wouldn't mind that lifestyle, would she?"

"Sounds pretty good." Morton nodded, thinking about his high maintenance wife. "But do you really think this *Tejano* thing, as you call it, is going to work?"

Jake leaned. "It's working already. With the money you've already contributed we've helped Andrew Smith move closer to getting his party's nomination. Through *Tejano* we're choosing the straw man to run against Senator Creighton."

Dan Morton stared at Hardesty. "Hell. I still think this is a pretty damn weird way of doing things. I thought you said we were going to help Russell, not defeat him." He started to rise.

"Wait a minute. Hear me out." Hardesty's hand closed around Morton's forearm, holding him fast. "I told you when we first agreed to work together on this project. We are helping him, just indirectly. We prop up some dumbass straw man the Senator can easily run over in the general election. Why just play one side of the street when we can manipulate the whole damn process?"

Morton sat back down. "Go ahead. Keep talking."

Encouraged, Jake continued. "Remember, there are two candidates in the other party's primary, Warren McDonald and Andrew Smith. We simply pick the one Creighton can most likely defeat. Support that jerk, then pull the money out from under him when he gets the nomination. Senator Creighton is then free to focus his complete attention on his presidential campaign."

"So how do we get credit when our man reaches the White House?" Morton countered. "Just out of the goodness of his heart?"

"Of course not." Jake smiled. "That base is covered. The senator, or future president I should say, will know of our assistance. Trust me. We have connections high up in Creighton's presidential campaign. He'll know our help was given but I gurran-damn-tee he sure wouldn't want to know the details of our operation."

"But what if Creighton decides not to reciprocate?"

"Hell, Colonel. Nothing is for sure in life except death and taxes. And we're working on the taxes. I trust Russell Creighton to remember who his friends are. Payback time. That's the name of this whole fucking political game in the first place." Jake glanced at his watched and decided now was a good time to make his exit. He stood and placed his drink on the table beside his chair.

Dan Morton smiled, asking the next question though knowing the likely answer. "So how much more do you want from me?"

"I estimate we need to put another million into Smith's campaign," Jake calmly replied as the two walked to the elevator.

"One mil!" Dan exclaimed as he jumped to his feet. "Jeez. Do you expect me to write you a check tonight? Look, Hardesty, I might be doing all right, but I ain't Fort Knox. I don't have that kinda money to play politics with, especially with some cockeyed scheme like this. I've given you almost that much already and what do we have to show for it?"

Jake ignored the hard-to-answer question and pressed on. "I never expected you to fund it all, Colonel. You know powerful people in this country and around the world who can pitch in a few hundred thou each. They do it all the time to swing elections."

"It's possible. But are you sure this Operation *Tejano* is secure?" Morton asked as the two entered the elevator and proceeded to the ground floor.

"Very secure. I told you when we started, I established a Swiss bank account in the name of Triad Investments, a dummy corporation. A simple business transaction. You deposit to Triad, then I see to it that the money is transferred to correspondent banks in Texas and put it to proper use."

"But put to use for whom and by whom? You have never explained that part to me."

Once out on the street, the men arrived at Morton's waiting Mercedes. His driver opened and closed the rear door. Morton lowered the window and threw out his cigar, almost hitting Hardesty's boot.

Jake looked around. "This is not the time nor the place to go into that. Don't worry. I'm telling you, it's fool-proof. Sleep on it, sir. If it's all right, I'll stop back by in the morning, and we can go into more detail. A President Russell Creighton is who you need on your side and we can make that happen."

Morton motioned for his driver to put the car in gear. "Be here at nine o'clock. And, Jake, I'm not saying my answer will necessarily be affirmative. I want to be damn sure this is a winner, for Creighton and for me."

CHAPTER 7

▼

WIMBERLEY, TEXAS
SEPTEMBER 19

Jennifer Spencer felt relaxed and comfortable in her nylon running shorts and cotton tank top, hair hanging loosely about her shoulders. Her toes played with the golden buffalo and Indian switch grasses as she watched the late afternoon sunlight glistening on the slowly moving blue-green waters of the Blanco River. She admired the magnificent bald cypress trees towering above the north bank and the rough limestone and caliche ledge with ash junipers and live oaks comprising the south side. Her golden retriever, Lad, napped at her side.

Her gaze reluctantly moved back to Andrew Smith's Federal Election Commission reports. She had picked up the lists the previous day from Suzanne Chism at the McDonald for Senate campaign headquarters. Jennifer's brow wrinkled at the intimidating stacks.

"Damn," she muttered. "There must be hundreds of pages of contributions and expenses for this wanna-be US senator." She wondered how she could have ever thought this would be exciting.

"Penny for your thoughts."

Startled, Jennifer turned to see her mother standing behind her. "Oh, hi, Mom, I was just thinking about all the great times we had here."

"Yes, we've spent some splendid times." Savannah Spencer sat beside her. "I'm so pleased you invited me to join you for the weekend."

"Remember the time Justin chased me into the river with that dead water moccasin he found? Like to have scared me to death. I could have killed him."

Savannah laughed. "You and your brother were a sight to behold. Your father used to say it was worth the price of this place to be able to spend even a week a year here."

Jennifer pushed the reports aside, relieved to have another excuse to delay the analysis. "I guess Dad was too busy to come out."

"When isn't your father busy? I worry he'll never slow down. He was heading to the ER when I left. There was an awful auto accident north of Waco and an orthopedic surgeon was needed."

"I've been trying to remember how long we've owned S-4."

"Well, as you recall, your father coined that name for the four of us. Hmm, let's see, I had just completed my first session in the state senate. Then one more four-year term, so I guess about 12 now. Why do you ask?"

"I can't imagine not having this place. It was always great coming back in the summers while I was at UVA and a super hideaway to study for UT law school exams."

Savannah smiled at her daughter. "By the way, you never did tell me what you're doing. Is all this legal review for the depositions you have next week in that securities case?"

Jennifer shook her head. "Not quite. Actually this is the reason I asked you to spend the weekend with me. I need your political instincts and judgment."

Savannah thumbed through the papers. "Federal Election Commission. What on earth are you doing with these? And how could I help?"

"I could use your advice. You've got decades of experience in the hard-hitting world of Texas politics, everyone's favorite contact sport."

They both laughed, then Jennifer continued. "You remember my friend, Helena Whiteside?"

"Wasn't she your roommate at UVA your senior year from Dallas?"

"Yep, we were pledge sisters, hit it off immediately when we learned we were both from Texas. She's living in Houston and working for a law firm as a paralegal. Poor girl. She's thinking about going back to get a law degree."

"So what does Helen have to do with these papers?"

"One of the lawyers in her firm is Warren McDonald. This Warren McDonald." Jennifer picked up one of the FEC forms with McDonald's name at the top. "Helena invited me to a campaign fundraiser for him."

"Fundraiser, huh? Didn't know your new law firm was already that successful."

"I've been doing pretty well but not to the point where I can drop the big bucks for these kind of events. It was at some oil man's River Oaks swankienda. Thousand dollars a head. Helena got us comp tickets."

Savannah flashed a knowing smile. "Always helps to boost the crowd. Makes for a good showing."

Jennifer nodded. "I'm beginning to believe appearance is as important as reality. Matter of fact, I guess in a way in politics appearance is reality."

"Yes, until the ballots are counted. That's when you get the ultimate reality check. Anyway, go ahead. So you went to some high roller fundraiser and...."

"And Warren made a terrific speech," Jennifer replied. "He talked a lot about public education, which you know is an issue of importance to me."

"So you hear a stem-winding stump speech and the next thing you know you're reviewing Federal Election Commission reports?"

"Not quite. I told Helena how impressed I was with the speech so she promptly took me up to meet the guy. Well, one thing led to another, and when he asked if I'd help out some on his campaign, I didn't know what else to say but yes."

"So tell me about this Mr. McDonald. He must have been really something for you to volunteer on the spur of the moment."

Jennifer looked across the river, focusing on a horse grazing in the pasture. "Yes, he is. Warren's about fifty, very handsome, six foot two, black hair, blue eyes, in great shape."

"I was thinking more in terms of what he believes in." She cupped her daughter's chin and turned her face toward her own. "Not whether he should be on the cover of GQ."

Jennifer blushed. "Helena says he's very bright, was editor in chief of the *Texas Law Review,* been with the firm about twenty years. He took a leave of absence six years ago to run for state attorney general but lost in the primary. I heard him speak once then and was impressed."

"Now I remember his name. I went to a meet-and-greet reception for him when he came through Waco while I was in the senate. He had the guts to question the conduct of the ATF and FBI in the Branch Davidian raid. I got your father to tag along and even he was impressed." Savannah raised an eyebrow and gave her daughter a quizzical look. "By chance is there more to your interest than public policy?"

Jennifer ignored her mother's inquiry. "Please, Mother, don't confuse me with some White House bimbo. His wife is a stay-at-home mom, raising two fine teenage boys. I've met all three of them at the campaign headquarters."

Savannah moved on. "So what are you doing on the campaign?"

"As you know, there're two sides to any campaign: politics and money. I'm not much into putting up yard signs or handing out bumper stickers, so I opted for trying my hand at fundraising. It's what makes a political campaign successful."

Jennifer stood and rubbed the back of her neck. "I started out working the sign-in tables at a few events, then moved to organizing call lists. About a month ago I got up the courage to begin making fundraising calls."

"I'm sure Mr. McDonald appreciates that but back to the reports. Where's the connection with all of this?"

"Warren knows a lot of people, not only in Houston, but around the state. He made a heck of a lot of contacts in that AG race, has some great supporters."

"Well, he better. It takes a lot of money to run a winning campaign. Frankly, I was a little surprised anyone else decided to get in that race."

"Me too. Warren announced first, and with one statewide race under his belt most people involved with the campaign didn't think anyone would challenge him. Plus, it will be hard as the devil for anyone to beat Sen. Creighton."

"You're right about that. Creighton has name recognition and certainly helped a lot of people over years of service in the Senate and House."

"I've talked with Suzanne Chism about that. She's Warren's campaign manager and really knows her stuff. She told me some things about Andrew Smith's background that make me think he could win this thing. The press has really seized on the idea of that East Texas schoolteacher driving around visiting all two hundred and fifty-four county courthouses. He garners more than his share of free media coverage."

Jennifer picked up a small tree branch and threw it into the yard. Lad was immediately on his feet to fetch it. "He's certainly become a contender."

"But you still haven't answered my question, Jen? Why are you looking at this guy's federal election reports?"

"Because even if I concede Smith has something going for him, the more I read in the papers and watch TV, the more it appears he is receiving a heck of a lot more money than seems warranted."

Savannah patted Lad on his head when he dropped the branch at her feet and lay down beside them. "I'm totally confused, honey. What do you mean?"

"We get press clippings at the Houston campaign headquarters every week on what both candidates are doing, where they're speaking, what groups they are appearing before. I'm telling you, this guy, Smith, is traveling all over Texas, from El Paso to Texarkana. He's spending big bucks, and it sure ain't just gas money for that little red pickup of his."

Savannah stood and moved to rub her daughter's shoulders. "So what do you think's going on?"

"I don't know, but I intend to find out. Warren deserves to be our next Senator. I want to see who is supporting Smith and find out how much he's raising and spending. I'm wondering if all of the income and expenses is being reported. And seeing as you're the professional politician of the Spencer family, I need you to help me search for answers."

Savannah looked back to the paper-strewn picnic table. "I'm certainly glad I didn't have to file these forms for my state senate races. The feds want to know it all, don't they?"

"Absolutely." Jennifer moved to the table and pulled a few of the documents forward. "You have to list the contributor's address, telephone number, occupation, and employer. And who cares except some bureaucrat in Washington who's got nothing better to do than flyspeck these damn things in order to keep a safe government job?"

"But why study all this? What is it going to tell you anyway?" Still standing, Savannah leaned over the table and replaced some of the reports in one of the transfer boxes.

"I don't know. I'm just thinking with all his activity, Smith has got to be receiving more financial support than Warren. This seemed the best place to start getting answers about his financial sources."

"Sweetheart, it's not going to show up on these forms. It will be off the record, off the books. You don't think if Mr. or Ms. Big Bucks is going to blow the cap and that the campaign would actually report it, do you? That would be a federal offense for both the candidate and the contributor. Same with the PACs. If the trial lawyer PAC, for example, gives twenty thousand, you won't find it here."

"Come on." Savannah pulled on her daughter's hand. Lad immediately rose to follow them. "Let's walk down to the rapids." With the retriever at their side, the two strolled to the water, then settled on the flat rocks to soak up the warm afternoon sun.

"I have a suggestion," Savannah broke the silence. "Smith is from Lufkin. Almost all of his big money should come from around there."

"I don't follow you. Why do you say that?"

"First of all, the Washington lobbyists don't know him and thus won't give him a dime."

Jennifer smiled. "More unwritten rules of the game, huh? Makes sense. The more I hear about this, the less I like any of it."

"Sorry, honey, it's a cutthroat, high stakes game for these guys, a real power play."

"So what should I do?"

"Since employers and addresses are listed on the FEC reports, why don't you take a legal pad and list the ones that fall outside the norm. That is, see if Smith is getting any big money outside of East Texas. Let's divide up the list. That'll speed up the process, and then we'll compare notes."

"Mom, that's brilliant." Jennifer gave Savannah a hive five. "Let's go back to the cabin and get started." With a game plan finally in hand, the nascent campaign volunteer could hardly contain her excitement.

"Wait a minute, I'm getting a reward for my ingenious idea. Fifteen minutes of solitude basking in the sun. You go and get started. I'll be along shortly."

Savannah reflected on Jennifer's success. Since trial work on the plaintiff's side was on a contingent fee basis, her daughter had acquired a nest egg in only five years. Savannah always hoped one of her children might eventually be interested in politics. This campaign could be a positive experience for Jennifer, and she hoped this sleuthing wouldn't lead her daughter down a path she would regret.

"I'll have to keep a watchful eye," Savannah muttered. After a few more minutes of solitude, she brushed herself off and re-joined her daughter.

CHAPTER 8

▼

MOSCOW, RUSSIA
SEPTEMBER 23

"Good morning, ladies and gentlemen. The captain has advised we are beginning our initial decent into Sheremetyevo Two. Flight attendants will be passing through the cabins...."

"Ohhh, my eyes," Kathryn Morton grumbled, removing the black silk sleep mask she wore on trans-Atlantic flights. "Feels like they've been scrubbed with sandpaper." She pulled out a silver compact and inspected her make-up after the 14-hour marathon flight from Dallas-Ft. Worth to JFK and finally Moscow. "Did you ever sleep, honey?" She brushed back her stylishly cut brown hair, dyed to cover the beginning traces of gray.

Dan Morton knotted his maroon tie and rubbed the stubble on his jaw. "Naw, never do." He glanced at his Rolex: 11 a.m. "It might be almost noon in Moscow, but my body clock says it's still two hours past midnight in Texas. Tell me again exactly what you'll be doing while I'm taking care of business?"

"Arranging an exhibition of the crown jewels and other works of art from the *Aruzheynaya Palata* located in the Kremlin. The board of the Fine Arts Museum felt that the Romanov crown jewels would really make an impact on the Fort Worth cultural community. I volunteered to make the initial contact."

An hour after their arrival, the Mortons retrieved their luggage and pushed their way through the crowded ill-lit lobby to the limousine arranged by Dan's secretary.

"*Tazi, tazi!*" the gypsy cabbies shouted. On earlier Moscow visits Morton had not minded taking potluck with one of the small, unmarked Ladas or Moskvitches. The fares were practically unregulated, except by a segment of the Russian Mafia, which controlled most facets of the local economy.

Initially, Dan had been impressed by the entrepreneurial spirit of the men using their private vehicles and bargaining for the best price. He subsequently learned drivers could not charge less than their bosses ordered, so profit was simply a function of a driver's persuasiveness. That had been his first encounter with the Russian Mafia, or "the company", as he now preferred to call the loose-knit organized crime syndicates.

"*Nyet, nyet, spasibo.*" Kathryn was polite but firm. She had been taking an introductory Russian course at Texas Christian University and found the language and its Cyrillic alphabet almost impossible to master.

"Welcome to *Moskva.*" Dmitri Krylov greeted them with a warm smile, then placed their luggage in the trunk of the Volga limousine. "Good to see you again, Colonel Morton." The thirty-two year old part-time student at Moscow State University had served as their chauffeur for the past five years.

"Hello, Dmitri." Dan removed his glove, extending his hand.

"How's the traffic?" Kathryn inquired. She shook his hand, then gave him a hug and customary kiss on each cheek.

"Not bad, Mrs. Morton. It should only take thirty minutes to downtown. Please," he gestured and opened the rear door.

The Mortons eased into the warm rear compartment, escaping the forty degree temperature. "These messages were faxed to your hotel this morning, Colonel Morton." He handed his employer an attaché and cellular phone through the privacy partition.

While Dan sifted through a stack of call slips, Kathryn perused the latest edition of *The Moscow Times.* "Oh look, Dan, *Zhizn' za tsarya* is performing at the Bolshoi. Why don't you check with the concierge and see if he can still get tickets for tomorrow night's performance?"

Dan put aside the call slips to look at the bustling city. He was pleased that Kathryn's cultural exchange provided the perfect cover for his clandestine meeting.

The clicking of Kathryn Morton's knee-high boots on the marble floor echoed through the lobby of the exclusive Metropol Hotel. While her husband checked in and Dmitri took care of their luggage, she gazed at the lavish interior with its chandeliers and Baroque gold leaf designs atop marble pillars.

Dan joined her as the head bellman escorted them to their usual suite on the eighth floor. A maid assisted Kathryn as she unpacked for their five day stay. Once she had departed, Kathryn turned to her husband, seated at a French writing desk reviewing a stack of documents taken from his brief case.

"Two o'clock. Let's see, I'm to meet Natasha Semenova just outside the Kremlin's Borovitsky Gate at five." Kathryn threw her gray herringbone tweed jacket on a nearby lounge chair and removed the matching wool trousers. "She has a list of suggested selections we're to see and is taking me on a private two-hour tour of the Armory." As she approached Dan, she noticed his gaze fall to her shapely legs. "Refresh my memory. What are your plans, sweetheart?"

"I have a 4:30 meeting with Yuri Potapov, the new General Director of Rosyvooruzhenize, the state arms monopoly. We are to meet at Lubyanka, the former KGB headquarters, a ten minute walk from here. How 'bout if I meet you back here for an 8:30 dinner reservation at Skazka? You've always liked that place."

"Perfect," Kathryn replied. "But what do we do now? You look exhausted. How 'bout a nap, and then down to the club for a massage and steam?"

Dan put the documents aside and looked admiringly at his wife. "Sounds almost perfect, but I think you have that out of order." He gently pulled his wife to the long narrow windows covered with organza sheers. Unfastening the tiny pearl buttons on her black cashmere sweater, he opened it and lightly ran his finger tips over her lace bra. "I suggest massage first, nap later."

Kathryn smiled, then took a sip of the chilled Stolichnaya the maid had poured before leaving. She lit a cigarette from the nearby pack, letting Dan take a long draw before she did likewise. "And I suppose you want me to be the masseuse?"

"No point in you doing *all* the work, my dear." Dan finished his vodka shot and poured another. With that, he jerked shut the royal red drapes and guided her to the king-size four-poster bed.

At four o'clock Dan dressed and quietly slipped out of the suite. Before departing, he left a 4:30 wake-up call for his wife. He hated lying to Kathryn but had no choice. There was no meeting with General Director Potapov, in fact, he didn't know if such a person existed. He was meeting at Lenin's Tomb in Red Square with former KGB officer turned capitalist, Boris Volkov.

A gray cloud cover had dropped the temperature several degrees, and a light drizzle was falling as Dan walked toward the northeast wall of the Kremlin. His attire made him stand out in the crowd of bundled-up Russians, but that caused a perverse pleasure. He had taken Kathryn's advice and packed his rough-out range jacket with sheep skin lining and Stetson. He was proud to be a Texan and an American.

"Greetings, Colonel Morton. Welcome to Mother Russia." Volkov's husky voice invaded Dan's thoughts.

"Greetings to you too, Boris Volkov." Dan replied, as he shook hands with the retired KGB officer. Volkov gave him a hearty bear hug, and Dan detected the bulge of a pistol under the man's heavy topcoat.

Morton stepped back and eyed the affluent Russian businessman from head to toe. The beginnings of a gray-flecked beard covered his chin and cheeks. The arms dealer wore rugged military-style boots and heavy gloves.

"Come, let us walk. It will only get colder standing here at Lenin's resting place."

The men walked eastward toward the multi-colored onion domes of Saint Basil's Cathedral, awash in the warm glow of floodlights. It was a stark contrast, Dan thought, to the ruby red stars adorning the towers of the Kremlin's grim walls off to their right.

"So, Colonel Morton, what can you tell me about this Project *Tejano,* as you call it?"

"I am pleased to report all goes well. The rubles you supplied two months ago have been put to good use."

"And exactly how is that?"

"Your funds were routed to one of the two candidates running for the privilege of being defeated by Sen. Creighton. The school teacher, Andrew Smith, is campaigning across the state of Texas, getting excellent news coverage."

"It still seems strange, supporting the opponent of the man you want to win. Even here we are not that clever in our political conduct. And Sen. Creighton? How is he doing?" Volkov slowed their pace. "I have seen much of him on CNN, traveling the United States on his presidential campaign. How does that race look?"

"Excellent. Our plan leaves Creighton free to travel the country. Only one other candidate, the governor of South Carolina, has announced for President, and our national press corps has already written him off as a non-starter."

Volkov exhaled the strong cigarette, the smoke mixing with his visibly chilled breath. "But with no primary opponent, how does Creighton get any press attention?"

"Easy. He is free to stay on his message and chide President Templeton every chance he gets. Templeton destroyed the recent Middle East peace talks with his crude remarks two weeks ago. Creighton seized on that. There's a new issue every week, dramatizing why the fool shouldn't be re-elected."

Volkov guided Dan across Red Square, away from the Kremlin walls. They slowly strolled past GUM, the four story galleria of small stores and kiosks. "Excellent. I am glad we can work together to bring change, you and I. We need a new American president. One who will be friendly to our wants and needs."

Morton nodded in agreement. "This president and the Congress are weak. They do not understand that arming Americans and citizens of other nations will produce less terrorism, not more."

"We once had strong leaders, Khrushchev, Brezhnev. Stalin especially knew only the strong survive."

"And your country will be strong again. With the right American president in office, my company will export the handguns your people need to protect themselves. And you can be the one to supply them. By the way, how is the security business?"

"Butov is fine," Volkov said, referring to the private organization he operated with several other ex-KGB officers. "We have our ways of convincing new businesses they need us for protection."

"From whom?"

"The gypsies, the street people. For a nice percentage of their income, our clients are permitted to operate in peace. If they don't use us, they suddenly find they have major problems, if you understand what I mean."

Dan knew quite well. He had heard that mafia bosses like Volkov worked both sides of the street, taking a cut from the gypsies, then fire-bombing or sabotaging kiosks and other retail establishments if the proprietors didn't produce sufficient protection money.

Morton decided to broach the real subject of their meeting. "I appreciate all you have done for *Tejano*. But I have come to request another contribution to the fund."

General Volkov turned and stared coldly at the American. "How much this time? We have already contributed twenty million rubles to *Tejano*. That's almost seven hundred fifty thousand US dollars."

"I know, General. I ask for only two hundred thousand dollars more this time. To show my good faith and confidence, I have invested another five hundred thousand US dollars. I have the telephone number of our Zurich bank. You can call right now, if you wish to confirm. I have given instructions to respond to your inquiry."

They walked toward Manezhnaya Square. "That will not be necessary. My business associates here in Moscow and in St. Petersburg need handguns, pistols like your company manufactures. I can buy all you can make. Change the laws and we can prosper like you Americans."

Volkov stopped and turned to face Dan. "Have you ever been to *Ogni Moskvy*?"

Dan frowned. The Russian seemed to ignore his request for additional funding. "No, I don't believe so. 'The Lights of Moscow'? What is that?"

The former KGB officer pointed to the top floor of the Moskva Hotel. "Come, let us view the lights of Moscow. Have some vodka and espresso. There we will discuss your financial needs."

Minutes later they were shown to a secluded table on the eighth floor of the gray concrete structure. After the waiter had taken their drink orders, they sat in silence gazing at the lights.

After polishing off his second vodka, Volkov looked at Morton, who sat quietly. "Your thoughts, my friend?"

"Just that it's hard to believe thirty plus years ago I was in a hot, steamy jungle directing an armored cavalry troop of tanks and personnel carriers north to the Ho Chi Minh trail tracking VC and NVA, all equipped with Soviet-made weapons. Now I comfortably sit in downtown Moscow a block from Red Square looking through rain at these lights illuminating offices where decisions were made to provide arms used against me and my troops."

"Times have changed, haven't they? Both of our governments have changed." The Russian downed his vodka shot and took a bite of black bread. "I agree, Colonel, that we should work together. You want your gun laws changed to allow more arms sales in America to fight the terrorists. I need your weapons to help maintain peace on the streets of Moskva. And that is not all. With the aid of your government, there is much potential here in my country."

"I know, Boris. Loans by the Export-Import Bank, the World Bank, the IMF, they all need to be resumed. Stronger business for Russia not only helps your fellow citizens, it helps you and Irina and those two sons of whom I can tell you are so proud."

Dan pressed on, allowing Volkov to think. "About the *Tejano* funding, General. Can I count on you again? We must ensure that our mission is successful."

"I don't know. Can I be sure no one will learn of my participation?"

"Absolutely." Although he had promised Jake Hardesty not to reveal project details, he needed the additional money from the Russian. "We established an offshore corporation called Triad Investments."

"What business does this Triad Investments conduct in your country?"

Dan laughed. "It does nothing. It's a shell, a dummy corporation. Merely a vehicle to open an offshore bank account in Zurich, then funnel money to fund *Tejano*."

"So it is in Switzerland that Triad is incorporated?"

Perhaps the vodkas, cigar, the entire atmosphere were affecting his judgment, but Morton felt he needed to draw Volkov into his confidence. "No, in Mauritius."

"Mauritius? Never heard of it." Boris laughed. "Did you make that up too?"

"No, it's a small volcanic island in the Indian Ocean off the southeast coast of Africa."

Volkov was intrigued. "Why Mauritius rather than the US?" he asked.

"Simple. Confidentiality. The Republic of Mauritius has strict laws against disclosure of principals and shareholders, that type of thing. Most importantly, we aren't required to file annual reports on our accounts. So what do you say? Are you in for more?"

The two rode the cramped elevator to the street level, stepped into the cold night air and strolled toward the Metropol. "I don't know," Volkov mused. "We could be financially ruined. It is dangerous to interfere with foreign elections, especially after the most recent terrorist attacks on America. Your country's laws are stringent. One could spend much time in your federal penitentiary and pay enormous fines."

Morton cleared his throat. "Why don't you think about what I've said and take your time. Call me in a couple of days. But I must tell you, without an increase from you, I will have to make arrangements elsewhere."

Volkov studied the retired military man in the street lights on Ulitsa Volkonka. He knew Dan Morton had connections throughout the world. Still holding Dan's hand, Volkov shook it again. "No, I need no more time." He handed Dan a business card. "Call my office in the morning with wire transfer instructions."

"Thank you. Thank you very much. I assure you the money will be put to its highest and best use to bring about the change you and I both want to see."

"In politics, Mr. Morton, I know you can not guarantee Sen. Creighton's re-election to the Senate much less election to the presidency. But I do ask that you guard against my participation ever being revealed. If Creighton wins, I know we will all profit in our own ways. But for now, forget *Tejano*. You and Mrs. Morton enjoy our beautiful old city. Please, give her my very best. If you need anything, call my office."

"*Spasibo.*"

"*Bcevo dobrovo,*" the general replied. "Good night. Keep me advised." He turned and opened the door to the back seat of a black Chaika sedan that had seemingly appeared out of nowhere.

As the driver pulled away from the curb, Morton pulled out a fresh cigar and lit it. He walked the five blocks back to the warmth of the Metropol, replaying every aspect of the meeting with his Russian partner in *Tejano*. Though he was pleased with his day's work, he was late for dinner and knew Kathryn would be angry. He would think of some excuse and promise to make it up to her with another expensive trinket.

A few minutes later the doorman bowed slightly and pulled open the shiny brass handle of the Metropol's lobby doors. An apology from the lobby phone might ease the infliction of Kathryn's wrath before rejoining her, he thought.

"Where in living hell have you been for the past six hours? I've been worried to death about you," came the caustic reply over the house phone.

Worry was better than anger. That he could manipulate. "The damn guy could talk the ears off a dead man," Dan responded. "I was at General Director Potapov's office for a while, then he took me to some flea-bitten bar for a couple of drinks. Guns, guns, and more guns, that's all he wanted to discuss. But I think you can count on a couple more minks as a result of the meeting. A very profitable visit if I do say so." Deception came so easily.

CHAPTER 9

▼

MOSCOW
SEPTEMBER 23

Vladimir Kiriyenkov pushed the tiny button on the luminous dial of his digital watch: 10:15. He had anticipated hearing from his partner by 10 p.m. Surely Boris Volkov's business with the American would not take much longer.

At 55, Kiriyenkov felt out of place among the youth who milled around the Midnight Express bar and gyrated on the strobe-lit dance floor. He was here for business, not pleasure. Kiriyenkov made nightly rounds of at least four bars and restaurants checking on Butov security guards. Five muscular Georgians patrolling the sidewalk with Stechkin machine pistols kept the waiting patrons in order. If they wished to enjoy continued good health and freedom, all customers knew to stay in line..

Vladimir made an audit of the records of the bars' weekly income and expenses, informing the managers how much he expected to collect on his next visit. The accounting courses he had taken at Columbia University while a KGB deep cover in New York City helped immensely in his new business endeavors.

Kiriyenkov's attention to a couple spinning to the Latin beats emanating from the sound system was interrupted by the vibrating of his cell phone. Boris, he confirmed, checking the number. "*Da?*"

"Volkov," the curt voice answered. "Where are you, Vlad?"

"Midnight Express. And you?"

"Outside the Moskva. The American just left."

"How did it go?" Kiriyenkov cupped his free hand over his ear to muffle the disco music and background noises.

"I will give you a full report shortly. Meet me at Aragvi in fifteen minutes. One more thing, did you bring the Yazkov dossier?"

"Yes, it is in the car."

"Bring it in with you. I want to see it again. It is time to relay further orders. I don't trust these fool Americans."

Before Kiriyenkov could say another word, General Volkov hung up. Once in the car, he flipped on the back seat reading light and reviewed the file on their agent in Texas, Sergei Davidovich Yazkov.

Boris Volkov nodded in recognition to three Butov employees, who were attired in company-issue black jumpsuits and combat boots and snapped to attention when he exited from the limo, entering Aragvi.

"General Volkov, it is so good to see you again. It has been too long. Your colleague is at your table." The maitre d' snapped his fingers and a waiter instantly appeared and ushered the guest to a private room where Kiriyenkov stood, warming himself in front of an enormous fireplace.

The restaurant had the ambiance of a hunting lodge. Dining chairs and tables were hewn from heavy pine, the place settings of pewter. Wall paintings depicting hunting scenes of ancient Georgia reached to the tall ceilings. No wonder it had been Stalin's favorite hangout, Volkov mused.

"Greetings, Vlad, sorry to have taken so long. Traffic on Tverskaya was heavier than I expected. Come, sit."

Two waiters helped the men with their coats, then pulled out their chairs and quietly departed. A moment later, an elderly woman brought two chilled glasses and a bottle of Volkov's favorite vodka, followed by a platter of caviar, sturgeon, hard cheese and black bread.

"So, it went well?" Kiriyenkov asked as he spread caviar thickly on the bread.

"Yes, I had to play the role of the dumb Russian for a while to get the information I wanted, but it did not take long."

"You are satisfied with what you learned?"

"All is well." Volkov told of his meeting with the American arms dealer.

"Have we made a wise investment?"

"Yes, I think so. But who can say if Creighton will win? Their system of democracy might be much older than ours, but certainly not as predicable as the outcomes here. But this American can provide the respectable access we need."

"What of Byreley and Trumwell?" Kiriyenkov referred to the New York law firm he had come to know while working at Chase Bank. "They have an excellent lobbying office in D.C."

"We could still use them too once the project is completed and Creighton is elected. Plus that public relations firm you suggested in New York. We will need all the contacts we can buy to get those fucking Americans to part with their almighty dollars and support business in this country."

"When will you talk with Colonel Morton again?"

"The big ox will call bright and early in the morning, wanting to know how to get more of our money."

"What will you tell him?"

"I will arrange a contribution of one million US dollars from our Nauruan bank account. Are you sure the money is still there?"

Kiriyenkov had attained a bank license from the Republic of Nauru, a small South Pacific island located north of the Solomon Islands, south of the equator. He had made an initial deposit of twenty-five million dollars. "Yes, I visited with International Communications, our service company, only last week. All is well."

"And our identities are still secure?"

"Without question. Andrei checked them out thoroughly before we chose to use their facilities." Andrei Balusov, another former KGB agent, had also worked deep cover in the United States. After the reforms he had chosen to stay in America. "He went to their offices in Chicago and met with the principals personally. If our business gets fucked up, he knows exactly who to take care of."

"Excellent. Has Andrei been to this bank of ours?"

"There's no reason to go since there is not even a bank building on the damn island. All is done with computers. Planes only go there twice a week. The Nauruans don't care to see us any more than we want to see them. They just want to see our money on their ledgers and collect the exorbitant fees we had to pay to get the bank charter and to keep it updated."

Volkov slapped his colleague on the shoulder, and poured another shot before their waitresses served them. "I am proud of you, Vlad. Your time at Chase was well spent."

"Thank you, General. I had a feeling while going to Columbia night school that working there would prove to be of value."

"Doesn't someone in the Nauruan government have to have names, even in a God forsaken place like that?" Boris continued, increasingly impressed by the business acumen of his partner.

"InCom had to pay a local to be a bank director for us. We call the bank Baltic Federal. Andrei gave his InCom contact some false passport information for the other directors. You and I are the only ones who can make withdrawals or deposits. InCom makes it all very simple."

"We can get our money back to our bank here in Moscow at anytime?"

"Absolutely. All done by wire transfers. I have taken care of the necessary bank officers here as well to keep our banking operations confidential."

"That is why I don't trust those Americans. They are fucking amateurs when it comes to these matters. Listen to this. Some friend of Morton's, Jake I believed he called him, learned about offshore corporations and bank accounts from a provider on the Internet!"

"Who is their service company, the goddamn FBI?"

"Who knows, maybe the CIA. I think they might be getting in over their heads. If this operation is ever uncovered, I don't want our involvement to surface."

Kiriyenkov nodded in agreement. "So that is why you wanted the Yazkov file?" He picked up the brown envelope lying on the chair next to him.

"Exactly." Volkov took his glass and the half full bottle of vodka, and went to stand in front of the fire. "Tell me about our man in Texas."

"Sergei Davidovich Yazkov is forty years of age. A former sergeant in the Special Forces. Twenty years, Army service. Native of Smolensk. Older brother, Ruslan, was also regular Army and was killed in Afghanistan in the mid 1980s. He blames Ruslan's death on the Americans and vows revenge because of their support of the Afghans."

"Married?" Volkov took another sip, this time directly from the bottle.

"Single. We recruited him for Butov five years ago. He has an outstanding service record in Afghanistan and fighting the Chechens. Fifteen kills as best we could determine."

"How does he feel about Americans?"

"He hates them and all things American. He believes they are ruining our country, destroying our culture and the old ways. He complains of stupid Americans forcing their way of living on Russians. Once he said he would kill the next Russian who tried to sell a Michael Jackson CD instead of a folk ballad of the motherland."

Volkov nodded. "I am convinced we were right in sending this man, Yazkov, to protect our investment. I don't trust Morton and his associates to keep a fucking secret. They might get sloppy and waste our money."

"Yazkov will prevent that," Vladimir said. "All we have to do is give the order."

"Get word to him to increase surveillance. Do it now. We do not want this so-called *Tejano* operation uncovered, even if it means eventually eliminating the good Colonel Daniel Augustus Morton." Volkov's voice was hard. "Instruct Yazkov to make his next move and proceed as we discussed with him before he left."

Vladimir Kiriyenkov punched a series of digits on his cell phone and waited for the international call to go through.

"Andrei? Vlad here. Contact our asset through the arranged method. Message: Move to stage two with H-L in that order."

CHAPTER 10

▼

SAN ANTONIO
SEPTEMBER 28

"Roommate wanted in Austin: single, black female. If interested contact Box HL."

Sergei Yazkov peered at the *San Antonio Express* classifieds. He had been searching for the ad every day for the past week. After his recruitment, General Volkov had explained that he was to monitor the United States Senate campaigns of the two candidates and look for instructions via the classified ads. The order of surveillance was given by the code HL. "H" for Houston, hometown of Warren McDonald. "L" for Lufkin and Andrew Smith. According to these veiled instructions, he was to proceed to Austin and contact the Houston candidate's campaign.

As he packed, Yazkov thought back on Volkov's discussion concerning his mission in America. While Volkov and others were funneling money into Smith's campaign, he was to infiltrate the campaign and watch for any unusual activity. Under no circumstances could the Russian's involvement be discerned. If anyone acted suspicious of the burgeoning funds, he was to convince them in the strongest terms to ignore such activity. If they persisted in attempting to uncover the operation, his orders were simple: termination.

After the killings in South Texas, Sergei had driven to the San Antonio airport where he abandoned the stolen pickup. He theorized that when authorities found the truck they would assume he had taken a departing flight. Instead, he headed for a cheap dive where he would go unnoticed.

With Austin only eighty miles north, Sergei decided to travel by bus. He had staked out the nearby bus station for several days, and, as anticipated, the Texas Department of Public Safety and San Antonio police had the terminal under surveillance. This challenge was part of his game, hide and seek.

Since coming to San Antonio he had made the necessary purchases, a battered fatigue jacket at a surplus store, a pair of wooden crutches at a medical equipment store, and disguise materials from a costume shop to alter his appearance.

White watching news reports and reading the headline stories of the brutal killings along the border, Sergei gloated in his cleverness. Local officials in Maverick and Uvalde counties had called in the famed Texas Rangers to coordinate their investigations. He watched as Ranger Lt. Juan Falcone briefed reporters. Under intense questioning, the young Hispanic officer conceded there remained uncertainty as to the murderer's whereabouts, why he had killed or whether he was still in the state.

He knew investigators would calculate height and weight similarities, since changes of clothes had been taken from both men. The crutches would throw them off as to height. Yazkov scissored the top of his hair, then applied cream to closely shave the crown. He glued on a shaggy, graying beard and long hair under a faded cap to complete his disguise.

Sergei glanced at the two large canvas bags and hesitated due to the risk of being searched. In addition, on crutches he found it difficult to carry the bags, which contained weapons and equipment. He decided to ship them to a post office box in Austin.

That afternoon a ragged, disabled veteran on crutches boarded a crowded Greyhound bound for Kansas City, with an intermediate stop in Austin. Weary San Antonio police and DPS troopers paid scant attention when another vagrant hobbled aboard yet another bus leaving for Austin and points beyond.

A few hours later, Sergei walked two blocks from the Austin bus station to the Salvation Army to rest and freshen up. He tossed the crutches to a legless beggar sitting on the floor of the soup kitchen. Alone in the restroom, he removed the facial disguise and tossed it in the trash. Fifteen minutes later a slightly balding man in his mid-thirties boarded a University of Texas shuttle headed for campus, confident he would now blend into the international community of fifty thousand students.

At the Student Union cafeteria, Sergei ordered a sandwich and studied *The Daily Texan*, the campus newspaper. The classifieds yielded Yazkov a list of eight potential residences. He called each one, inquiring not only about monthly rates, but also location and access to the university and city bus routes. It took five tries before he found one that was perfect, a furnished one bedroom garage apartment, three blocks north of the law school.

Sergei politely smiled as an elderly woman cautiously opened the front door. "Hello, my name is Francisco Alvarez. I'm responding to an ad I saw in *The Daily Texan* about a room for rent. Is it still available?"

Learning of the man's intentions for appearing on her door step, Inez Kolby opened the door wider. "Yes, it is. If you'll walk around the side of the house and down the driveway, I'll meet you at the back door and show it to you."

Inside the garage apartment, Sergei looked about with satisfaction. "Very nice."

"Thank you. It's clean and quiet. Will you be living alone or with a roommate?" Mrs. Kolby opened and closed the closet doors, then traced her finger across the breakfast table's white metallic top, indicating an absence of dust and grime.

"Alone. And I am a very tidy housekeeper. I am a student from Monterey, Mexico," he said, using his Spanish accent. "I am in your country temporarily for a graduate program in American studies at the university."

The handsome young man seemed mature, therefore not likely to cause problems. "You are in luck, Mr. Alvarez. A first year law student dropped out of class last week. I guess the stress got to her. She left behind her television and all of her linens. I don't care what you do or how often you're even here, just so long as the rent's paid at the first of each month."

"How about if I take care of that now?" Sergei pulled out a roll of bills and began counting out twenties. Inez Kolby relaxed and smiled as three months of cash rent crossed her palm.

"Good afternoon, Warren McDonald for United States Senate campaign headquarters."

"Hello. I am calling to get information about volunteering for Mr. McDonald's campaign."

"Certainly. One moment please." The young man transferred the call to the volunteer coordinator.

"Hello, this is Dixie Thompson, may I help you?" The harried young woman continued looking over a small stack of pink call slips.

"Yes, my name is Francisco Alvarez. My thesis is on the practical aspects of campaigning in the United States, as compared to the process in Mexico and other Latin-American democracies. With your permission, I would like to volunteer for your campaign with the hopes of incorporating some first hand observations of the day-to-day operations of your headquarters and of learning about the candidate."

Dixie thought a moment, setting the call slips aside. "I'm not sure what you'd gain by just observing."

"Oh, I'm sorry, I did not make myself clear. I would like to actually help out if I could. I have heard you run the best volunteer organization in the state," Yazkov lied.

The flattery had its intended effect. "Well, I try to run a tight ship. Why don't you stop by and we'll visit. If I'm not in, I'll leave word of our conversation with whoever's in charge. It'll be no problem ... now you said your name was Alvarez?"

"Yes, Francisco Alvarez, I will stop by this afternoon after class."

"Well, how are *yew*? You must be that Francisco Alvarez that Dixie told me about. My name is Jo Lynne Cutberth. I'm from Carthage, over in East Texas," the twenty-one year old co-ed drawled. "We're so glad you're here to help us elect Warren McDonald to the United States Senate." She extended her hand.

"*Buenos tardes, señorita.* Thank you for allowing me to be of service to your Señor McDonald. I will try to do whatever you need of me," he added, making a melodramatic bow.

Yazkov's jet black wig and pencil-thin mustache made him glad he had spent the extra money to buy the more expensive disguise material. As she stared at him, Sergei was satisfied the young woman could not detect the ruse.

"Oh, my goodness," Jo Lynne twittered, batting dark lashes. The East Texas beauty queen acted as though she had met a true to life, in the flesh, Latin lover. "*Muchas gracias* to you too, Señor Alvarez. Welcome to *Tejas*, I mean Texas."

"Are you the campaign manager?" Sergei smiled.

"Heavens no, I'm a senior poly sci major at UT, but I'm thinkin' 'bout going on to law school."

"So who is the campaign manager?" Sergei inquired.

"Suzanne Chism, but she's not here right now. She's in Lubbock with the candidate on a South Plains swing. We expect her back tomorrow night."

"Everyone seems quite busy. Is it like this all the time?" Yazkov counted ten individuals at desks around the crowded room. All were talking on telephones, writing on notepads, referring to strategically marked maps and up-dated itineraries.

Jo Lynne stopped at a desk where a young man dressed in a burnt orange sweat shirt and faded blue jeans hung up a telephone and was poised to place another call.

"Excuse me a second, B. J., this is Francisco Alvarez, our newest volunteer. He's going to help with calls for the fundraiser. Would you please get him started on that phone over there? If he can raise us three thousand by five thirty you get a pay raise."

"Right. Two times nuthin' is still nuthin," B. J. replied with a laugh as he greeted his new assistant. He pulled out a well-used sheet of paper and blank legal pad, then took Sergei to a nearby desk. "This is what we call the pitch sheet. It gives all the pertinent details of the event. There's an introduction here as well. All you do is get the sucker on the line and read off the sheet. If he takes the bait, fine, if not, move on to the next one. Easy as pie."

Yazkov studied the single piece of paper, then glanced over a list of names the young man handed him. "And what is this?"

"It's a call list of those who're apt to spring for the fundraiser. I'm told they're all rich enough to pay the freight, but none have ponied-up yet." B. J. pointed to a blue Styrofoam cooler on the floor in the far corner of the room. "Make yourself at home. There's all the bottled water you can drink. I think we have a few soft drinks in there too. Holler if you have any questions or problems. Good luck, *amigo.*"

At first a cacophony of sounds, ringing phones, buzzing equipment and constant chatter distracted Sergei. He watched a steady stream of paper going into and coming out of the fax machines. The copy machine regularly begged for more paper as it produced fliers containing news of various stops on the upcoming tour.

Sergei looked around, surveying the scene of organized chaos. "No smoking" signs were prominently displayed on the bright orange and white walls. Paper plates with leftover pizza, half empty coffee cups and a couple of hardened doughnuts from the morning shift littered the work area.

Sergei studied his pitch sheet and call list and commenced the solicitation process. If the response was "no," he moved to the next prospect.

By 6 p.m., Yazkov had made fifty calls, reached six people and gotten four to contribute a total of three thousand dollars. Jo Lynne Cutberth was beside herself with his productivity. "Francisco, you are just real, real good at this, ya know? I do hope you'll come back tomorrow. Wanna go get a beer on Sixth Street with some of us and sorta unwind a bit?"

"Thank you for the compliment, Señorita Cutberth, but I shouldn't. I have some studying to do and a paper I must work on tonight. But I will try to return later this week."

Three hours later, over a steaming bowl of potato and bacon soup and a length of sausage with cheese and crackers, Sergei Yazkov congratulated himself for the ease with which he had been accepted into the McDonald campaign office.

CHAPTER 11

▼

WASHINGTON, D. C.
OCTOBER 2

Jake Hardesty wiped a heavy mist from his face. York insisted they meet outside in a public place to ensure they were not being followed or taped. Jake decided it was not worth protesting. They agreed to approach the Lincoln Memorial from opposite directions within ten minutes of each other.

Jake approached the Vietnam War Memorial, a sight that rarely failed to move those who fought in the conflict and even those who could only imagine what it was like. He visited the site infrequently, spending most of his waking hours on nearby Capitol Hill or entertaining congressmen in expensive downtown bars and restaurants. On weekends he liked to escape to Annapolis on the Atlantic seashore or to the Virginia countryside. He had no interest in mingling with more tourists, he got enough of that in the Capitol rotunda during the week. And, as time went by he found it harder, not easier, to come to this hallowed ground memorializing his comrades. The conflict hadn't ended for him. Often when he closed his eyes at night, it was as if he were back in the boonies humping through the drenching monsoon rains of Southeast Asia.

Jake walked to the front of the Wall and, like others near him, felt compelled to touch it. This is my panel. He reverently pressed his palm to Panel 33F where the names of his platoon mates filled lines 82, 83, and 84. Tears welled in his eyes. He could not contain them, nor did he try. Pangs of guilt surged through every fiber because it was their names, not his, on the Wall. Closing his eyes, the past and present blended together, decades only a breath away.

There was a chill in the air but not enough to distract him or the others from contemplating the dark facade of the cold, black granite. Other vets, many in old fatigue jackets and jeans, aging parents, widows, children and grandchildren comprised the crowd, all mesmerized by the Wall and the names it held. It pleased him that tourists respectfully remained on the pathway of black brick pavers when they came to honor those who paid the ultimate price.

Jake pulled up the collar on his combat fatigue jacket, with its olive drab name tag and Sergeant E-5 stripes and adjusted the fatigue cap covering his salt and pepper gray hair. He had stuffed his jeans into combat boots acquired in Vietnam with o.d. fabric on the sides. Unlike many, he chose not to wear his Purple Heart and other medals, which many of those who fought considered "out of uniform."

America's version of the wailing wall, Jake thought, watching and listening. A place where family and comrades come to remember the 58,132 dead whose names are engraved on the black granite panels in front of him. But for the grace of God and some damn good nurses and chopper pilots, his name might be up there as well. Looking at the names, he realized he could also see his reflection. The water streaming down seemed like tears. It's like the Wall is crying, crying for me and the other survivors.

The pungent smell of rotten carnations and roses mingled with the heaviness of the late afternoon mist. Jake looked at other mementoes resting at the base of the memorial which he knew were regularly collected by the National Park Service, cataloged and stored in a warehouse in Lanham, Maryland. Jake suspected that back in 1982 when the Wall was constructed, no one imagined that more than a quarter of a century later such sacraments would still be placed honoring the American dead of Vietnam.

Slowly, Jake walked toward the Lincoln Memorial, turning from the Wall toward veterans squatting on the hillside, lost in thought within the seclusion of the tree line. He glanced at the darkening sky, hearing the roar of distant jet engines as a plane approached Reagan National Airport. The air was filled with the whirling sounds of rotary blades of Marine One, President Templeton's helicopter, approaching the helipad on the west lawn of the White House. Suddenly past and present seemed as one. What was then and what was now? Where the hell am I?

In the approaching darkness he vaguely made out the silhouettes of three nurses treating a wounded soldier. One's head was turned up toward what Jake thought were sounds of an approaching Huey medivac. He looked up and saw the door gunner manning the M 60 D machine gun, clearing Viet Cong from the landing zone. The sporadic ten second bursts from the front-mounted Gatling guns rang in his ears.

Overhead flares lit the darkness. Voices in his head were yelling: "Hot l.z.! VC! Get down! Hit the deck!"

Jack ran through the mist toward the nurses and the GI a few yards from the Wall. One nurse was coming toward him. When they reached one another Jake took her in his arms and flung her to the ground, covering her body with his. He noticed the bars and medical corps insignia on her jacket. "Get down, Captain." Jake gently but firmly pressed her head against the grassy terrain.

After a few seconds the woman struggled to a sitting position, patting Jake's back. "It's okay, sergeant. We're all right. You're home. We are all safe," she whispered. "It's over. It's all over." The stranger rubbed his head, then delicately shook it to clear the cobwebs and bring Jake back to reality.

Like a broken ammonia ampoule, the sweet smell of her perfume filled his nostrils, awakening him from a surreal encounter. Jake realized no woman would be wearing perfume in a hot combat zone. Looking up he saw strands of gray in her golden blonde hair. The military style steel-rimmed glasses couldn't hide her angelic face.

As the officer pulled Jake to his feet he noticed that a small crowd had gathered, some vets in wheel chairs, others on crutches, many dressed in partial battle garb. He smiled with embarrassment. "I'm sorry, Captain. Still get flashbacks every now and then. Nightmares too. They just seem to come and go."

The nurse knowingly smiled, squeezing his arm. "I understand. We call it post traumatic stress. Most all of us have had it in one form or another. When I got back I treated a lot of vets at Walter Reed and more recently at the VA hospital in Maryland."

"Thank you for what you did for us over there, ma'am. All of you," he added, looking at the nearby Women's Vietnam Veterans Memorial. He could see the outline of one of the statues holding an i.v. bottle over a wounded GI, a tube running to his arm.

"You're welcome," the captain softly replied. "It was our job. We were proud to be there for you guys."

"It was more than a job and you know it. It was a calling. It was a mission of mercy." Tears welled again but he managed to salute the officer. Though her lips were now trembling, the nurse returned the salute. Jake stepped closer and placed his arms around her. With immense satisfaction and gratitude he stepped back, turned and walked toward the Lincoln Memorial with a renewed sense of commitment to his mission. He was convinced fellow vet Russell Creighton would never lead this country into another Vietnam-like quagmire. Jake vowed he would do all he could, no matter the cost, to help the senator reach the White House.

Bill York briskly mounted the steps leading to the statue of Abraham Lincoln. The lobbyist crossed to the north side of the cavernous space and studied the president's second inaugural address. Out of the corner of his eye he noticed Jake Hardesty trotting up the steps on his right, heading towards the Gettysburg Address on the south wall.

Jake stared up at Lincoln, who appeared to be looking down on the crowd assembled at his feet. Bill joined the group admiring the marble likeness. Hardesty looked across the length of the Reflecting Pool to the Washington Monument.

Moments later Bill York moved to his side. "Hey, Jake, my man, good to see ya' again. We're gonna have to stop meeting like this or people are gonna start thinking we've got a thing for each other."

Jake grimaced. "The last thing I'd ever do is get matched up with the likes of you."

York held out two Styrofoam coffee cups. "Let's go over to that park bench by the Reflecting Pool."

Minutes later the two lobbyists were seated. York casually peeled off the lid and blew on the steaming coffee. "Let's get to it," Jake said. "Tell me about Rebecca Durham. What's been happenin' with AGOA, and what do y'all have planned for the next few weeks? Short hand it for me."

"I met with her two weeks ago." York wiped his mouth with the back of his hand. "I had no idea they have so many chapters around the country. I'm here to tell ya', Jake, Ms. Rebecca Scott Durham is on a mission. She idolizes Sen. Creighton, as much as she hates Templeton and wants to help get our man in the White House ASAP."

"How 'bout Texas? Has she recruited from any of the gun owner chapters down there?"

"Oh yeah, there's big time representation in Texas. Fortunately for us, AGOA is especially strong in East Texas around Smith's hometown"

Jake was wary. "She's not going public about AGOA members' support is she?"

"Hell no. She's too savvy for that. It will never surface."

"Sounds good." Jake said. "Let's walk toward the Washington Monument for a few minutes. What else has she got working back home?"

"She's plugged in with county officials all over the state, county judges, commissioners and sheriffs. Hell of a network, I promise you that. Ever seen a pot-bellied county sheriff who didn't want to be appointed US Marshall by the president? They all fancy themselves as the next Wyatt Earp. Most all of 'em are Association members. She's working with them behind the scenes to endorse Smith and already has coordinators in about seventy-five counties."

"How 'bout McDonald down in Houston? Won't Durham put some of her true believers on his program? Surely there's somebody she could use."

"No way. She's still pissed at McDonald for some comment he made in his attorney general race a few years back."

Jake stopped. "About what?"

"I don't really know, except that he supported the ban on assault weapons and the Brady Bill. Those were federal issues, and she felt he didn't have to comment on them in a race for state office."

"You haven't mentioned my name, have you?" Hardesty resumed walking. "This is still contained, as far as she sees it."

"Right. She knows someone else is involved on the money side, but not who."

"No idea about Morton either?"

"Nope, she only knows that somehow the finances are being taken care of. I'm tellin' ya, she gets off on the idea of screwin' up the process. It's all a big game with her."

He checked his watch. "Damn, Jake, I gotta go. Quick, tell me 'bout Colonel Morton. What's he up to?"

Jake pointed down the Mall toward the Capitol, the stark white edifice awash in floodlights. "He's up to making the next so-called Million Mom March look a hell of a lot different than it has the past few years."

"That's welcome news. He and the other gun manufacturers can't afford to have the suburbia soccer moms continue to come up here every year whining for more gun control. They're apt to put him out of business, even if we do get Creighton in the White House."

"Yeah, that damn 'wall of death' was the clincher last year. I still can't believe that many school kids died of gunshot wounds. That's gonna be different next time, and *Tejano* money will help make it so."

"What's he going to do?"

"You're gonna love this. He's set up a Section 527 Committee under the FEC regs called 'Citizens for A Safer America.' Such a political committee isn't required to report its funding sources."

"So, what does that have to do with *Tejano?*"

Jake smiled. "Simple. All the money comes straight from our Zurich bank account, and thus, from whoever in the world our bagman, the good colonel, has hit up for money. This citizens' committee will then fund our own group of moms with strollers who will protest the next Million Mom March, pointing out access to guns makes for a safer home place. Also that teachers need to be armed."

"But how does that help us select a weak candidate for Creighton to run against?" York asked.

"I confess it doesn't do that, but what the hell, Morton's sugar daddies aren't exactly in a position to call the FBI and complain that their money's being illegally used. And as you pointed out, it helps keep our funding source in business."

"You got a point there. I like it. Have you actually seen the 'ol man lately?"

"Yeah, I went back to Fort Worth three weeks ago to brief him again on the operation. You'll be happy to know he's deposited a million in the Triad Investments account in Zurich."

"Jesus! Where did that come from?"

"Hell if I know. 'Don't ask, don't tell,' that's my motto."

"Well, if we get Creighton elected to the White House, much less re-elected to the Senate, we're all gonna have friends in high places. Does he have any idea about Rebecca or AGOA on my side of the operation?"

"Of course not," Jake replied. "As we've said a hundred times, this is a contained operation. Morton only knows that I have to be reaching out to others, but he hasn't got a clue as to who they are. You're safe, Durham's safe, and it'll stay that way."

Chapter 12

▼

Sao Paulo, Brazil
October 15

Inside their rococo mansion overlooking the expansive city, Juan Carlos Rojas and his wife, Adriana, sat with Dan Morton and Jake Hardesty. While Juan Carlos and Dan engaged in pleasantries, Jake relaxed and let his eyes explore the surroundings. The interior design reminded him of a university research library with hundreds of leather-bound, gold-engraved volumes lining two of the walls. An 18-foot mahogany bar was reflected in a mirrored wall.

Morton had briefed him about their dinner companions. Rojas was an attorney and international entrepreneur who invested the income from his lucrative corporate law practice in the stocks of his client companies. His wife spent her time on the tennis courts or disposing of her husband's hefty income in fashionable boutiques.

"Where do you go when you leave Sao Palo, Jake?" Adrianna inquired.

"We hop over to Rio tomorrow for two days, then on to La Paz for the same and wind up in Santiago for the weekend before heading home." Jake openly admired Adrianna's low-cut gown, and pearl and diamond choker. Her bleached-blonde hair was pulled back, revealing diamond earrings.

Adrianna coyly smiled as she took a cigarillo and lighter from the coffee table. "And what is so important for you to make such a whirlwind tour of our continent?" Offering Jake the lighter, she leaned forward revealing ample cleavage.

"Oh, nothing that would interest you, Mrs. Rojas. Colonel Morton...."

She lightly touched the palm of his hand with her fingertips. "I like to think we've already become friends, Jake. Please, call me Adrianna." She exhaled a ring of smoke that lingered over them like a cloud.

"Whatever you say, ma'am, I mean Adrianna. Colonel Morton owns an arms manufacturing company in Texas. We're making sales calls on some of his clients."

Observing his wife's usual seductiveness, Juan Carlos turned to Jake. "Mr. Hardesty, are you aware of Brazil's fine art collections? Nowhere else in the world are gathered so many Renoir, Van Gogh, Goya, and of course, Degas sculptures. They are my favorite. And you, sir, do you prefer modernists, traditionalists, or impressionists?"

Hardesty redirected his attention to his host. "Well, sir, truth to tell, I've always been partial to Russells and Remingtons."

Though Colonel Morton's Washington lobbyist might feign airs of a hill country redneck, given his base of operation in his nation's capital, Adrianna seriously doubted he felt out of place. "Would you like to see our private art collection, Jake? It's quite impressive."

"It'd be my pleasure, ma'am."

Adrianna stood, took Jake's hand and escorted him from the library.

Once his wife and the lobbyist left the room, Rojas dispensed with good manners. "Four hundred thousand dollars I have invested in Operation *Tejano*, Colonel. For that much I'm entitled to a guarantee Senator Creighton wins both his senate and presidential campaigns."

"Damn it, Juan Carlos, I wish I could guarantee a victory, but my country isn't some damn banana republic. We've funneled your money plus that of others into Andrew Smith's campaign. At this point we're scheming to pick Creighton's opponent for the general election, not get involved in the damn presidential race."

Juan Carlos' voice was low. "But can the money ever be traced to me and my associates in Bogota?"

"Never. That much I can guarantee."

"I need to hear details from your man Hardesty. How is he pulling off such an operation? That is why I requested this meeting in the first place."

Adrianna and Jake returned to the room. Before they could be seated Morton asked, "Juan Carlos, why don't you tell Jake about that restored art museum? I believe it's my turn two see your private collection."

Dan had alerted Jake to Rojas's probable request for details on Operation *Tejano*. Although they had originally agreed to keep all information on a need-to-know basis, Morton had instructed now was the time to placate Rojas with a few specifics.

Rojas ran his hands over his dark, pomaded hair. "Sit down, Mr. Hardesty. You are probably in need of a rest after your private time with my charming wife. I know Colonel Morton has informed you of my participation in *Tejano*. Now he is seeking even more money. Before I commit, I need information on how you are utilizing the funds."

"I understand your concern, Mr. Rojas. Here's how it works. After your funds are deposited in a Zurich bank account, it's split up. Most of it comes across the Mexican border into Texas in the back of produce trucks."

"What? Produce, in trucks, across the border? That's the craziest thing I've ever heard!"

"So crazy that no Border Patrol agent with drug sniffing dogs is going to be snoopin' for greenbacks among the lettuce. Plus, their focus now days is elsewhere."

"Elsewhere, what do you mean ... elsewhere?"

"What I mean is the US Treasury Department is focusing on money laundering. Customs Service agents have been instructed to concentrate on halting bulk shipments of cash being smuggled out of the US."

Rojas smiled and leaned back. "Ahh, now I see. They check for money going out of country but not for money coming in."

Jake clinked his glass with Juan Carlos'. "You got it, pardner. We slip right on through."

"All right, but once the money comes in, what becomes of it?"

"Once in, we divvy up the money and distribute it to our political operatives in key counties throughout South Texas. Let's just say, come election day there'll be plenty of street money to pay off *hombres* who go to the polling places. They will know exactly who to vote for, if they know what's good for 'em."

"Your South Texas sounds like our South America. I have renewed appreciation, Mr. Hardesty, for how you manipulate your political system. I always felt you *Americanos* too often left the important business of elections to chance. Tell me more."

"We also transfer some cash to bank accounts in Dallas and Houston, to legitimate sounding companies formed to do international business. Certain people then get paid for services rendered. We refer to them as 'straw donors'. The understanding is it would be unhealthy if they did not also contribute an equal amount to Andrew Smith's campaign."

Rojas's eyebrow arched. "But what if someone checks out these donors?"

"Not to worry. The FEC doesn't have enough staff to do that. After all, we're talking about a party primary race in one state. No telling how many house and senate elections will be on ballots around the country."

"But what about someone from McDonald's campaign, a newspaper or some interested person? What's to prevent them from snooping around?"

Jake laughed. "So what if they did? Without some extensive background investigations they wouldn't see anything other than law abiding citizens taking part in democracy. The Smith campaign would report the names, addresses and employers on the FEC forms, just like all the other federal campaigns."

After several more revelations about the operation, Juan Carlos glanced up, noting his wife's and Morton's return. "I am satisfied with what you have revealed. You do good work, my friend. I will talk to the colonel regarding further investments in Operation *Tejano*. Maybe I cannot cast a vote in the United States, but with your help, I will have significant influence in selecting the next President of the United States." The Brazilian political investor rose and guided Hardesty toward the dining room.

Three hours later, a limousine delivered Morton and Hardesty to the Hotel Moffarrej. Walking to their rooms Jake said, "With all due respect, Colonel, I don't like informing complete strangers about *Tejano's* operations, especially some guy in Brazil of all places."

"I understand, Jake. Usually I feel the same way, but this had to be an exception. I can assure you Juan Carlos is no stranger to me. I've known him many years."

"That right? Well, if it's all so damn-fired important, I'd appreciate it if you'd let me in on why this dude gets VIP treatment? Why does he get info on how *Tejano* actually functions?"

Morton paused and faced his partner. "First, let me say the evening was very successful, in no small part due to your disclosures. I thank you for that. Juan Carlos agreed to wire another eight hundred thousand Brazilian *reals* to Zurich within the week. That's approximately a half million US dollars. In return he insisted we reveal some of the operation to him in case he needs to relate it to his money sources in Colombia."

"Colombia? What the hell! There's no one in that God forsaken country but cocaine dealers and crooked politicians bought and paid for so those drug czars can make a killin' dealing dope. Damn it, what's the fucking deal?" Jake's chest heaved.

Morton reached over and patted Jake on the shoulder. "Calm down, my man. We, that is you and I, are not dealing directly with any Colombians. Only Juan Carlos is."

"I guess that makes it all okay. I'll be sure and tell the DEA and FBI when they come knockin' on my door. Being brought up on federal conspiracy charges by the Bureau's Campaign Finance Task Force was not part of my original game plan."

Morton shook his head and smiled. "Relax, partner. I doubt that's going to happen."

"You doubt?" Jake replied, raising his voice. "Can't you be just a bit more encouraging than 'you doubt'? Just who the hell are Rojas's contacts? More importantly, why would the Colombians give a rat's ass about what we're doing?"

"You don't want to know nor do you need to know the name of his sources. As a matter of fact, I'm not even sure myself at this point."

"I don't know, Colonel. What if *Tejano* is uncovered, especially this foreign money shit?"

"Don't worry, I'm telling you, there's no paper trail. And why they are investing is none of our business. As a matter of fact, I don't want to know."

Jake wiped his face with his hands. "I've had about all I can stomach for one night. I've got to sleep on this. I think things are getting out of hand."

"I don't like it anymore than you do, Jake. Frankly, when I first contacted him, I had no idea Juan Carlos would be using Colombian money."

"Sounds like ol' J.C. is a laundry man himself. Just another middle man in the food chain."

"I do have a comfort level, Jake. As I said, I've known Juan Carlos a long time, and I trust him." As Jake unlocked his door, Morton placed a companionable arm around Hardesty's shoulder. "Listen, go get some sleep. We've got a lot more traveling do tomorrow. Let's meet for breakfast at eight."

Dan Morton stepped into the hotel's penthouse suite and passed through the living room and briefly stopped at the bar in the dining room, where he poured a final nightcap. In the bedroom he slipped out of his tuxedo and into the hotel's bathrobe the maid had laid out on the king size bed. He went out on the balcony to relax before retiring.

Except for the Spartan living conditions, he missed the Army since his retirement. The money he made back then paled in comparison, but the power he once had was his greatest reward.

It felt good to be in charge again. This time not just in command of a company or a battalion of troops, but of a developing world-wide network that would influence not only American but international politics.

But now there was the potential problem of Mr. Jake Hardesty, lobbyist extraordinare. Was his partner in crime going soft on him? It was Jake Hardesty's ingenious idea in the first place to run this scam. Shit, the whole thing was as illegal as hell and Jake knew it. If it were uncovered, the FBI and Justice Department would run out of paper setting forth all of the federal campaign election laws they had violated. High risk. High reward. That's what made this game exciting.

So why was the fucking guy suddenly getting so self-righteous about using a little drug money? No telling what Hardesty would think if he knew about the Russian Mafia participation. Hell, all offshore campaign contributions are illegal, even if they've been given by the Russian Orthodox Church or the Vatican. He finished off his drink and headed for bed.

Five floors below, Jake Hardesty threw his tux jacket on the floor and struggled in frustration to remove the pearl studs from his cuffs. Stripped to his boxers, he went into the bathroom to get ready for bed. Eye drops burned as he tried to ease the irritation from a night of smoking and drinking. After brushing his teeth, he grabbed for the aspirin and blood pressure meds.

Hardesty struggled to recognize his own face in the bathroom mirror. "God, what happened to my original idea? What the hell is Dan Morton doing?"

Flicking off the lights, he let his weight collapse onto the bed without taking the time to pull back the covers. His stomach churned. Jake quickly sat up to avoid regurgitating the acidity from the rich food and alcohol. A bottle of antacid on his night stand provided some relief. Jake sat, clutching the bottle and thought about the evening's revelations. He listened to his heavy breathing for a while, then laid back down.

After what seemed like hours of tossing and turning, he awoke, covered with sweat, his thoughts only on *Tejano*.

CHAPTER 13

▼

AUSTIN, TEXAS
OCTOBER 22

"And that, ladies and gentlemen, is why I want to be your United States Senator. I want to represent you, the people of Austin here in the heart of Texas and the folks in Amarillo up in the Panhandle. Those out in Alpine in the Big Bend. And the folks in San Augustine County over in the East Texas Piney Woods. I want to speak for all Texans, not for the fat cat Washington lobbyists. Not for the special interests groups feeding at the public trough."

Jennifer Spencer vigorously joined in the applause that persisted in interrupting Warren McDonald's speech.

Just like I wrote it, Suzanne mused. She turned to Jennifer standing next to her in the crowded ballroom of the Driskell Hotel. "Well, you came and you saw. The question is, did you conquer? After your in-depth study of Smith's FEC reports, did you arrive at any startling conclusions? Are aliens from Mars or the Mafia funneling money to our little school teacher?" Stuffing a copy of McDonald's speech in her well-worn attaché, the campaign manager made no attempt to hide her smirk.

Suzanne's nonchalant attitude was irritating, but Jennifer refused to let her emotions show. Her eyes focused on McDonald concluding his well-rehearsed speech. "Andrew Smith is collecting and reporting pretty big bucks, with a lot of money coming out of the Dallas-Fort Worth area and Houston, but I still think he's spending more than his contributions justify."

Suzanne's gaze drifted over the crowd, noting a number of local lobbyists clapping begrudgingly. Even though they disagreed with him on the issues, these well-heeled men and women banked on McDonald being the likely winner of the party primary. Damn the issues. He was a big time Houston corporate lawyer who had come close to being elected attorney general in the last election. He had the contacts and should be able to raise enough money to make a decent television buy in most of the state's twenty media markets. Picking the winner was the only thing that mattered to these pros. "So, my dear Jennifer, just what are you saying?"

"I don't think all of Smith's commercial airline travel, meals, hotel bills, advertising and staff expenses are showing up on his FEC reports. For all the campaigning he's doing, he's got to be spending and raising more than he's reporting to the Feds."

Suzanne's interest was piqued. "Hmm, maybe he's getting it in cash. Or someone with his campaign staff is."

"He's also getting a lot of max-out givers, and their addresses are in the big cities. Some are from out of state, LA and New York to name just a couple of places. Why, pray tell, would they give to an unknown, untested public school teacher?"

Suzanne smiled and waved at some of the volunteers, leaving now that Warren had finished. Maybe Spencer was onto something after all, maybe there was something shady going on. "Let's go get a drink." She motioned that they follow the hangers-on into the hotel's lobby bar.

Once settled onto the richly upholstered bar stools, Suzanne motioned for a waiter. "Bourbon on the rocks. What about you, Jen?"

"Just a glass of water," Jennifer told the bartender.

"I understand your concern about PACs giving to Smith. It's unusual they'd be backing an unknown like Andrew Smith," Suzanne said. "How 'bout Warren's list? Any of the same names on his reports?"

"Nope. Hell, he's lucky to be getting half of what that teacher is reporting. Oh, I know he's got the support of a few of his lobby friends here in Austin, but none of the heavy hitters outta D.C. Most all of our money is coming from his Houston buddies and those in other parts of the state who supported him in the AG race." Jennifer chewed a handful of spicy peanuts, then washed them down with several swallows of ice water before hastily ordering a gin and tonic.

"Tell you what, Spencer, why don't you take some time off from your law practice and go up to the Dallas-Fort Worth area. Contact a few of the people who've given to Smith. Make up something about doing an independent survey. Say it's for a college political science course or some bullshit like that. Find out who they support and why. Do some one-on-one interviews. Talk to as many as you can, then let's get back together in a week or so and see what your amateur detective work has yielded."

"You mean you believe there might be more here than meets the eye?"

"I don't know about that, but I do find it pretty weird anyone would be throwing that much money Smith's way. It doesn't follow political logic, but let's not jump to conclusions yet."

"I say, is this seat taken?"

Jennifer and Suzanne had been so engrossed in conversation they hadn't noticed the man who had come up behind them. Suzanne looked at her companion then shrugged. "Be our guest, it's a free country."

Forcing a pleasant smile, Seregi Yazkov extended his hand. "Good evening, ladies. I'm Jonathan Hyde-Bourke. And whom might I have the privilege of meeting?" he asked in a clipped British accent before signaling the waiter for another round.

"Chism, Suzanne Chism." She stretched across Jennifer to shake his hand. "I'm campaign manager for the future United States Senator in the ballroom. The one who just made a world class speech, thanks to yours truly. And this is Jennifer Spencer."

Sergei shook and held Jennifer's hand. "What a delightful coincidence. I read in the student newspaper that Mr. McDonald would be speaking, so I came to listen and learn more about your political system. I'm a graduate student at the London School of

Economics, but I'm here for the semester studying at the University of Texas Business School. You are quite right, it was a jolly good talk." He released his firm grip and smiled at the attractive young woman seated inches away.

His stare made Jennifer uncomfortable. "Well, he's our man," she finally remarked. "We expect him to win, the Senate, the White House, and who knows, before long Warren will be speaking to your Parliament."

"I was very impressed," Yazkov replied, working hard on the British accent.

Suzanne interjected, "Well, in that case, come over to the campaign headquarters and lick some stamps for us. Hell, who knows, you might even get to meet the candidate himself. Tell the staff I sent you."

"That would be quite exciting. Thank you. Perhaps in the next week or so. I'm frightfully busy right now, studies and all, you know. Might I see you there, Miss Spencer?"

Jennifer blushed slightly. The man's close proximity and the aroma of his cologne were almost overwhelming. At first, she thought he was bald but on closer scrutiny, decided his head had been shaved, leaving only a thin rim of graying hair at the temples. He had a closely cropped brown mustache and piercing blue eyes. He was smartly attired in a brown suit and dark blue shirt open at the neck.

"It's possible. I'm usually there when I come to town." When his thigh brushed hers, she immediately wiggled her barstool away.

"Come to town? So where might home be?"

"I'm just a volunteer, I have to work for a living."

"And what would that be?"

Her forehead creased, her mouth frowned. "Let's just say I have a pretty demanding job. And speaking of that, it's getting late. I gotta hit the road. Nice to meet you, Mister Bourke."

She pushed a ten dollar bill into Suzanne's hand and kissed her on the cheek. "Here's for the drinks, keep the change." Jennifer managed a polite smile, giving her hand reluctantly when the man extended his. She had taken only a few steps when suddenly she snapped her fingers. "Oh, Suzanne, I almost forgot. I'll run up to Dallas as soon as possible and do that checking you suggested. I'll call you at headquarters and let you know what I uncover. Thanks for the advice. *Ciao.*" She turned again and hurried toward the hotel exit.

Sergei watched Jennifer depart, then redirected his attention to Suzanne. "An impressive young woman you have volunteering for Mr. McDonald. Smart and very attractive, I might add."

"Yeah, she's a gal with a mission." Suzanne tossed some bills on the bar, then reached for her attaché.

Sergei handed the money back to her. "No, no, my treat, I insist. This has been an unexpected pleasure to meet you both. And what mission might the fair Ms. Spencer be on?"

"Thanks very much. Next time it's on me." Suzanne stuffed the bills in her wallet. "Oh, she's got a theory about Warren's opponents and some unusual looking fundraising she thinks might be going on. She … aw, never mind. I don't think you'd find it very interesting. Pretty boring stuff, actually."

Realizing she had blurted more than she intended, Suzanne changed the subject. "Say, I was serious. Why don't you come by headquarters and give us some help. It ain't Number Ten Downing Street, but it'd give you a chance to learn something other than dry business theory. You can use that sophisticated accent of yours to do a little call time and fundraising for Warren. Who knows, that pretty young lawyer from Houston might come back while you're there."

"Oh, a barrister. Now why doesn't that surprise me?"

"Damn it," Suzanne exclaimed under her breath. "What the hell. The fact I told you she's a Houston trial lawyer ain't gonna tear up the world. Listen, I'm sorry, but I have to go too. Nice meeting you, Mr. Hyde, or Mr. Bourke, or however you say it." She extended her hand. "I've got another long day tomorrow on the campaign trail. No rest for the weary, the old saying goes."

Once she departed, Sergei Yazkov ordered a black Russian and thought about what he had learned about Warren McDonald's campaign. He had hoped to meet McDonald's campaign manager at the event. That was precisely why he came. The chance introduction of Jennifer Spencer had proved even more intriguing. What unusual fundraising was it she thought was going on? Had this Jennifer Spencer stumbled on the project? Perhaps this Houston lawyer merited closer investigation.

CHAPTER 14

▼

CHICAGO
NOVEMBER 29

After tightening the belt on his trench coat, Bill York held onto the snap-brim hat that shielded his face from Chicago's wind-whipped mist. He was in town for two meetings, one with Rebecca Durham, the other with a noted Northwestern University economics professor, who would testify later in the week in opposition to tax legislation effecting e-commerce. Several of his clients vigorously opposed the measure and, having arranged for an expert witness, York wanted a last-minute review of his testimony. He needed no surprises.

Settled on the commuter train from the Evanston campus, he flipped through the *Chicago Tribune*. A headline caught his attention. Senator Russell Creighton had made a weekend stop in Gary, Indiana, where he laid out a ten-point program for economic re-vitalization of the nation's inner cities. He had gained endorsements from ten mayors in the Illinois-Indiana region.

"Madison Avenue," a recorded voice matter-of factly announced over the public address system, as more passengers boarded for the remaining twenty minute ride downtown. While brown brick apartment buildings and retail stores whizzed by the train windows, York thought of Rebecca. He was anxious to learn how the Dan Morton-financed political operation was progressing. At the Chicago Avenue stop, York and a throng of other pedestrians ascended the steep steps into the bustling city.

He spotted Rebecca waiting in front of the Water Tower on Michigan Avenue. "Hope you haven't been waiting long." Bill gave the politically correct air kiss and hug. "How's the Gun Owner's regional conference going?"

"Fine, our opening session just let out. I only had to walk a couple of blocks. Speaking of walking, let's do it. Keeps the blood circulating."

York took Rebecca's arm as they jaywalked in front of cabs and city buses lining the curb lane. "You know, it does me good to get out here to the heartland of America."

Rebecca lifted the hem of her coat to avoid a film of mud that was forming on the ground. "And why is that, may I ask?"

"Because it confirms my theory of the political process. I doubt very seriously that the people I saw on the train or these around us have any interest whatsoever in politics. Do you think it really matters to any of these jerks who'll be the next president of the United States?"

"You don't know that. What did you do, take a poll?" Rebecca challenged. They both ignored a Salvation Army band performing while a woman dutifully rang a small bell beside the customary iron pot hanging on a tripod.

"I don't have to commission a damn poll to know that. I can tell by just looking at 'em. They're only thinking about what they can waste money on, selecting some damn trinket for a relative or friend who has no need for it and who'll probably give it away next year."

Rebecca pulled on York's coat sleeve, directing him back across Michigan Avenue. "Well, I care about politics and so do you. The people at my AGOA meeting care. And it's our job to see that these people care, that they want Russell Creighton to be their president."

"Yeah, that's right, I do care." York gained a tighter grip on the briefcase clutched under his arm, protecting it from the crowd. "I love it, but not for the same reasons as you. It's kinda like playing a game of chess. These local yokels are pawns we move on the game board of national politics. The congressmen and senators are the knights and bishops. The king is the White House to be protected or captured, and the queen, she's the *numero uno* piece to be manipulated, the candidate. We win this game and we win big time."

"Speaking of the game, I need more cash for our Texas project."

York stopped and turned. "You what?"

Rebecca raised a hand. "Don't start on me just yet, Bill. At least hear me out on this."

"So how much more do you need?"

"Thirty thousand."

"Thirty grand? How in the hell do you intend to spend it?"

"My operatives will be paying kids to leaflet cars in shopping centers for the next several days, leading up to Andrew Smith's big Galveston shindig on December 7th. I'll distribute most of it to get a crowd out for the event."

"Thirty thou just for that? I've already given you more than two million from the Zurich account."

"Tickets are a hundred bucks a pop, five hundred for sponsors and a grand for patrons for the big do. Plus, I came up with a great fund-raising gimmick that will raise money as well as a hell of a lot of national press attention."

"And just what is that, people paying big money to watch little Andy make a fool of himself? That shouldn't be too hard for him."

"No, better than that. A raffle. I got a handgun manufacturer in Fort Worth to donate one of his prize pistols to be given away. One of my guys persuaded Smith it's a great idea. He'll be a literal preacher of our constitutional right to bear arms or at least handguns against the terrorists."

"So who did you get to donate the weapon?" York asked, his voice filled with trepidation.

"One of our allies on Capitol Hill, Dan Morton. I was surprised how little it took for one of my Dallas members to convince him to do it, almost like he was already on board with our program."

In keeping with his deal with Jake Hardesty, York had not told Rebecca that Morton was the source for their funding and now was not the time or place to get into it. "So if there's a raffle, why do you need more money?"

"Simple. I intend to send people from Houston, maybe some from the Beaumont-Port Arthur area. A lot of the money you give me will be spread out across the upper Gulf coast so that they can go and give. I think it's a gangbuster idea."

"But is it safe? That's a hell of a lot to drop at one event. Are you sure there's no way the money can be traced to us, especially with this gun-give-away crap? That's really going to attract attention."

"No problem." Durham checked her watch. "My operatives have been careful in spreading out the dough, both for the raffle as well as for contributions to the campaign for tickets. Some will report in their own names, others will give in the name of relatives. Smith's FEC reports have got to be pumped up. He's got to prove that the high rollers as well as the commoners are supporting him."

Rebecca waited for a comment, then grew angry at his continued silence. "Listen, York, don't flake on me now. This damn thing is working and Smith's leading in the polls. Isn't that what you wanted in the first place?"

Bill York stopped walking and pulled the attaché from under his arm. Pulling out a large manila envelope, he handed it to the AGOA political director. "Okay, you got it, literally. Here's fifty grand. I figured you wanted this meeting to ask for money, not for a re-play of our nice time together in San Diego." He cast a knowing smile. "That's all for right now. But, Rebecca, please be careful. We're throwing a hell of a lot a money around, and now with this goofy gun raffle idea, we don't want to raise any eyebrows."

Rebecca kissed him full on the mouth. "Thanks, sweetheart, and I'm truly sorry I don't have more free time for us. Listen, don't sweat the political stuff, I have no more intention of this becoming public than you. After all, I'm a hell of a lot closer to the action." She squeezed York's hand. "I gotta get back to the conference before I'm missed. Thanks so much. I'll be in touch."

CHAPTER 15

▼

GALVESTON
DECEMBER 7

Wearing a wind breaker and khaki pants, her shoulder length hair mingling with the East Bay's damp breeze, Savannah Spencer could easily have passed for one of Jennifer's contemporaries. The sky was overcast and at half past twelve, Jennifer felt they were in for a cool afternoon and evening on Galveston Island. Her mother's advice had proven helpful weeks earlier, and Jennifer suspected that she would have insight about anything gleaned at the Andrew Smith campaign event they would be attending. "Are we having fun yet?"

"Sure," Savannah cheerfully replied. "It's always great to be with you, wherever and whenever. You know this weather reminds me of the trip your father and I took to London three Christmases ago. I imagine old Charles Dickens would appreciate the city's annual 'Dickens on the Strand' festivities." She pointed at a group of high school students roasting chestnuts on a barbecue grill and bagging them for sale, while carolers in period attire performed nearby.

"Look at this." Jennifer handed her mother an 81/2 x 11 sheet of light green paper plucked off a parked car's windshield. "It appears

Warren's opponent is pretty well-organized. Those teenagers are placing these fliers on every parked car."

Savannah read the leaflet. "Come meet the next United States Senator for the Great State of Texas—Andy Smith will be in the Hotel Galvez Ballroom at three p.m., Saturday, December 7th for a handgun raffle to benefit his winning campaign. Win a Morton Nine Millimeter, plus be a part of the Galveston County Welcoming Committee. Meet the candidate as he strolls Broadway between two and three p.m.."

Jennifer's eyes widened. "What kind of political event is this? Have you ever heard of a more bizarre idea, raffling off a handgun of all things!"

"I'm more intrigued by what's not printed. I wonder who created these?"

"The Smith campaign, I imagine. Who else would be doing it?"

"If that's the case, they're breaking the law. Look down here." Savannah pointed to the bottom of the flyer.

Jennifer shrugged. "I don't see anything."

"That's my point, there's no political disclaimer telling who printed and paid for it."

"Damn, you're right. Some detective I am! You'd certainly think that little school teacher's campaign staff would at least know the state and federal laws. Let's ask one of those kids where he got these."

"Big white dude over on Broadway," the youngster replied to Jennifer's inquiry. "He's paying us, and he also give us money to pay people to go line Broadway when that guy Smith comes to town at two."

With a more complete description of the money man, Jennifer and Savannah drove ten blocks south and surveyed the crowd. Fifteen minutes later Jennifer spotted their target.

"Yeah, I paid the kids to hand 'em out and get up a crowd. So what?" A large man sporting a shaggy beard and unkempt hair walked the street handing out flyers as he answered Jennifer. He wore a red shirt and coveralls. "Nothing wrong with that, is there? Ain't breaking no friggin' law."

Jennifer smiled, took a flyer, neatly folded and stuffed it in the back pocket of her jeans. "Didn't say you were. Just curious. Have a nice day."

"Fuck you, damn nosy broads," he muttered under his breath.

Once the two women were a hundred yards down the sidewalk, the man opened the door of an '85 Eldorado parked at the nearby curb and tossed the flyers into the driver's seat. He punched in a number on his cell phone. "Ms. Durham, Red Davis here. I'm in Galveston. You said call if anything came up."

The political director for the AGOA could barely hear her operative over the phone static. "What's the problem?"

"Just thought you'd want to know, two dames were asking about the leaflets." He gave Rebecca their descriptions. "Definitely not cops. Maybe from another campaign. No, they didn't give any names or identification. Sure, no problem. I'll get a couple of my boys to tail 'em and take care of that. I'll call ya back when I've got more info. Ten four."

Rebecca Durham hung up the receiver in her Falls Church, Virginia, office. *Damn, I wonder if they noticed there's no political disclaimer? Who are these two women snooping around, asking questions anyway? Federal Election Commission? Texas Secretary of State? Doubtful. Neither elections enforcement office have enough field staff for such activity. McDonald campaign staff? Possible. It would be just like Warren McDonald to dispatch political spies trying to catch some foul-up, especially since Smith is so far ahead in the polls.*

Rebecca Durham despised the Houston lawyer and would not put such tactics past him. The truth would be known soon enough. She would decide what action to take once she knew with whom she was dealing.

Two hours later, Jennifer and Savannah stood by the low wall in front of the Galvez lobby watching supporters and curiosity seekers push through the entry. The sun had set, and a gentle breeze coming off Galveston Bay chilled them.

Savannah made out the crude lettering of a hand-made sign carried by a man silently parading in front of the entry way, "Andy Smith Sticks To His Guns."

The Spencer women watched another Smith supporter locked in vehement debate with a gun control protester a few yards away. "Andy Smith needs to be elected to the United States Senate for only one reason," the supporter exclaimed. "He stands up for the Second Amendment to the Constitution. He believes what I believe, that the Second Amendment establishes an absolute right to own a handgun. People must be able to protect themselves from the terrorists."

The protester, a young woman Jennifer estimated to be in her mid-twenties, cradled an infant on her hip. "Well, I'm sorry, sir, but I think this raffle is utterly tasteless. I think it's terrible for Mr. Smith to raise money for his campaign through the sale of something that has been used to assassinate schoolchildren in growing numbers the past few years."

"Yeah, I agree." Another man shouted at the sign carrier. "It's insensitive, down right abominable. Remember this, championing the Second Amendment requires that you get nominated first, and I don't think this sort of thing will appeal to the majority of Texas primary voters."

A few minutes later, using fictitious names, Jennifer and her mother signed in and picked up Smith for Senate circular stickers to wear on their jackets. They paid cash for the entry fee and merged into the crowd. Savannah purchased cocktails at one of the five cash bars located around the perimeter of the noisy ballroom, while her daughter made her way to the seafood buffet in the middle of the room. Watching people elbow their way to get to the iced shrimp and crab fingers, Jennifer concluded it was the food, not the school teacher, who attracted much of the capacity crowd.

Jennifer introduced herself as Mary Jo Dixon and her mother as her aunt, Lou Beth Stewart. They worked the crowd, eliciting vital information, then smoothly moved on to the next unsuspecting interviewee. Savannah approached a man in line to order a beer. "Excuse me, sir. Can you tell me what Andy is giving away at this raffle?"

"Oh, yes, ma'am." The man respectfully took off his Stetson. "It's a nine millimeter Morton handgun. I figure it's worth about five hundred dollars. The Morton Nine is flat and solid as granite, like a polished black tombstone, no heavier than a good 'ol cowboy boot." He held up his hand and motioned toward the ceiling as if squeezing off a round. "It's a semiautomatic—squeeze-squeeze, bang-bang, no pausing to re-cock, really popular with law enforcement and the military."

"And why is that?" Savannah paid for the man's beer in return for his mini-lecture.

"'Cause of what they call 'stopping power.' To put it bluntly, it'll knock a terrorist dead on his ass with one shot. Excuse the language." His face flushed with embarrassment.

Savannah smiled. "Don't worry about that, Mister Roper," she replied, glancing at his name tag. "I wasn't born yesterday. I have a son in the Navy stationed in the Persian Gulf and a husband who loves to hunt." She surveyed the crowd and estimated nearly five hundred people packed the ballroom. "Looks like this little gimmick, uh, I mean raffle, has turned out the supporters."

With a free beer in hand, the stranger was now equally free with his comments. "Yep, I read in this morning's paper that Andy even set up an Internet website. Once the word hit the political chat rooms, raffle tickets for the gun give-away began selling around the world. It's not only a chance to win a great little firearm, but to make a political statement as well."

"What do you mean, make a political statement?"

Mr. Roper turned admiring eyes on Jennifer. "What I mean, honey, is that Texans are tired of the gubment tryin' to take away our basic freedoms. By our actions here at this raffle we show 'em we are willin' to put our money where our mouth is. Look, here he comes right now. Don't he look great?"

Before Jennifer could ask another question, Roper had rushed to join a group gathering near the stage for the candidate's stump speech. Andrew Smith came to the podium dressed in a western-cut outfit, a six-shooter in one hand and the modern nine millimeter in the other. "My fellow Texans, during the roaring twenties there were no muggings or rapes. Individuals were polite to one another. That was because every man who walked the street had a gun. Just like here in Texas, *all* Americans should be able to walk the streets with concealed handguns."

Roper and a few others were the first to start the round of applause, interrupting Smith. After a few seconds, Smith grinned and motioned for silence so he could continue. "Gun control is a slippery slope. One thing leads to another, and in the end you lose your right to defend yourself, your home, your family. I'm telling you, my friends, if more Americans were armed, if more people could carry concealed handguns, crime would plummet. The terrorists and other criminals wouldn't know who was packin' heat and who wasn't."

A man Jennifer estimated to be in his seventies shouted: "That's right, Andy boy, tell 'em like it is." Again the crowd broke into rousing cheers.

"As you know, before I started this campaign I was a high school civics teacher in Lufkin. I've talked with my fellow school teachers around the state during this campaign, and they all say the same thing, if they are allowed to carry concealed firearms, school violence will decrease, maybe even be prevented all together. Where I come from, if a teacher could lay his handgun on the desk to show he meant business, we could maintain school discipline."

Savannah turned to watch a wildly cheering woman hoist a homemade poster marked "Teachers for Andy—Andy for teachers."

Grinning with satisfaction, the candidate again motioned for silence. "I want to be your United States Senator and go to Washington for you. But I must tell you, I don't trust the government. If the government knows who has guns, one day there could be another Hitler." Smith dramatically pointed to a couple in the front row. "There could be a knock on your door in the night and some uniformed bruiser saying, 'You have two guns, we want 'em.'"

The gray-haired lady to whom Smith pointed, clutched her husband's forearm as if the Gestapo in hob-nailed boots was standing in front of her.

"And let me say this to our friends in the news media." Smith turned and stared directly at a young man holding a television camera. "We don't use the word 'weapon.' Why? 'Cause it's a bad ol' buzzword.

A baseball bat is just a baseball bat until it's used as a weapon. Use the term firearms. You call a guy who likes cars a car 'buff' but one who likes guns a gun nut. Gun control is communism. A government for the people and by the people doesn't fear an armed populace. If strict gun control made a place safe, the District of Columbia would be the safest place on the planet. Even down here in the great state of Texas, we sure know that ain't the case."

The crowd roared with raucous laughter and couldn't contain itself as thunderous applause filled the ballroom. "Thank you for coming, ladies and gentleman. Help put Andy Smith in the Senate, and God bless Texas!" Smith waved farewell as the brass from one of the local high school bands trumpeted "The Eyes of Texas." He stepped down from the stage and plunged into the enthusiastic crowd.

Jennifer whispered under her breath behind a cupped hand. "Mom, can you believe this reaction? Maybe there's something seriously wrong with me because I agree with the protesters outside. This Smith guy's scary. If he gets the nomination and beats Russell Creighton, America will look even more like the wild and woolly west. There'll probably be gun-fights in every bar on Saturday nights. I hate to think about the increase in number of the cases of road rage on our overcrowded freeways."

Savannah held a finger to her mouth. "Shhh … it's time for the raffle. This ought to be even better, or worse, depending on one's point of view."

The crowd, pumped by Andy Smith's self-righteous speech, hooted as Donna Sue McKitrick, the Galveston county campaign chair, stepped onto the stage. Decked out in a Lone Star flag of Texas outfit and dangling Texas earrings, the buxom blonde reached deep into a barrel filled with thousands of ten dollar raffle tickets. She pulled one out and handed it down to Smith who studied the handwriting on the winning ducat. "And the winner of a brand new Morton nine millimeter is none other than Mr. Jimmy Bob Huntley of Vidor over in Jefferson County." Holding the handgun high above his head, he called out like a TV quiz show host, "Jimmy Bob, come on down and claim your grand prize!"

"Well, I'll be damn." The retired refinery worker hoisted his enormous frame onto the stage to rub up against Donna Sue. "I ain't never won anything in my life, 'ceptin' a trip to the casino over in Lake Charles." He caressed the pistol with beefy hands. "Don't mess with Texas, and now don't no one be messing with me is all I gotta say … and oh yeah, let's send Andy Smith to Washington!"

The crowd cheered. Television cameras and reporters from around the state crowded in to record for posterity the latest twist in grassroots fundraising.

"Mr. Huntley, what's your reaction to being the winner of this first-ever political raffle of a weapon?" a reporter shouted.

Jimmy Bob pulled on a strap of his coveralls and pondered the weighty question. "Well, I'm a strong believer in our right to bear arms. That's why Davy Crockett and all them other boys died at the Alamo for us."

An Hispanic reporter bit her lip and tried to focus on her job. "Could you explain that last remark for our viewers?"

Jimmy Bob scratched his crew cut with the nine millimeter. "Hmm, not sure I can right now, with all this excitement. But I can tell you this, me and the missus got us a sign in our front yard I made myself. It says 'Never Mind the Dog, Beware of Owner.' I painted a picture of a gun pointing straight at the trespasser." Huntley put the Morton in the pocket of his coveralls and jumped down from the stage where he was surrounded by those wishing they held his winning ticket. "That's all I got to say for now," he yelled back.

From in front of the stage, Smith shouted over the noise. "Friends, this is not just about raising money. This has given those who feel their rights under the Second Amendment are being eroded a chance to make a statement. Someone is finally willing to stand up for what they believe in. If anything, this raffle might make 'em more active in our campaign to take back Washington for the people."

With his final remark, the candidate returned to working the crowd and the obligatory baby kissing.

Some supporters wore crisp white shirts and ties, others were in more casual weekend attire. Jennifer noticed that a number of them wore baseball caps with the American Gun Owners Association logo.

She wedged in close enough to overhear Smith paraphrase the Bible to one admirer. "Those gun grabbers are drunk with wine and we're filled with the spirit. We're the ones doing the Lord's work."

Smith then turned to a reporter from one of the national networks who was standing next to Savannah. "This is not a gimmick, sir. I believe in what I'm doing here. Back home in Lufkin, I'm an honorary Angelina County deputy sheriff, and I got a badge out in my pickup to prove it."

"But, Mr. Smith, what do you say to your critics who contend that handguns such as this Morton nine millimeter are used to commit crimes and kill school children?" a reporter shouted above the din of the crowd.

"I say that this raffle is nothing more than law-abiding citizens transferring legal property to another law-abiding citizen. It's not like we're walking down the street handing out guns left and right."

Jennifer turned to her mother, but spoke loud enough for others around to take notice. "These people want to make a statement, well, I have a statement for them. Hold a child's body after a nine-millimeter blows a hole in her face. I'm offended and ashamed that a U.S. Senate candidate could take what killed a little boy, like the one last week in the school shooting up in Fort Worth, and raffle it off as a prize. Let's get out of here. I've had about all the politics I can stand for one evening." Jennifer turned to leave, with Savannah hurrying to join her.

"That was the damnedest thing I've ever seen," Jennifer exclaimed as she headed her convertible north across the island causeway and onto the mainland.

Savannah tightened her seat belt. "As the old saying goes, 'that's politics for ya.' Now we've seen with our own eyes why we're supporting Warren McDonald over Andrew Smith."

She turned on the map light to study her notes. "So, let's see what we've got, information-wise. We have leaflets paid for by some undisclosed source, most likely the same folks who paid those boys to get people to line the streets to greet the candidate. Then we have this one-of-a-kind raffle thing."

Jennifer kept her eyes on the road as she headed across the Gulf Coast lowlands. "Did anybody admit they'd been given money for the raffle?"

Savannah perused her notes. "Not exactly. About twenty said someone had given them tickets. Whether those had been paid for or had been distributed by the campaign, I have no idea. That would be impossible to determine at this point."

Jennifer whizzed past a slow moving eighteen-wheeler, then eased back into her lane. "Same with me. Ten or so said they'd been given free tickets to get in the place. We don't know if the Smith campaign comp'd them in, or someone else paid."

Savannah set her notes aside and crossed her arms. "Personally, I think the place was papered with starving dupes."

Jennifer momentarily took her eyes off the road and glanced at her mother. "What do you mean by that?"

"Just what you were referring to, complimentary tickets. That's a term we used in my day, when it was a big fundraiser but a lot of the crowd got in free. 'Papered' meaning freebies given to folks just to show up and make it look good for the press and the true believers."

"It was worse than that tonight," Jennifer said. "Many were obviously paid to be there or given money to contribute. I think it's possible Andy Smith and his campaign staff might not even know a thing about the illegalities."

"Why do you say that?" Savannah asked.

"Simple. First, the flyers had no disclaimer indicating who printed them. Surely Smith's not that dumb, although all that gun talk makes me wonder. Second, if Smith really wanted to raise money with that stupid raffle of his, why use his own funds to do it?"

"Maybe you're right, but we still don't know who the culprit is. I doubt the brains behind it is that guy who would barely talk to us out on Broadway. And what's more, why would anyone choose to illegally support Smith anyway? Your man Warren has a better chance of defeating Senator Creighton in the general election next fall."

Jennifer stared at the lights of the downtown Houston skyscrapers gleaming in the distance. "Maybe that's the point. Maybe someone is supporting a loser, some joker who hasn't got a snowball's chance in hell to be elected to the United States Senate. If he, she, they, whoever, can give money, they could just as easily cut it off at any time, if Andy Smith wins the party nomination."

Savannah pondered the theory before replying. "That's pretty far out, sweetheart. Your unknown contributors would have to be pretty well-heeled to be propping up some strawman for Russell Creighton to knock over in the Senate race."

Jennifer drove several more miles before breaking the silence. "Don't forget, Mr. Creighton also wants to be his party's presidential nominee. If he winds up with a weak opponent in his senate re-election race, he can focus on the national campaign and feel safe and secure back in Texas."

"So are you suggesting Creighton is behind the leafleting and other money you think's going to the Smith campaign?"

"Could be. Damn, I don't know, mom," Jennifer replied in frustration. "Maybe there's nothing here to start with. Maybe everything is legit. Maybe Smith is pumping up his own campaign to make himself look good. Maybe Creighton is behind it all, or then again, maybe he doesn't know a damn thing about it."

She slammed a fist against the steering wheel. "This is just so much bullshit! Warren's getting his ass beat, and now I'm beginning to think the funding of Smith's campaign might be connected to Creighton and his presidential ambitions. Frankly, I don't know what to think, and at this point I'm too tired to try and figure it all out anyway."

Savannah Spencer reached over and patted her daughter's arm. "Don't be jumping to conclusions yet, honey. Forget about it for a while and pay attention to the road. Let's get back to your apartment and relax. It'll all be there tomorrow for us to try and figure out."

Thirty minutes later Jennifer and her mother got out of the car and climbed the stairs to Jennifer's apartment. Once at the door, Savannah shook her head at the sound of a dog's ferocious barking.

"Lad must think he's a great guard dog," Savannah said as the golden retriever reared on his hind legs, licking Jennifer's face once the two women stepped inside and locked the door.

"Yeah, I love him. I'm really glad I got him last year. Don't know about the guard business, I think his bark's worse than his bite." Jennifer pushed the large animal to the floor, commanding him to sit.

"Why don't you take off your shoes and relax while I take him outside." Jennifer walked through the small two-bedroom apartment, returning with the dog's leash. "All is well, looks like he hasn't made a mess. Good thing we were only gone a few hours and got back when we did, though."

Savannah stood at the door and called after her daughter. "By the way, I'm glad you selected this apartment complex. It seems pretty secure. Even if Lad is not the best watchdog in the world. I don't think there's a lot to be worried about."

Two men sat in a car parked in front of Jennifer's apartment complex. "Yeah, I got the license number." The driver spoke into the cell phone. "I saw them go to apartment 204, where a big fucking dog greeted 'em at the door. The young one just took the dog out for a crap, I guess. Anything else you want us to do while we're here?"

Red Davis sat in Big Al's Bar B Q in Galveston. "No, you done good, boys. I'll report to the chief and we'll see what's next. Call it a night and come on back. There's a stash waitin' for you for your efforts."

The longshoreman snapped the cell phone closed and wiped white powder from beneath his nostrils. He would try and chill a while before reporting the latest development to Rebecca Durham.

CHAPTER 16

▼

VIENNA
JANUARY 9

Kathryn Morton soaked her lithe body in mineral oils and knew if she relaxed much longer she might doze off. Yesterday, she and Dan had experienced a tranquil ten-hour train ride through the snow-covered countryside of Germany and Austria. When Dan spoke of their reservations at the Palais Schwarzenberg, she had been delighted. The hotel, a former palace built in the early eighteenth century, was situated in a formal park, giving it the feel of a country estate.

Kathryn gently rested her head against the cool marble, bubbles engulfing the tips of her shoulder-length hair. Sipping a second glass of champagne, she listened to the strains of a Chopin waltz coming from the gardens outside their bedroom window. She and Dan would soon be in bed, and the thought of making love in the afternoon aroused her.

She heard the downstairs hallway door gently open and close. "Up here," she called to her husband, returning from his jog around the hotel grounds.

Moments later, Dan Morton entered the marble-tiled bath carrying a beer in one hand and an open champagne bottle in the other. His lean, muscular body glistened in sweat and his breathing had not returned to normal. "Well, you certainly look comfortable." He reached over and refilled her glass, then set the two bottles on the edge of the tub. "Looks like you've had a rough afternoon."

"You should try it sometime. This would be good for you. Thank you again for booking us here. Nothing can measure up to this."

Dan stood beside the oversized tub and gazed down at his wife. "A place fit for a queen they advertise, and a pretty damn good-looking one at that, I might add."

Kathryn reached over and gently massaged the front of his running shorts. "Mmm ... why don't you get in. The water's perfect." She gently tugged until she felt him react, then playfully reached out with both hands and slowly pulled his shorts until they fell to the floor.

Dan stepped into the bathtub, standing over her. "This European ambiance certainly brings out your very liberal arts side."

"Just you wait and see. I said thank you for bringing me here. Why don't you let me demonstrate my appreciation?" Seductively, she rose to her knees, gently kissing his chest.

Jake Hardesty stood in the warm sunlight, taking in the sights on the plaza outside the opera building across from the Bristol. He listened with amusement as costumed men and women made sales pitches to passing tourists for various evening performances around town. He glanced at his watch, almost two-thirty. He expected the Texas high roller to arrive shortly.

"Well, well, Mr. Hardesty, greetings and a warm welcome to the city of classical music."

Jake turned at the sound of Colonel Morton's familiar voice. His finger flicked at the feather in the Austrian mountain hat.

"Here's your ticket. We should be boarding in a few minutes."

"Ticket? Ticket for what?"

"I thought we'd kill three birds with one stone. Talk a little business, plus see the famous Vienna Woods. They do actually exist you know. That forest green touring car over there is ours."

Jake looked across the plaza to the limo marked Vienna Sightseeing Tours. "Well, I'm game for just about anything. So what's the third bird we're killing?"

Dan motioned Jake onto the waiting vehicle. "Don't worry, you'll find out soon enough. Just a little surprise I've arranged."

Their tour guide, Konrad, cheerfully welcomed them and commenced a steady narrative. As they passed nineteenth century apartment buildings along the Little Danube, a branch of the famous river of the same name, Morton got straight to the point. "Bring me up to date on *Tejano's* progress. Am I still getting my money's worth?"

Assuming *Tejano* would be the topic *du jour*, Jake had reviewed Rebecca Durham's report over breakfast, and was fully prepared for the briefing. "Yes, you can be assured of that, although we could always use more funding. Our main political operative has devised a great plan to help Andrew Smith's campaign. And Smith still doesn't even know what we're up to."

"Well, don't keep me in suspense. What's got you so excited?"

"We've hired a webmaster and moved into cyberspace. We're operating a covert campaign that is off the Federal Elections Commission's radar screen and will ensure Smith gets the nomination. Even if they did find out what we're doing, it is completely legit."

Jake began reciting key points in the Durham report. "To maintain secrecy, I'll simply refer to our political operative as the webmaster." He saw no reason to reveal Rebecca's identity to Morton. "Basically, we have two Internet campaigns. One uses e-mail, the other uses what is called a fan site."

"I know what e-mail is, so why don't you take me through that one first."

"It's really pretty simple. The webmaster has accumulated thousands of names and e-mail addresses of registered voters throughout Texas and combined them into various group lists. She then developed a very effective chain letter program."

"So what does she do with these groups?"

"Everyday she sends out notifications to each group and has them sorted in various ways."

"What do you mean, sorted?"

"She has organized them geographically. For example, if she knows Andrew Smith is traveling to a particular city for a campaign stop, she posts the information to an e-mail in a specific geographical area. Let's say Smith is going to Amarillo for a fundraiser next Thursday evening. She can spam it to Amarillo only, or to Potter and Randall counties, or to the entire Texas Panhandle if she wants. She encourages recipients to attend the event, and if they can, give money to Smith's campaign. Then she requests that recipients forward the message to friends and family using their personal e-mail address book."

"Interesting. Do you have any idea if it's effective?"

"Hell, yes, it is. We've heard from our snoops in his campaign that Smith is amazed at the size of the crowds he's seeing. We probably have a better electronic mail list than his campaign office."

"Pretty impressive."

"Yeah, you can say that again. Typically a person pays to have a website listed on a search engine, but we haven't gone that route for fear of detection. What we've done is put a link to the website in each e-mail we send out. Just point and click and bingo, you're there. The webmaster's received thousands of hits on the site every day by using the e-mail link."

"Isn't all of this regulated by the Federal Elections Commission? Sounds to me like you're doing something that could blow our cover."

Jake shook his head. "That's another great factor. The FEC has ruled a homemade web site is a form of volunteer political activity, specifically stating a fan site, as it's referred to, is not considered a financial contribution that has to be reported. Candidates have no control over it and no way to discover who set it up."

A broad smile crossed Morton's face and he slapped his partner on the back. "Good work. Damn good work, Jake. I'm real proud of you." He looked out the window to check his bearings. "Tell you what, why don't you save the rest for later. Let's sit back and enjoy the countryside." Morton faced forward, indicating he had heard enough for the time being.

The ancient buildings and heavy traffic were left far behind and Jake peered out the window at snow-capped mountains. As the car neared the quaint community of Baden, Konrad advised that in the eighteenth and nineteenth centuries the imperial family of Austria retreated here for the summer, bringing along their entourage. Some of Austria's most wealthy, he said, now called the area home.

Once in the small town, Jake was surprised when the car made an unscheduled stop at a wine tavern and picked up another passenger. Dan greeted the newcomer, introducing him to Jake as Urs Kaelin, an Austrian businessman.

"Herr Kaelin is a long time business colleague of mine," Dan explained, "and he's very interested in learning about Tejano."

Jake was startled at the mention of the word but closed his eyes and listened to the soothing intercom music. "Yes, go on."

"Actually, the real reason I asked you to come to Austria, Jake, was to talk to Herr Kaelin about *Tejano*."

"I must say you picked quite an unusual place to do it. Was there anything wrong with a dinner meeting in Vienna or a stroll in a city park? Why in the world go to this much trouble?"

"Herr Kaelin lives in the Baden area, and out of respect I decided we should come to him. Second, I don't want Kathryn to know we're meeting. If we were in the city she might discover our clandestine appointment. She was upset enough when I told her I was coming out here with you."

"With me! You told here that? Damn, and I guess that also means you told her about *Tejano?*" He leaned across the seat. "Would you excuse us for a moment, Herr Kaelin?" He then had the driver raise the privacy window.

"Why don't we take out an ad in *The Washington Post,* Colonel? Wanted: volunteers to engage in international conspiracy to illegally influence presidential and U.S. Senate elections. You do not have to be qualified to participate, only willing to tell as many of your friends as possible … and be willing to go to federal prison for at least twenty years.'"

"Wait just a minute, Jake. I did not tell Kathryn what we'd be talking about or that we'd be meeting with Urs. Listen to me," a note of anger now sounding in his whispered tones. "Urs Kaelin is Austria's leading handgun manufacturer and exporter. I believe he can be persuaded to help us, but he wants to know details that I can't explain. You're the only one who can supply that information.

"When you first explained your project to help Russell Creighton, the idea instantly appealed to me. It still does, now even more so," Morton soothed. "You know I'm on board and I've collected a hell of a lot of money from around the world to fund your little scheme. When Smith gets his party's nomination and we shift the political and financial support from him to Creighton, he can virtually ignore the Senate race in the general election and concentrate on his presidential campaign. Next stop the White House."

"That's the idea, and so far it's working like a charm. But what does all that have to do with the 'Tales of the Vienna Woods'?"

"I'll tell you what it has to do with it, my friend." Dan looked Hardesty in the eye. "More money, pure and simple. I am not a single-handed bottomless pit of wealth. We need the financial backing of men like Herr Kaelin, the Colombians and, well, let's just leave it at that."

"Wait just a damn minute. First, tell me why your Austrian friend here would want to pitch in big bucks and second, who the hell else have you cut in on the deal and why?"

Morton decided divulging the involvement of German, Russian and other American financiers would only further exasperate Hardesty. "You can ask Urs yourself about his motivation. As for any other players, you can be assured funds are being raised and mouths are sealed shut.

"Urs Kaelin is a man of immense wealth, Jake. I told him a few aspects of the project and he's interested in becoming involved. He's very cautious when investing the amount of money I'm asking. Please tell him about the political operation, no more than you have to divulge, but gain his confidence, and his money will follow. Like the South Americans, he wants to hear it from the operations man. You can close this deal."

"And if I don't, then what?"

"There will be no more money, and you will not have accomplished your mission. It's that simple. All you've done will have been for naught. Hear me loud and clear, Jake, I am tapped out. I cannot and will not provide further personal funds to finance your scheme. But I can get men like Urs Kaelin, with your help."

Jake replied, "I want to think about this for a minute before we move on. I don't like so damn many people in on *Tejano*. I didn't intend to access the United Nations to the White House, no matter how much money it means we get."

"Yeah, you think about it. But then do it. Not just for me but also for a certain friend of ours back in Texas who would like to reside at 1600 Pennsylvania Avenue. And think about what is best for your country too. Please, trust me on this one, Jake. One more time."

Dan signaled to the driver to lower the privacy window. Jake looked out the rear window, not ready to broach the subject of *Tejano*. He stared out the window at the deep forest and could only hope everything would work out as he had originally planned. Another international player, another possible leak, and, more importantly, someone whose motivation for participation he did not share. He was in too deeply to do anything but go along with Dan Morton. "Well, Herr Kaelin, what would you like to know about *Tejano?*"

Chapter 17

▼

El Paso
January 12

Looking out over the Chihuanuan Desert and Franklin Mountains from his motel window, Sergei Yazkov found it hard to believe he was in the same state where he had spent the last four months. The state's westernmost city was a stark contrast to the humid East Texas piney woods where he had monitored Andrew Smith's campaign. Nor could the yucca and prickly pear cactus of the Trans-Pecos alkali flats compare to the lush forests of his Russian homeland. This was the Texas he had envisioned, having watched numerous westerns on video since *perestroika* and the invasion of Western culture and its economy.

Tonight he would attend a fund-raising reception for Andrew Smith. He understood it would be the traditional *pachanga:* a Mexican buffet and all the beer and margaritas the boisterous supporters and freeloaders could consume.

Sergei had been constantly involved in the McDonald and Smith campaigns, volunteering at their headquarters and attending myriad campaign events. Of the two candidates, Smith appeared to have the broadest range of support. No doubt the money of Operation *Tejano* was a significant factor.

As Yazkov put on a *guayabero*, the traditional Mexican wedding shirt appropriate for such functions, he pondered the amount of support the front-runner had garnered in this far corner of West Texas. Although no one knew him, Yazkov decided to portray himself in a Hispanic disguise, just to play it safe. Checking himself one last time in the mirror, he pulled on his boots and headed out the door.

Jennifer Spencer trudged across the plaza toward the law office of Ramon Sanchez, a local McDonald supporter. She lugged her carry-on and should bags filled with campaign literature and files across the uneven cobblestones.

Suzanne Chism had asked her to make initial contacts for a McDonald fundraiser to be held in February. Calls made for the last two days from Ramon's offices left her apprehensive about receiving many commitments of support. Jennifer had been told the local congressman, Carlos Berlanga, Would endorse Andrew Smith at a reception held this evening at the home of a local automobile dealer. The congressman had done a stellar job of nailing down the traditional power brokers for his candidate. She would be lucky to gather a steering committee of those willing to stick out their necks for some corporate lawyer from far-off Houston.

Jennifer reached the storefront office and struggled to get her belongings through the crowded waiting room. She gave a good morning greeting to the receptionist and proceeded to her temporary office.

She had succeeded in persuading a handful of attorneys to endorse Warren McDonald, but their support was in name only and lukewarm at best. Due to the statewide teachers' union endorsement, other local labor unions were lining up behind Andrew Smith, who had been in town two weeks earlier. Any crumbs of political and financial support she could pick up would be a blessing.

After dropping off her bags beside her assigned desk, Jennifer proceeded to the small kitchen where she poured a fresh cup of coffee and took one of the sugar coated Mexican pastries from a basket on the counter. She hoped a shot of caffeine and the rush of sugar would energize her for making more cold calls.

Even though more than 500,000 Texans resided in El Paso, she would definitely advise Suzanne that Warren should come to this oasis only once for editorial board interviews and possibly a *pachanga*, assuming she could persuade enough locals to even organize one. Given the impact Smith had established, her time would be better spent soliciting money on the phone in Houston than flying almost 600 miles to woo a few voters and contributors.

After nine hours of virtually worthless telephone calls, Jennifer completed her list and packed up to leave for the airport before calling in her status report to Suzanne at the Austin headquarters.

"Well, kid, how is it out on the West Texas plains?" Chism lit her umpteenth cigarette of the day and tried not to cough directly into the receiver.

"About the only good thing I can say is that I've seen some beautiful desert I had never laid eyes on and probably never will again. I suggest you save Warren a trip out here, unless you want to reserve a telephone booth for the site of his El Paso County political rally." Jennifer couldn't hide her feelings of dejection, given the response to her efforts.

"That bad, huh? Sorry to hear it. I was hoping Ramon could at least line up some of the trial lawyers out there. Even if we had to drag the bag through a bar near the courthouse on a Friday after work, I'd be willing to schedule the candidate to go out there next month if he could raise five or ten thousand bucks."

"Ramon might be able to, but you'll have to confirm that with him. I suppose the radio and TV stations and newspapers would give Warren some free press coverage. We can talk about it more when I get back."

"Speaking of coming back, when are you booked to return?"

Jennifer glanced at her itinerary. "I've got a flight that leaves for Houston Hobby at nine-thirty tonight."

"Good, that leaves you a few more hours to make more calls and shake the trees for money."

Jennifer rolled her eyes. "Thanks but no thanks, I would just as soon bear-hug a barrel cactus. By now everyone has left their offices, assuming they were even in today. Based on the number of call-backs I left, it seems like no one is even in town, at least not for the Warren McDonald campaign."

"Well, cheer up. It could be worse."

"Really? And how would that be?"

Suzanne was silent for a moment. "I can't think of any way right now, but give me a few hours and I'll come up with something."

"I couldn't make more calls now anyway. Ramon offered me a free margarita on the rocks and some spicy nachos. I accepted his invitation, though I don't particularly care for the venue."

"Damn, now I wish I were out there with you. Where are you headed, to that little hole in the wall cantina he likes over on the square?"

"Nope, he wants to stop by a big *pachanga* the Smith campaign is having at one of his supporters' haciendas on Mount Franklin."

"A party, huh? Sounds like a hell of a deal. You can do a little undercover work, kinda like going behind enemy lines. Assess the quality and quantity of the crowd plus take in a great view of the city lights."

Chism attempted to put as positive a spin as she could on what sounded like an otherwise dismal trip. "Go and have a good time, Jen. Make some notes about the Smith event on your return flight. Something interesting might yet come out of your little excursion."

"My fellow El Pasoans, I don't care what they say down in Austin, this is the heart and soul of Texas. And, my friends, it is good to be back home, deep in the heart of Texas. Let me add, it is also nice to be off the Potomac River and away from all those pointy headed federal bureaucrats in Washington, D.C."

For the fifth time in the span of only ten minutes the crowd of almost two hundred interrupted the introductory remarks of Congressman Berlanga. Jennifer observed the enthusiastic crowd. "Damn, Ramon, I feel like a fish out of water," she whispered as the two diplomatically joined in the applause.

"Ah, don't sweat it, Spencer. Nobody knows you out here. I see a lot of folks who know me, though," the lawyer observed, waving to a friend. "I'll just introduce you as my long lost cousin on the gringo side of the family. Let's listen."

"*Mi amigos*, I am blessed to recommend Andrew Smith. He knows El Paso and the Trans-Pecos area. Why, his grandparents ranched a couple of hundred miles east of here near Pecos. I tell you, my friends, Andrew Smith appreciates our wide-open spaces and the issues that concern all of us here tonight. Please join me in welcoming your next United States Senator, one of my good friends, Andrew Smith."

Once again, as if on cue, the crowd responded. The candidate approached the microphone and delivered his standard stump speech.

Five minutes later Ramon whispered, "Hmm, I gotta tell you, that guy can talk."

"Yeah," Jennifer grudgingly replied. "Say, let's go over by the wall and catch a view of the city lights before you take me out to the airport. I've heard enough illegal immigrant bashing for one evening."

They made their way through the throng as Smith continued. The shrill tone of a cornet kicked off the music and the boisterous supporters cheered once more. Ramon accepted two margaritas from a roving waiter, and acknowledged numerous howdys from friends and acquaintances.

"Keep moving, please," Jennifer urged. "I would prefer not going through the meet and greet phase again. I deplore putting on a facade."

The sun was setting, and the strings of multi-colored party lights and *luminarios* arranged around the large patio of the palatial residence provided festive illumination. The chatter from inside grew louder following the speeches. While the *cervezas* and fajitas were being served, *mariachis* dressed in broad-brimmed sombreros, traditional black Spanish suits with red and green piping entertained the crowd with Spanish music. When they reached the patio's waist-high wall, Jennifer turned from the crowd and focused on the wide-open spaces.

"Nice view, isn't it?"

Suddenly Jennifer realized a stranger standing nearby was speaking to her. In the darkness she hadn't seen him approach. "Oh, yeah, great.

The lights of Juarez and El Paso with the mountains as a backdrop are spectacular. I've heard so much about it."

"I take it you are not from around here. May I introduce myself … my name is Raphael Martinez." Sergei Yazkov smiled and nodded slightly.

"Oh, hello. I'm Jennifer Spencer from Houston. You must be used to this view, living here in El Paso."

"Actually, I am not from here either. But I live closer than you. I own Los Lobos, a cafe in Sierra Blanca, about an hour and a half drive east of here. Pretty much all desert. What brings you all the way out here? You must be quite the committed Smith supporter."

Ramon had turned to speak with a friend and Jennifer realized she was flying solo. "Yes, I am, I mean, no, well, what I mean is I am a lawyer, and I'm working on a case with my friend over there. I do support Andrew Smith, but it's the lawsuit that brought me out here."

Having recognized Spencer from their brief meeting in Austin at the McDonald campaign party, Yazkov knew she was lying. He was glad he had worn the disguise but decided not to press his luck.

Jennifer looked intently at the man as she sipped her drink and engaged in small talk about the scenery and their work. There was something about him that troubled her. He looked vaguely familiar, but she couldn't place him. Something about his good looks. His speech pattern made her doubt that Raphael Martinez prepared tortillas and poured *cervezas* for a living.

After a few minutes Sergei shook her hand. "I really must be going. I have a long drive. Perhaps we will meet again." He turned and melted into the crowd.

"Who was that?" Ramon asked, returning to her side.

"I don't know. Just met him. Some guy from Sierra Blanca. Says he runs a restaurant over there … Los Lobos, I think he called it."

Ramon Sanchez took another margarita from a passing waiter. "Don't think so, my friend. Chuy's is the only cafe in that one horse town for as long as I can remember. I stopped in there for lunch about two weeks ago when I went over to the Hudspeth County courthouse for a hearing. For whatever reason, I think your new friend was pulling your leg."

Jennifer peered into the crowd, but the man was gone. "We'd better get out of here." She tapped her watch. "My plane leaves in a little over an hour, and it'll take a while clearing security."

As the two lawyers hurried for the exit, Jennifer thought again of the stranger from Sierra Blanca. She felt certain they had met before. There was something about the smile or the piercing eyes that seemed familiar, and the mustache didn't appear quite natural.

CHAPTER 18

▼

ROME
JANUARY 13

A few wispy clouds in a sapphire blue sky made for a perfect day on Piazza Navona. It was a balmy 63 degrees in the Italian capital, unusual for January. Cathedral bells struck twelve as workers from nearby shops filled the popular landmark. Laborers in overalls snacked on sandwiches brought from home, while the business set paused to enjoy a lengthy lunch at various sidewalk cafes.

Francesca Rosario, single and in her mid-thirties, was a striking Italian beauty, olive complexion, perfectly shaped lips and high cheekbones. She meticulously watched her diet and exercised daily at a club close to her family's business offices near the Pantheon. Stylishly attired in a leather blazer, tailored fuchsia silk blouse, straight suede skirt with ruffled hem and black kid boots, she set aside the menu, choosing to wait for her father. It would be a sign of disrespect to order, plus she was in no hurry on such a beautiful afternoon.

Moments later, she felt hands gently placed on her shoulders as a husky voice greeted her. *"Buon giorno, carina."*

Without turning, Francesca reached up and patted her father's weathered hands. "*Buon giorno*, papa. Welcome back to *Roma*." The young woman rose, hugged her father, kissing him on both cheeks.

Francesca admired her father's appearance. Maurizio Rosario wore a hand-tailored navy blazer, accented by a paisley handkerchief flared from the breast pocket, charcoal slacks, and a white silk shirt open at the neck. Tinted glasses hid his dark brown eyes from the noonday sun, and his coal-black hair belied his seventy-three years.

A waiter brought an additional menu. "That will not be necessary. Nothing heavy for me today. I must drive back to *Napoli* and I don't need to be dozing at the wheel." He turned to his daughter. "Would antipasti and salad be enough?"

Francesca spread the napkin in her lap and nodded. "Certainly. I'm going to the club after work and the last thing I need is to exercise on a full stomach. How about the *Caprese* and a carafe of the *Frascati.*"

When the waiter left, Francesca dutifully inquired about the health of her mother, aunts, uncles, and cousins in Naples and Sorrento. The conversation soon turned to business.

"So how are things at Lupio?" Maurizio referred to their wine distribution company, a subsidiary of Rosario Enterprises, the family-owned conglomerate.

"Quite well. Profits were up ten percent for the last quarter, and I anticipate more of the same this year."

"That comes as no surprise. You are an excellent businesswoman, Francesca. Now that I have given up some of my duties and am spending more time with the family, you know I rely on you to run the company. Your years at the offices in Florence and Catanzaro prepared you well to manage the family business."

After their meal was completed, the waiter brought cappuccinos. Maurizio leaned closer to his daughter. "There is something important I have come to ask of you. There is an American couple vacationing in Venice, a Colonel and Mrs. Daniel Morton. We have had mutual interests for many years."

"I remember going to Washington years ago and meeting Colonel Morton. He introduced us to several Italian-American congressmen. As I recall, he is successful and very handsome."

"He is also married and twenty years your senior."

Francesca's gaze lowered. "Yes, Papa. So what about this Colonel Morton? Has he the resources and connections to help protect our enterprises in the States?"

"Of that I am certain, but that is not my main interest at the moment. Two weeks ago he called to discuss a political project to assist Senator Russell Creighton in his presidential campaign. He solicited our financial participation."

"What did you tell him?"

"I told him this would be violating his country's laws prohibiting candidates from seeking contributions from foreigners. He responded that his project, called *Tejano*, did not contribute directly to the senator's campaign fund and assured me it is carried out with the utmost secrecy. I want you to go to Venice, Francesca, listen to what Colonel Morton has to say and make a decision as to our participation."

"But why me? It should be you."

"The time has come for you to make these political and investment decisions. I will not live forever."

Francesca pushed aside her cappuccino. "Don't talk like that, papa. You know that is the last thing I want to hear."

Maurizio shook his head. "I don't think it wise that I go North now. Though I am sure they know the source of our income, the *carabinieri* in the south and even here in *Roma* let us operate freely. In the North, it is different. We have no control in that part of the country."

"How much is Colonel Morton asking?" Francesca toyed with her wine glass.

"Five hundred thousand dollars."

"I realize we've helped to finance the campaigns of several U.S. congressmen, and I've been pleased with the results. But this is different. Getting involved in a presidential campaign could mean big problems if our contributions were discovered."

"Yes, that's why I want you to meet Colonel Morton and determine if his proposition is worth the risk." Maurizio paid the bill and stood to leave.

Francesca rose and took her father's outstretched hand. "Assuming we did contribute, what could we expect to gain from the investment?"

"If Senator Creighton becomes President, we would have access through Dan Morton and the lobbyists he hires. More importantly, I think we should do everything we can to defeat President Templeton. He is threatening to de-certify Italy for foreign aid and World Bank loans because of our increased drug traffic. If there is a crackdown, it would have a devastating effect on our operating capital. And if our country doesn't get the foreign aid, our president will be crippled. We've made a substantial investment to get Antonio in office, and we need to keep him there."

Francesca thought of Antonio Borcelli and the contributions the families had made to his campaign. He had quickly won the hearts and minds of a majority of the Italian people with his nationalistic views and charismatic leadership. In addition, he had kept his word and not made an issue of fighting organized crime. Many Italians had gradually accepted the families as a part of the culture, a necessary evil.

"Antonio has certainly performed for us as he said he would. He is an emblem of the new generation of politicians in Europe."

"You are right. Borcelli is a smooth, effective public speaker who was not a party to the corruption scandals that weakened previous administrations. He has recognized those concerns and speaks to them."

"Yes, but some of his critics liken him to Mussolini's ghost in a fancy suit."

"They are just jealous because he led a populist backlash against globalization and the trans multinational corporations which have usurped the prerogatives of the nation-state. Borcelli disdains being dictated to by the European Union. I couldn't agree with him more on that. We need a U.S. president who will not publicly disagree with him on that issue."

"Even if what you say is true, I'm not sure it is reason enough to take the risk of being caught in the criminal activity of funneling money into the American presidential campaign, no matter how covert or indirect it is."

Maurizio's lips thinned. "*Mi cara,* since when have any of our business endeavors been totally legitimate? The gun sales, prostitution, drugs, money laundering, do you think any of that could stand the light of day?"

"No, but contributing to presidential elections in America is entirely different. Our family has been involved in these other activities for decades. And, as you pointed out a few minutes ago, our well-paid friends in the *carabinieri* look the other way."

Francesca held out her arm, bringing her father to a halt to allow a scooter to speed through the narrow alleyway. "I don't know, papa, it all sounds very risky."

"That is why I want you to go to Venice and meet with Colonel Morton. He can explain it much better than I."

"I admit our participation does make some sense," she replied after a period of silence while they continued walking toward the river. "Certainly our funds have helped in other countries in which we have taken an interest. We have our friends in the Congress. But to have access to the President, how can I judge such a thing?"

They stepped onto a footbridge crossing the Tiber, drawing closer to St. Peter's. When they reached the crest of the bridge, Maurizio stopped and turned to face his daughter. "It will be totally up to you to decide how much we should invest now and how much later."

Francesca gazed down the river. Many criticized the fact that their livelihood came from illegal activities, she reflected, but money is money and it had provided the good life and power. If there were a demand and money to be made, she would make available the drugs, handguns, gambling or prostitutes. Getting further involved in the American political system was just a necessary part of doing business. She turned back to her father. "If this is your wish, Papa, you know I will go. When and where does Colonel Morton expect me?"

Maurizio brought his daughter's hand to his lips. "*Grazie*, Francesca. There is one last matter. He expects me, not you, to meet him at the Excelsior Hotel on the Lido this coming Friday at noon."

She arched an eyebrow. "But will he even talk to me about his project? He will want and expect you. You are *domo* in the Rosario family. And a woman? The family does not allow women to deal like this."

"Don't worry, *mi cara*," her father replied with a smile. "You are the buyer. He wants our money or else he would not be coming. If you do not like the deal, do not negotiate. And as for being a woman, times have changed around the world, and it is time they changed in the family as well."

"I love you, Papa. Thank you for your confidence. I promise to earn it."

"I know. And I also know I want it to be Francesca Rosario who is the one with access to the next President of the United States."

The two turned and walked toward the massive St. Peter's Cathedral to pay respect and to pray the rosary.

CHAPTER 19

▼

VENICE
JANUARY 15

The water-taxi ride from the San Zaccaria dock on *Canale di San Marco* to the island of *Lido Di Venezia* had taken Dan Morton fifteen minutes. He sat on the patio observing young women lounging in front of the Excelsior Hotel. Although the International Film Festival had concluded two days earlier, a number of actors and other movie moguls seated around him had extended their vacations.

Dan's daydreaming was interrupted by the sound of a full, throaty female voice. "Colonel Daniel Morton, I believe." He looked up to find a striking young woman standing beside his table.

The retired Army officer stood immediately. "Yes, I'm Dan Morton. And to whom do I owe the pleasure?" Once he had regained his composure, he liked even more what he saw, a woman of elegance with a slender, well-proportioned figure who blended in naturally with the international jet setters scattered throughout the crowd.

"I am Francesca Rosario, vice president of Rosario Industries." She took the American's hand in a firm, business-like grip. "I believe you know my father, Maurizio."

"Yes, of course. As a matter of fact, I'm here to meet him. I presume he is with you?" Dan glanced past Francesca toward the open French doors.

She ignored the inquiry. "I believe our discussion deserves a bit more privacy." Motioning for the waiter to clear Dan's tab, she paid the bill, leaving a generous tip. Francesca had taken charge before Dan had the slightest opportunity to protest.

The couple passed through the lobby of the huge, turreted Moorish style building and onto *Lungomar Gugliemo Marconi.* "I know you were expecting my father, but I came as his emissary."

Dan was mildly troubled at the unexpected development, wondering what the reason must be to justify a change in Maurizio's plans. "I hope he is not ill."

"No, he is in the best of health and asked that I extend his warmest regards. He told me what little he knows of your political operation, *Tejano,* I believe you call it, and requested I meet with you to learn more."

Once they had stepped onto the sands of Lido beach, Francesca removed her heels. "Assuming I decide to put Euros in the clandestine account, what do I get in return?"

When Francesca offered her hand for balance, Dan removed his shoes and socks. He felt a tinge of electricity running from her palm to his. Then, as quickly as it had happened, she withdrew her grasp. Dan reiterated what he had told Maurizio about the access her father would have, once Senator Creighton reached the White House.

"That access," Francesca corrected, "will not be my father's, it will be mine."

"But of course, however he wants it."

"No, not the way my father wants it. It is the way I want it." She paused to let the point sink in. "And I presume Senator Creighton will know of our aid in his election efforts?"

"Yes, but we'll be discrete about it. As I'm sure you understand, he wouldn't want to know the details of our involvement. But I can assure you that at the correct time our next president will know Francesca Rosario aided him in his quest for the White House, if that's what you wish."

As they passed beach cabanas, Dan spoke freely of the way in which the *Tejano* money was being withdrawn by Jack Hardesty and passed on to the other participants in the conspiracy. He told her far more than he had revealed to the other financial partners whose confidences he had labored to gain. He surmised that he wanted to see more of Francesca Rosario, and her participation in *Tejano* was as good an excuse as any.

"You ask for a very large sum of money, Colonel Morton," Francesca finally remarked. "I will have to think about it." She slipped her shoes back on, indicating the meeting had drawn to a close. "Why don't we take the ferry back now? I am staying at the *Cipriani* at the east end of Guidecca. Why don't you come for coffee or tea around ten-thirty in the morning, and we can discuss the security aspects in greater detail. Following our meeting, I will give you my answer."

Forty-five minutes later, Kathryn Morton stood at the San Zaccaria dock awaiting her husband. He had told her he was meeting with a businessman from Naples.

Kathryn's temper flared. "Sorry if I'm interrupting something,"

"Oh, Kathryn, I'm surprised to see you here, darling."

She stomped out her cigarette, grinding it into the stones of the dock. "That's rather obvious."

"Kathryn Morton, please meet Ms. Francesca Rosario, daughter of my good friend, Maurizio. Ms. Rosario, my wife, Kathryn. Maurizio is, uh, still on the island. I just met Ms. Rosario on the ferry. She was coming over to do some shopping."

"Right, sweetie, whatever you say. What were you meeting her father about?"

"Oh, just boring business matters. Some investments Francesca, I mean Mr. Rosario is interested in making back in the States." The surprise of being in the presence of Kathryn and the woman he had arranged to meet the next morning momentarily frazzled Morton.

Pigeons scattered as they made their way across San Marco Piazza. "What kind of investments? Real estate, oil and gas, stocks?" Kathryn paused, waiting for an answer and when it was apparent none was forthcoming, continued. "What's wrong, darling? Cat got your tongue?"

"No, I mean yes. What I mean is yes, real estate. They are looking to buy some property adjacent to the 610 Loop in Houston near the Galleria. Isn't that what you said, Ms. Rosario?" Dan averted his eyes from Kathryn's stare, hoping Francesca was more adept at deception than he.

"Yes, that is correct. My uncle was at M.D. Anderson Cancer Center last fall for prostate surgery. While Papa and I were visiting him, we were quite impressed with how that part of Houston is developing." Francesca took the hand-off in stride, noting that her reply seemed to mollify Morton's wife.

"This is the street to our hotel, Ms. Rosario." Kathryn turned and extended her hand. "My pleasure, I do hope we meet again."

"Oh, I'm sure we will," Francesca replied with a knowing smile. "I believe the family will return to Houston again this year, and when we do, I'll give you a call. Perhaps we can fly up to Fort Worth and take the two of you to dinner."

Dan smiled and shook her hand, impressed the young woman possessed the self-confidence to so artfully manipulate the brief conversation.

"Quite an impressive young woman." Kathryn watched Francesca Rosario head down the alleyway lined with quaint shops and cafes. "Something tells me she probably gets just about whomever or whatever she wants."

He dismissed the remark with a light kiss on Kathryn's check. "Yep, kinda reminds me of a strong-willed woman from Texas I know pretty well."

CHAPTER 20

▼

GRAND PRAIRIE, TEXAS
FEBRUARY 5

Jennifer sat deep in concentration at the Warren McDonald for Senate Metroplex campaign office, surrounded by 20 FEC reports and two yellow legal pads filled with names and telephone numbers. Casually attired in a burnt orange University of Texas sweat shirt and jeans, she could pass for a typical college co-ed, rather than a woman on a mission. She had identified contributors who donated five hundred dollars or more to Andrew Smith and was randomly calling the list asking who they were supporting. If they identified a candidate, she would ask why.

"Hello, my name is Jennifer Spencer. I'm calling for TIPR, Texas Independent Polling Resources," she lied once again. "May I please speak to Roger McKeithen?"

A puzzled female voice replied from a number called in Garland, a Dallas suburb. "No, not unless you're having a séance and are a mystic or somethin'. My husband's been in the grave almost three years now."

With that Jennifer gently replaced the receiver and made a tick mark in a column on the border of the legal pad. At this rate the number of dead bodies was catching up with those who had never heard of Smith. She massaged her neck and shoulder muscles, tense from cradling the receiver for four hours. What the unusual responses meant would have to be resolved at a later date. Perhaps Suzanne would have some brilliant idea, since this project was her idea in the first place.

Jennifer tried to ignore the Activity around her and proceeded to her fifty-eighth call of the day. "Hello, this is Jennifer Spencer, may I speak to Lou Dell Roberts, please?"

"This is Lou Dell. May I help you?"

Damn, I've finally gotta live one. Jennifer breezed through her pitch.

"Yes, I gave Mr. Smith a thousand dollars just like I was supposed to, so what?"

Like taking a deposition, listen for every word, every nuance. "Like you were supposed to? And what do you mean by that?"

"My husband, Jimmy Don, is a dep'ty sheriff here in Kaufman County. His boss done give him a grand in cash and told him we wuz supposed to go to a fundraiser for this guy Smith over in Mesquite."

"So it wasn't really your money?" Jennifer tried to confirm with a leading question, hurriedly making notes on the list.

Lou Dell Roberts hesitated. "Hell yes it was our money. Bubba Cummins give it to us. Say, who'd you say this is?" Not waiting for an answer, she yelled past the receiver. "Jimmy Don, put Junior down and git off your lazy butt and come talk to this nosy bitch."

This I do not need! Jennifer slammed the receiver into the cradle. The stress and frustration of the day's cold calling had gotten to her. She had learned enough about little Lou Dell, Jimmy Don, and Sheriff Bubba anyway. She took several deep breaths to regain her composure before proceeding to the next name.

Two hours later the smell of cheeseburgers and fries being consumed by volunteers caused Jennifer to question why she was holed up in a stuffy campaign office on a beautiful winter afternoon. Having placed almost ninety calls throughout the Dallas-Fort Worth area, fatigue coupled with severe writer's cramps were beginning to set in.

Several TCU students arrived and were making reminder calls concerning Warren McDonald's visit. Their chores near completion, some were on their way to a TCU-Rice basketball game, leaving Jennifer to her tedious project.

"Hello, may I please speak to Denise Rosenthal?" She absentmindedly circled the next name on the call list. "Ms. Rosenthal, my name is Jennifer Spencer and I'm conducting a public opinion poll …"

Six minutes later, she added another name to the growing list of people categorized as contributors to Andrew Smith but who seemed to have no clue who the man was. Was it possible someone was putting money in Smith's campaign without this many people having any clue as to what was going on? Who would do such a thing and why?

"May I please speak to Marcus Stowers?"

An irritated voice on the other end of the line in nearby Crowley responded that her brother had moved to California two years earlier. Sandra Stowers added, "I've never heard of Smith and can't imagine why my brother would be listed as a contributor since he only lived in Texas for a year before moving on and could care less about politics."

Yet another unexplainable large donation.

"Morton residence. May I help you?"

"May I speak to Kathryn Morton?" Jennifer identified herself and explained the purpose of the call.

"One moment please." The maid put the caller on hold on the kitchen extension and went into the Mortons' handsomely decorated, cherry-paneled study.

Kathryn Morton nonchalantly pushed the flashing light on the telephone console. "This is Kathryn Morton, what can I do for you?" She collapsed into a plushly upholstered lounger, unbuttoned the top two pearl buttons on her cashmere sweater and rubbed her throat.

"Ms. Morton, my name is Jennifer Spencer." She propped her running shoes on the paper-strewn desk and began her rote inquiry.

"Andrew Smith? Are you kidding?" Kathryn retorted when confronted with information that she was listed on the FEC reports as a contributor. "There must be some mistake. I've never heard of the damn guy."

Intrigued by the interrogation, Kathryn stepped over to an antique writing table and flipped on the desk lamp. Taking a pen from the silver inkwell, she jotted down the telephone number of the incoming call that appeared on caller ID. "Bullshit! Heard of him but never met the guy, and I sure as hell wouldn't waste good money on some politico."

"Then why would your name be on his Federal Election Commission report?" Jennifer leaned forward and drew several large stars around Kathryn Morton's name.

"Wait just a sec, there's another call I need to take." Kathryn put the caller on hold and using another line, called the number she had written down.

"Warren McDonald for United States Senate Campaign. May I help yew?"

"Yes, could you give me your address please? I'd like to come by and pick up some bumper stickers and yard signs."

"Yes maam, we're at 12033 Westgate Drive in Grand Prairie. Do you know where that is?"

Having heard enough, Kathryn returned to her interrogator. "Well, Jennifer Spencer, I tell you what, how 'bout if I just saddle up and come on over to the Warren McDonald headquarters in Grand Prairie so we can continue with this little detective work of yours in person?"

"Holy shit!" Jennifer collapsed back into her chair and stared at the telephone.

CHAPTER 21

▼

AUSTIN
FEBRUARY 11

Juan Falcone pushed away from the steel-cased desk at the Department of Public Safety headquarters and rubbed his bloodshot eyes. He had been studying file material on the Crosser murders all morning but had only succeeded in developing eye strain and frustration from the growing futility of his daily routine.

"Hey, Lieutenant, *como esta?*" Sgt. Ray Maxwell, returning from the coffee machine, paused at Falcone's desk. "How long's it been now since those two killings down in South Texas?"

"About five months." He feigned concentration on the file folders open before him, hoping the fellow Ranger would move on without further interrogation.

Maxwell took a sip of the fresh coffee. "Any leads?"

"Not really," Juan reluctantly conceded. "I've run computer checks on other homicides across the state and Southwest, but nothing has proven helpful. Not having a suspect sure doesn't help matters."

Maxwell patted his shoulder. "You might as well close the file, buddy. The perp's probably long gone. Kinda like that rail-car killer investigation we worked a few years ago. Maybe your man will strike again, and someone in another state will pick up his trail."

Juan looked down at his notes. "I'm afraid you might be right, but I hate like hell to think the bastard got out of Texas. He's killed two people in our jurisdiction, and I'd like to nail his ass before he kills again here or moves out of state."

Maxwell nodded. "Plus, if he moves on, you've got that hassle with getting a governor's warrant and possibly a *habeas corpus* hearing if they challenged all that extradition bullshit. Good luck, and holler if I can help." He turned and headed toward his desk.

"You got it, appreciate the offer." Before Juan could return his attention to the papers spread before him, the intercom buzzed. "Falcone here."

"Call on line three, Lieutenant."

He punched another button. "This is Lt. Juan Falcone, may I help you?"

"No sir, but maybe I can help you. This is Sgt. Ricardo Gomez with the Stolen Property Division, San Antonio Police Department. I think we have something down here you might be interested in. Got a pen?"

Juan flipped to a fresh page on his legal pad. "Sure, Sergeant, go ahead."

"We made a collar on an eighteen year old last night. Picked him up on a B&E of a private residence. No driver's license or other ID, but the perp says his name's Freddie Martinez. 911 received a call after someone heard noise coming from the yard next door. Fortunately, we had an unmarked patrol car in the area, so we had the kid followed and made the bust at Martinez's apartment over on the west side."

Juan didn't see any connection to his investigation but, as a matter of professional courtesy, tried to sound interested. "Did you recover any stolen property?"

"Yes, sir, some expensive stereo equipment taken from the residence. Also, at his crib we found three shot guns and some fancy jewelry reported missing after several other recent burglaries."

Losing interest, Juan made crude drawings of the stolen property before putting the pen down. "Excuse me, Sergeant, but what does this have to do with me? I'm working a double homicide, not trying to nab a petty thief."

"I know that, sir. I'm calling because of the state-wide bulletin you released. I thought you might be interested in the vehicle the dude was driving, a '91 Chevy S-10 pickup, four-wheel drive, metallic blue, gun rack, over-size wheels. I think, Lieutenant, we might have arrested your cop-killer."

Juan's palm slammed the desk top. "All right!" His cry startled another Ranger working nearby. Except for the color, the truck fit the description on the bulletin. "Got a tag or VIN number?"

"Both. Texas plates GQU 9873. The VIN is JNXAY2105VM400935."

Juan quickly cross-checked his notes. Wrong license plate number but a match on the VIN, which was definitely more important. They had found Roberto Salazar's truck!

"Have you run the truck for prints or vacuumed it yet?" Falcone anxiously inquired.

"Not yet. We'll start on that in about an hour."

"This could be very important, Sergeant. Call our local DPS office and tell them, on my order, to have our best man come out and do the print job. In the meantime, don't touch a thing in the cab or truck bed. Do not, under any circumstances, leave new prints. Understood?"

"Yes, sir, whatever you say."

Juan glanced at the wall clock. "It's nearly ten thirty. I'll run out to the State Aircraft Pooling Board, catch a plane and be in your shop by noon. Fax me the kid's rap sheet so I can study it on the plane. Line me up an interrogation room and tell Martinez to call his lawyer. If he doesn't have one, talk to the District Attorney's office and have them go to court and get one appointed. I don't want any foul ups on this. And hey … good work, *compadre."*

Theresa Herrera inhaled deeply on a cigarette and passed it to Freddie Martinez. "My client has nothing to say to you, Lt. Falcone. I don't know why I'm down here on such short notice. I was in the middle of a critical suppression of evidence hearing in a sexual assault case. You could have saved the State of Texas a tank of jet fuel and yourself some time."

She looked down at the badge affixed to the pocket of the western cut white shirt, then to the empty holster and tooled leather belt strapped to the lawman's hips. "Surely a big-time Texas Ranger has better things to do than fly down from Austin due to some allegedly stolen stereo equipment. What's this really about?"

"I believe you're the one in the big time, Ms. Herrera, not me." Juan removed his hat and placed it, along with his aviator style sunglasses, on the conference table separating them. As a standard precaution, he had checked his gun in the munitions room. Ignoring her cross-examination, he continued. "Sgt. Gomez told me a little about you on the ride in from the airport. I understand you were a damn good assistant DA for seven years and have now made a truckload of money putting to use what you learned representing the bad guys."

Theresa smiled, accepting the backhanded compliment. "You know the old saying, everyone's entitled to the best defense money can buy. You still haven't told me what brought a Texas Ranger to the Alamo City."

Juan took a chair across the table from her and stretched his legs. "You're right, the State of Texas doesn't pay me to go looking for stolen goods, no matter what their value." He coldly stared at Martinez. "You better hope this up-standing young citizen has stolen enough property to pay you a hefty retainer for defending him on two murder indictments, one being that of a peace officer. The latter being a capital offense, I'm sure the Maverick County DA will seek the death penalty."

Juan sat in silence, letting his remarks sink in while he studied the opposition. He detected a slight twitch in her facial muscles when he mentioned the death penalty.

Intended as a silent sign of confidence, Herrera placed her attaché on the table but chose not to open it. "Go on, you've got my attention."

"There were two gruesome murders committed a couple of months ago, one in Maverick County, the other about the same time near Sabinal in Uvalde County. The first was of a deputy sheriff patrolling the Rio Grande. The second was some dirt poor cowboy. Given the circumstances, the two county sheriffs asked for assistance from the Rangers."

"What does all that have to do with my client? I've represented Mr. Martinez before. He and all his family live in town, and I seriously doubt he's ever been out of San Antonio."

"Simple. When Martinez was arrested he was driving the pickup belonging to Roberto Salazar, one of the victims. I'd say your guy has some serious explaining to do."

"I'm sorry to hear about the fatalities, but you still haven't connected the dots for me. Do you have Freddie's prints at the scene of the crime? Any witnesses eyeball him committing the act?"

"Maybe we can't put him at the scenes, but I know one thing, Freddie might beat the rap, but he won't beat the ride. And it will be a long, expensive one. Why don't you have the kid come clean and tell me all about the pickup and the murders?"

"With all due respect, I don't see that we have anything to discuss." Herrera stood to leave.

Juan held up his hand to halt her movements. "Wait a minute. I apologize. I was out of line. I'm sorry. I guess this case is getting to me." He stood and pulled out the chair for her. "Please, Ms. Herrera, take a seat." He flashed a modest smile of contrition as the lawyer slowly resumed her chair and defiantly crossed her arms. "I don't like having a dead fellow officer and an innocent cowhand who left a wife and three kids, especially when they're both *Tejanos.*"

Theresa softened a little as she stared at the handsome young officer and waited to find out what else he had to say. Perhaps she had rushed to judgment because of the man's tough-talking exterior. "Tell you what, let me talk with my client in private. Give me twenty minutes. I'll see what I can do to help both him and you. As I said, I know Freddie and his family well. Freddie might not be the brightest bulb in the family package, but he's not a stone-cold cop killer."

Juan called for the jailer to unlock the door. "I'll be upstairs waiting in the Stolen Property Division. Take your time, and call me when you're ready to talk."

Back in the interrogatioin room, Falcone found Marinez sitting in silence, nervously puffing another cigarette.

"Do you swear to tell the truth, the whole truth and nothing but the truth, so help you God?" the court reporter droned.

"I do." Freddie Martinez gave the cigarette to Theresa, then sat with his hands folded on the table.

After the requisite preliminary questions establishing the man's age, residence and background, Juan decided to try a fatherly approach and shifted to Spanish. He leaned back in his chair in order to eliminate any feeling of pressure the suspect might have. "Can you show proof of ownership of the pickup truck you were driving at the time of your arrest last night?"

Freddie glanced to his lawyer. After Theresa spoke a few words to him in Spanish in a low reassuring voice, he continued. "No, sir, I can't 'cause I don't own it."

"Who did you take it from? When did you take it and where was it at the time?"

When Freddie's brow furrowed, Theresa counted out the questions using her fingers. "Who, when and where? Try to remember, Freddie. Answer the officer honestly."

"Who? I don't have any idea. Where? From the parking garage out at the airport. And when? It was about four or five months ago."

Falcone knew he had no choice but to trust that the young hood was telling the truth, but didn't like what he was hearing. The time frame fit in with the date of the deaths, but it also meant the chances of lifting a good set of prints were slim.

Continuing in Spanish, Juan turned to Theresa. "Come on, counsel. I could use a little more cooperative attitude here. Explain that to your client and ask him what he was doing at the airport and why he selected this truck?"

After Herrera spoke to him again, Freddie nodded and turned back to Juan.

"It was my buddy, Donnie Stevens' idea to go out there. He said people are sometimes in a hurry to meet relatives and friends comin' in on a plane or runnin' to catch one, and they forget to lock up. That way we don't have to use a slim jim or nothin' like that to get in."

Juan felt further dejection, an accomplice and at least one more set of prints to confuse the issue. "Go ahead, so was this one locked?"

"No, sir, we hit the jackpot. We went from car to car, tryin' the door handles. The keys weren't in it but I had no trouble hot wirin' it. We got in and made off like bandits." He smirked at his own humor. "But we had to pay a bundle to get it out of the parking garage."

"Do you recall how much that was?"

Freddie thought about that. "No sir. Donnie found the parkin' ticket in the visor and I drove it out like I owned the damn thing. Bein' as how this was such a fancy rig and all, we decided to hide it for a while. Donnie's old man runs a paint and body shop so we left it there for a couple of weeks. Then we had it spray painted, figurin' there was a good chance the owner would turn in a stolen car report. We switched plates with an old junker Donnie's dad had taken in to sell."

Drumming his fingers on the table, Juan tried to think what else to ask. His deal with Martinez' attorney hadn't gotten him much in return.

Theresa interrupted his thoughts. "Well, Lt. Falcone, may I go now, unless that is, you have additional questions."

"Yes, I guess that's it for now."

Theresa pushed back from the table. "You seem the savvy, persistent type, Lieutenant. I'd be willing to wager you'll get your man. You Rangers take pride in that."

"Not much to go on." Sgt. Gomez reviewed the confession transcript with Juan later that evening. "Most likely the killer bought a ticket for the next departure and hooked 'em outta town. How 'bout locally? Want to hold off for now?"

"Double the squad of men checking out the cheap hotels around the time the truck was taken from the airport. Use what ID we have on the guy in terms of height, weight, et cetera." Juan stood and snapped his briefcase shut.

"Done. I'll have a report for you in two days."

"Be sure and tell DPS to send whatever prints they lift to FBI."

"Why bring in the FBI? Do you think your man might have a federal record?"

"No, that's unlikely but I'd like to run any prints we find through AFIS," Juan replied, referring to the Automated Fingerprint

Identification System. "Also, tell them I want the prints run through INTERPOL. They exchange information with police agencies in more than one hundred member countries. The killer came across the Rio Grande River just before he killed the Maverick County deputy. My bet is he's either a Mexican national or from some other country."

Gomez gave a thumbs up. "Sounds good to me. Maybe this will lead to something for you after all, Lieutenant."

"I hope so. I've sure as hell been drilling a dry well so far. While you're doing all that, I'm going to stick around town and work the hotel survey with your guys. You know how to get in touch with me."

CHAPTER 22

▼

FORT WORTH
FEBRUARY 13

The shrill ringing of the bedside phone awoke Boris Volkov. Not wanting to awaken his wife, he groped in the dark for the receiver. "Hello," he growled.

Dan Morton sat alone in his office in downtown Fort Worth, the door closed and locked, routinely making calls updating his global financial partners. "Dan Morton here, General." He looked at the grandfather clock across the room. I realize it's a little after midnight there, but I thought this would be the best time to catch you at home. I apologize for disturbing you. Were you asleep?"

Volkov rubbed his eyes then looked at the luminescent dial of the table clock. "Of course I was, but you've ruined that for now." Volkov slipped on his robe and slippers and handed his wife the receiver. "I'll take the call in the other room. Hang up when I tell you and go back to sleep."

A moment later, he took a seat behind his desk in the study and switched on a small reading light. "What the devil do you want this time of night, Colonel Morton?"

"I'm going out of town for a few days and didn't know when I'd be able to catch you, given the different time zones and my business schedule. I wanted to let you know *Tejano* is running smoothly. Andrew Smith is climbing in the polls. Your investment is paying dividends. I'm confident he will win his party's nomination and we will have ultimate victory."

Volkov lit a cigarette. "This is good news, worth being disturbed for. And I presume no one knows of our operation except those who are a part of it, correct?" Volkov detected a long pause. "I am correct, am I not, Colonel Morton?" He leaned over the desk and awaited an answer from the other side of the world.

"Uh, yes, I think you are safe. We ..."

"What! You *think*! Don't you know for certain all is secure?"

"Yes, I know we are."

"Then why did you hesitate in answering?" The Russian businessman stood as if somehow his authoritative figure might be transmitted through the phone lines.

"I don't think it's anything, but yesterday my wife told me she received an unusual call while I was out of town. Some woman wanted to know why my wife had contributed to Smith."

"Who called?"

Morton briefly explained his contribution in his wife's name and the call Kathryn had received from Jennifer Spencer. "Several days have passed and Kathryn has heard nothing further. I think Spencer is some nosy volunteer in Warren McDonald's local campaign office. I'm sure we've heard the last of her. I'm always honest with you, Boris. Don't worry about it. I'm not."

Volkov sat down and hastily scribbled Jennifer Spencer's name on a pad of paper. "You idiot! Why the hell did you make contributions in your wife's name? You moron! I have told you, if anyone uncovers my involvement in *Tejano*, I will hold you personally responsible, especially if it is due to some fucking blunder on your part. Call me in seven days at ten in the evening my time and give me another update. I will make a point to be home to receive your call." Without waiting for some weak excuse for the American's screw-up, Volkov abruptly hung up.

Seconds later, he dialed another number. After one ring Vladimir Kiriyenkov flipped open his cell phone. "Where are you?" Volkov asked.

"I am on the Garden Ring Road, nearing Gorky Park. I am inspecting one more club before I return to my apartment. What do you need?"

"Contact Sergei Yazkov. Give him the name Jennifer Spencer. She is somewhere in Texas, possibly in the Dallas or Fort Worth area. She has been asking questions about campaign contributions. Tell Yazkov to find out who she is and let us know if we have a problem. *Do it now.* Tell him to report back to you in three days," he said as he slammed down the receiver.

Volkov turned out the light and sat in darkness finishing his cigarette. It appeared his decision to send Yazkov to Texas was a wise one. He would know how to deal with this woman.

CHAPTER 23

▼

SAN ANTONIO
FEBRUARY 15

Ricardo Gomez studied the contents of a hand-delivered package received thirty minutes earlier. "This is the craziest damn thing I've ever seen."

Officer Dwight Sibley glanced up from a stack of burglary reports. "What have you got there, Sergeant, another ring of car thieves operating on the South side?"

"No," the senior detective replied, "nothing like that. Get a hold of Lt. Falcone for me at Ranger headquarters in Austin. If he's not at his desk, have him paged."

Two hours later Juan sat in front of Gomez's desk at the SAPD. "So what's so important?"

"We dusted Roberto Salazar's pickup for fingerprints and did everything but tear it apart looking for something that might connect it to the killings."

"Anything turn up?"

"Nothing except fingerprints."

Juan perked up. "Tell me what you found."

"As you might expect, Freddie Martinez's and Donnie Stevens' prints were all over the place."

"Then why did you call me?" Juan stood to leave. "I've run into enough dead ends."

"Wait a second, Lieutenant. Please sit down. Per your request, we called the tech from the Department of Public Safety, and he found a set of prints on a corner of the tailgate. They were smudged, but he thought they might be good enough to work with. We ran them locally and through FBI."

"And ...?"

"Nothing matched. But then we had them run through Interpol like you instructed. Believe it or not, they came up with a perfect match. We apparently have a Russian visitor in the state of Texas, by the name of Sergei Yazkov."

A big smile spread across Juan's face, and he raised his hand to exchange a high five with the detective. "Damn! That's the best news I've heard in a long time. A Russian? Now you've really got my attention."

Gomez pushed a thick overnight express package across the desk to the Ranger. "Take a look at this. I received it just before we paged you."

As Juan opened the envelope, he noticed the return address, INTERPOL General Secretariat Office, 26 Rue Armengand, St. Cloud, France. He summarily glanced through the INTERPOL papers. "These forms are a little hard to interpret," Juan said. "Does it say what kind of criminal record this guy Yazkov has?"

"That's the interesting part. None." The police detective reached across the desk and pulled out a single sheet of paper. "He's got an excellent military record, and I don't see any mention of trouble with the law in Russia or elsewhere."

Juan pushed the file aside. "How can I get more info on our visitor?"

Gomez looked at his watch. "I assumed you would want more. While you were on the way into the department I asked the local FBI agent to call their office in the Embassy in Moscow." Gomez looked at the wall clock. "Arrangements have been made for you to talk with the Special Agent there about thirty minutes from now."

"Damn, you've done good, Sgt. I'll bring a DPS application form next time I come back to San Antonio. The Rangers can use someone like you."

Sgt. Gomez beamed at the compliment. "Thank you, sir. I might take you up on it one of these days. In the meantime, let's get some coffee and see what our counterparts in the Russian police department have to say."

Juan heard the nasal twang of the SAPD operator. "Lt. Falcone, I have Special Agent Patrick Stevens on the line for you. You may go ahead with your call."

Over a slight static came a flat mid-western tone. "Lt. Falcone? Can you hear me all right?"

"Yes, sir, excellent connection."

"I'm in the office of Colonel Ivan Kapkov of the Moscow Militia. We have you on speaker phone. I've told Colonel Kapkov what little I know about the two killings, and the fingerprints lifted from the pickup truck which match those his department filed with INTERPOL."

A heavily accented voice resonated from the speakerphone. "Lt. Falcone, this is Kapkov. I have heard much about the famous Texas Rangers. If there is anything we can do to help solve these crimes, we will."

"Thank you very much, Colonel, I appreciate that. From what I've been advised, this man, Sergei Yazkov, has no criminal record in Moscow. Is that correct?"

"That is true, none in Moscow or anywhere else in Russia."

"Do you have Yazkov's file there with you, sir?"

"It is being copied as we speak. I should have it back shortly. In the meantime, go ahead with any questions and I will try to answer them."

"If Yazkov has no criminal record, why do you have his prints on file? And why did you send them to INTERPOL?"

"Most of the so-called Russian Mafia provides uniformed security guard service to protect businesses from street thugs and other criminal elements. This is fine so long as they are not, what is your American word, 'screwing over' businesses and using it to cover extortion. The

Militia can do little to prevent this, but we can prevent hired criminals from standing guard at the front doors of business establishments with machine guns and blackjacks. We require the security guard companies to be licensed and to have fingerprint and background information on their employees. We work with INTERPOL to determine if they have a criminal record elsewhere."

"I take it then Sergei Yazkov is employed by one of these licensed companies?"

"Yes, he is." There was a pause on the Moscow end of the line. "Sgt. Petrenko, do you have that file copied yet?"

Juan heard a door open and close, then a muffled conversation taking place away from the telephone.

Juan placed his hand over the receiver and whispered to Gomez. "What the hell is the Russian Mafia doing in Texas?"

Kapkov continued. "I have the file now. Petrenko, wait by the door in case I need something else. It shows here Yazkov works for the Butov organization."

"Do you have a work or home address for him?"

"Yes, both are here."

"Colonel Kapkov, if you could locate this man, that in itself would be enough to prove there may have been a foul up on the fingerprints, we could move on to other leads."

"You can be assured that we will find this man, Sergei Yazkov, if he is in Moscow. Let us talk tomorrow Night at this time, and I will tell you what I have learned."

When the conference call ended and Colonel Kapkov indicated his services were no longer needed, Staff Sergeant Nikolai Petrenko excused himself. Making his way along the dimly lit streets, Petrenko reflected on what he had overheard. Perhaps the conversation with the American would be of value to another of his employers.

When the opportunity came to stop directing traffic on the cold Moscow streets and become personal assistant to Colonel Kapkov, Petrenko had leapt at it. He discovered wealthy businessmen paid for tidbits of information from his eavesdropping on phone conversations, idle gossip and scanning incoming and outgoing mail.

Stopping at a corner bar, he ordered a bottle of vodka and sat at a solitary table. "Butov, Butov," he muttered aloud as he poured.

Suddenly the connection came to him. He pulled out his cell phone and scrolled the address book, looking for a telephone number.

The phone rang only once before it was answered. Cupping his hand over the receiver, he turned away from the bartender. "Good evening, General Volkov, this is Sgt. Petrenko of the MVD. I believe I have some information you will find most interesting. Please tell me when and where I can meet you."

CHAPTER 24

▼

JEFF DAVIS COUNTY, TEXAS
FEBRUARY 17

Jake Hardesty glanced at his watch. He had been waiting at the Jeff Davis County courthouse in far West Texas only fifteen minutes, but it seemed like an hour. The previous day Dan Morton had tracked him down in D. C. and requested he catch the next available flight to Midland. When he arrived, a rental car was parked at the curb ready to roll for the three hour drive across the high plateau to the historic town of Fort Davis.

Jake had pressed Morton regarding the nature of the impromptu rendezvous but was politely refused details. "I think everything's okay, but we need to visit," was Morton's only reply.

A sudden honk from a luxury SUV heralded the gun manufacturer's arrival. After exchanging greetings, a broad smile crossed Morton's face. "Sorry to keep you waiting. I got tied up on the phone at the plant. I trust your travel arrangements were satisfactory?"

"First class all the way." Jake eyed Morton's faded jeans and sheepskin jacket, then looked down at his own rumpled business suit and tasseled Italian loafers. "Guess I could look a little more like a city slicker, but I'm not sure how."

"Don't worry about it." Morton good naturally slapped him on the back. "I've got casual clothes at the ranch that'll fit you fine. Come on, let's hit the road."

"What about my rent car?"

"Give me the keys. I'll radio ahead and have one of my ranch hands drive it out to my place. We can visit in my car while I show you the hot tourist attractions."

Racing across the barren terrain, Morton turned down the volume on the country music blaring from the CD player. "I guess you're wondering why I asked you to come all the way out here on such short notice."

"I confess the thought crossed my mind." Jake glanced out the widow at the distant Davis Mountains. "This isn't exactly the route I take home every day from Capitol Hill."

Morton slowed and pulled onto the grounds of Old Fort Davis. He came to a stop in front of the parade grounds, turned off the ignition and sat staring at the native stone dwellings and the red sandstone cliffs behind them.

Jake noticed on the entrance sign it was a national historic site. "Excuse me, but are we getting out here?"

Dan shook his head as though clearing his thoughts, then pressed a button on the armrest to unlock the doors. "Yeah, just for a few minutes to stretch our legs."

Once they reached the gravel walkway adjacent to the parade ground, the two men stood in silence, watching a hawk glide above the long abandoned barracks across the field. "I presume you want to know about the *Tejano* status," Jake said.

"Yeah, I'll get to that. I also want you to bring me up to speed on those damn gun control bills we've been trying to block. But there's something else that's been bothering me lately."

Jake turned to look at his financial partner and client. "And what might that be?"

"A few days ago my wife got a call concerning the Andrew Smith campaign."

"Oh, what about?"

Dan explained the call from Jennifer Spencer and of his suspicion she might be working for the Warren McDonald campaign.

"You think McDonald's campaign sent her out to do a little checking?"

By now the men had reached the opposite side of the field. The retired colonel waved at two park rangers dressed in period piece Cavalry uniforms sweeping the porch of the nearby officers' quarters. "Kathryn couldn't tell, and I don't know either."

As they headed back to the car, Jake picked up a loose stone and hurled it toward a sparrow sitting on a fence rail near the barracks. The small gray bird took flight and Jake squinted in the afternoon sun, watching it soar. "Do you want me to do some checking on Spencer. I know a good private investigator in Dallas who could at least find out where she lives, what she does for a living."

Morton shook his head. "I'm not ready to get into that kind of operation. Plus, I've already done a little investigating of my own." He pulled three sheets of paper out of his jacket pocket and handed them to Jake. "It's amazing what you can find on the damn Internet."

Jake started to glance over the papers but Morton interrupted him. "Let me save you the time. I practically know them by heart. You can take them with you."

Jake folded the papers and slipped them in his suit pocket. "Okay, fill me in on this Spencer woman."

"I found only four Jennifer Spencers in Texas, one in Albany, another in Brownsville and two in Houston.

"My bet is that Mrs. Morton's caller is one of those in Houston."

Morton nodded. "On one of the papers I gave you, you'll see one for an apartment number and address on Montrose Boulevard and another address on Louisiana Street, downtown."

Jake reclined the power seat and switched on the leather seat warmer. In the cozy warmth of the luxury SUV he felt himself about to doze off. He turned toward Morton to pay closer attention. "The downtown address might be an office for the same person."

Morton eased up on the speed and waved when a county sheriff's patrol car passed going in the opposite direction. "I thought the same thing. The office is in a building called the Lamar Legal Center."

Jake smirked. "Great, just what we need, a damn lawyer on our case."

Morton's car rumbled across a cattle guard and passed under the JRP brand. "Well, here we are. Now you'll get a chance to see what I'm trying to preserve."

Jake saw a squat, gray factory building surrounded by a large parking lot filled with pickup trucks. The plant was behind a tall chain link fence with concertina wire strung along the top.

Morton pulled into a reserved parking space near the front door and turned off the engine. "I went to the legal directory at the Martindale-Hubbell website. When I typed in Jennifer Spencer's name and office address, I got her complete bio." Morton covered the highlights of the information he had gleaned.

"Did you get any indication of what her specialty is?"

"Yep, but to get that I went to the website for her law firm. It's a small litigation boutique doing plaintiff business and personal injury litigation."

"More bad news." Jake shook his head. "Sounds like she's anti-establishment all the way. If she'd been born a few decades earlier she'd been burning her bra, marching in civil rights demonstrations and protesting the war you and I were fighting."

Morton laughed. "Don't jump to rash conclusions. To me it indicates she's probably a risk taker."

"Yeah, probably the aggressive, take-charge type. If it's the same woman who called your wife, at least we know she's a practicing lawyer in Houston and not a paid staffer for the McDonald campaign. She might not be connected to his campaign at all."

Their discussion of Jennifer Spencer was interrupted when a uniformed security guard opened Dan Morton's car door. "Good afternoon, Colonel. We've been expecting you. You gentlemen have any briefcases or luggage you need assistance with?"

"No, Ed, we won't be staying long. Mr. Hardesty works for Morton, Inc. in Washington, D.C. You don't have to worry about issuing a security badge. I'm going to show him some of the new products we're designing before we go the ranch house."

The guard held open the door. "Very good, sir."

After they were escorted into the building, Dan showed Hardesty into his private office. Jake marveled at the western paintings and sculptures. "Quite a layout you have out here, Colonel. If you're ever weary looking at these fine paintings, I'd be happy to take them off your hands."

Morton dropped into a lounge chair and propped his boots on the coffee table. "Not a chance. It's a hassle getting out here, but I love it once I'm here. Sit down a minute and let me finish telling you about what else I learned about Jennifer Spencer. I'll show you the production lines when we get through."

Jake sat in a strato-lounger and pulled out the footrest. "You still don't know if this Houston lawyer is the same person who called your wife."

"I'm convinced she's one and the same," Morton said. "I called Houston information and got a number for the Warren McDonald campaign headquarters. I called there and asked to speak to Jennifer Spencer."

Jake dropped the footrest and leaned forward. "And … did you actually talk to her?"

"No. The young man who answered said she wasn't there and asked if I had tried her law office. He gave me that number and sure enough, it was the same one I had gotten off the Internet."

"Nice work. But just because she has some connection to the campaign still doesn't mean she was the caller."

Dan smiled. "One more, and very important, fact. When I asked what her job was with the campaign this kid told me she was a volunteer fundraiser. That's enough for me. It all adds up."

Jake nodded and sat in silence for a moment. "Tell you what, forget the private eye. I'll go down to Houston and meet this gal. I'll think of some way to approach her without arousing her suspicions."

"No, not yet. Let's see if we hear any more from her. But I do think you should put her name out to your political operatives in *Tejano*. If she surfaces again, we'll take care of our inquisitive young lawyer."

Morton looked at his watch and stood. "Come on. Let's go down the hall to the assembly lines before they shut down for the day. After that we'll go over to the ranch house. The sun's gone down over the yardarm somewhere in the world. I'll break open the bar, then we'll enjoy some king size T-bone steaks."

"I'll drink to that." Jake stepped out into the hallway as Morton closed and locked the office door. "I'm surprised you were able to uncover all that info about Jennifer Spencer so quickly. I hope to hell we've heard the last of that woman."

CHAPTER 25

▼

SAN ANTONIO
FEBRUARY 17

Sgt. Gomez crumpled the aluminum foil containing the remains of a burrito and tossed it in the wastebasket. "So what's your guess, Lieutenant, about the information this Russian cop is going to have for us?"

Juan pulled the telephone console closer and awaited the signal from the department operator. "The fact this man Sergei Yazkov is employed by a company controlled by the Russian Mafia bothers me a lot. Nothing good can come from that." He glanced at his watch when the operator announced that Colonel Kapkov was on the line.

"Good evening, Colonel Kapkov. Sgt. Ricardo Gomez is here with me and we have you on the speaker. First, let me thank you again for conducting your investigation and arranging your schedule to take my call at this late hour. Were you able to locate Sergei Yazkov?"

"No, I could not. The only thing I feel confident telling you, Lt. Falcone, is that Sergei Yazkov is not presently working as a security guard for the Butov organization. For reasons I will explain, I believe there is a high probability Yazkov is not in this country."

Juan hurriedly jotted down the unwelcome comments. "Can you tell me more about what you were able to uncover?"

"Yes, but first, I emphasize, Yazkov is very dangerous, a trained killer. Given his background, it is certainly possible he could have easily killed the two Americans you spoke of." Kapkov summarized Yazkov's military career. "I will fax you his photograph and a complete copy of my investigation."

"Thank you very much. I look forward to studying your report, Colonel Kapkov. If I have questions after reading it, may I call again?"

"Certainly, at any time. I will try to learn more if you think it will be helpful to your investigation."

"Why can you say with such certainly that Yazkov is no longer working for Butov?"

"The people with whom I spoke at his apartment building said they have not seen him in at least five months. Each says he was there one day and gone the next, leaving no word of where he was going. The manager said he left money for the rest of the month and took all of his personal effects."

"Did you interview anyone at his company?"

"Yes, I spoke with one of his supervisors, a man named Vladimir Kiriyenkov."

"What did he have to say?"

"That part was most interesting. For some reason Kiriyenkov was hesitant to discuss Yazkov and would not do so until he had spoken to his boss, Boris Volkov."

"I take it from what you say, Boris Volkov is the one who owns Butov."

"He is one of the owners along with several of his former KGB colleagues. Volkov and his associates also have financial interests in other businesses, some of which simply serve as fronts for organized crime."

Juan could faintly hear the Russian police officer speaking to someone else in the room.

"I am sorry, Lt. Falcone, I must conclude our conversation. I've been informed we have some problems in the streets that require my immediate attention. Read my report and call if you have questions. I must go."

"Certainly. Once again, Colonel, I greatly appreciate what you have done. Good night, sir."

Gomez slumped back in his chair, mentally exhausted from trying to follow the man's English given the heavy Russian accent. "Man, what a story! Do you think you're really tracking a professional killer sent by the Russian Mafia?"

Juan nodded. "Sergei Yazkov is here for a reason. He's either accomplished the mission he was assigned and slipped back across the border or he's still here."

"But we don't know for certain he was sent. Maybe he decided to come on his own."

"I don't think so. Why would someone like that illegally enter this country? I would bet my next pay check he was sent by that guy Volkov. The question now is, why."

Juan spread the notes he'd taken out before him and picked up the receiver. "I'm going to call my boss. I want his direction on this. I think we're about to intensify the search for the Crosser, Mr. Sergei Yazkov."

CHAPTER 26

▼

MOSCOW
FEBRUARY 17

Driving down Novy Arbat, the chauffeur incessantly honked the horn of the black Mercedes, alerting other vehicles and pedestrians to move out of his way. To keep his job, the driver knew he must always have his boss to his destination on time, or he would find himself standing outside a Metro station begging for his next meal.

The Mercedes reached the Old Arbat, a street closed to vehicular traffic. The cobblestone streets, lined with bars and cafes, were filled with weekend shoppers. Women strolled arm in arm, families pushed strollers and toddlers bundled up like Eskimos against the cold The auto's passenger pounded on the bullet-proof privacy window and motioned for the driver to pull to a stop. Boris Volkov heaved his bulk from the warm interior and stepped into the cold. "It is almost one o'clock," he growled, glancing at his watch. "Be back here at one forty-five, and don't be a minute late."

Volkov slammed the door and tightened the belt of his expensive foreign-made cashmere overcoat. Pulling on a mink shapka, he looked up at the gray sky. With the temperature hovering in the high teens, another heavy snow was forecast.

The former KGB officer crossed Vozdvizhenka Prospekt and proceeded a short distance to his favorite cafe. As soon as he stepped inside, the acrid aroma of pungent Russian cigarettes filled his nostrils. He crossed the room to the fireplace and warmed his hands while searching for a table where he could concentrate undisturbed. The handful of men occupying the dining room glanced up when he entered, then returned to their conversations, disinterested in the newest customer.

Knowing Volkov would expect his usual, the manager hurriedly brought a bottle of vodka, a shot glass, caviar, butter, and black bread. "Good afternoon, General Volkov. Will you be having lunch? We have some excellent herring, or perhaps your favorite, the mushroom noodle soup and fresh pelmeni."

Volkov appreciated the meat-filled dumplings but was not in the mood to mix food with his alcohol. The red caviar and liquid lunch would suffice. "Not today, I must prepare for a meeting and do not want to be disturbed." With that he took off the overcoat and pulled a small notebook from inside his suit jacket.

He leafed through the pages, examining notes he had made about recent developments effecting his investment in the *Tejano* project. With a small pencil he drew a line connecting two names, Jennifer Spencer and Sergei Yazkov.

At precisely two o'clock, Volkov's driver stopped in the parking lot in front of Moscow State University at the overlook on Sparrow Hills. As he had anticipated, given the weather and time of day, the area was deserted. Only one other vehicle was in the lot, a dirty Lada he recognized as belonging to Vladimir Kiriyenko.

Volkov approached his associate's car and found it empty. Turning around, he spotted the man standing beside a low brick wall of the campus overlook. "What are you doing out here, trying to freeze to death?" He trudged across the snow-covered grounds toward Kiriyenko.

Vladimir shook his superior's hand and extended a greeting. "*Privyet,* General." He zipped his heavy ski jacket to the collar. "It is not that bad once you get used to it. I enjoy the solitude up here. The view of the university and the Kremlin is one of the best in the city."

Boris nodded in agreement, looking at the central building of *Moskovsy Gosudarstveny Universitet,* largest of the classic Stalin Gothic skyscrapers in the city. In the distance he could see the red brick walls of the Kremlin and the Moscow River encircling the core of the ancient city.

Volkov lit a cigarette and inhaled deeply to gain warmth. "You were early. Where have you been this time of day?"

"Making weekly rounds of the restaurants, collecting our cut of the profits. I just left the Agrave on *Leninsky Prospekt.*"

"That is good. You made contact with Sergei Yazkov like I requested?"

"*Da,* I telephoned Andrei in New York City. He said Yazkov had already met the young woman on more than one occasion."

Volkov found it hard to believe there had already been a connection made between the two. "But how could this be? Tell me what you learned."

Vladimir related in detail Yazkov's meeting with Spencer and Suzanne Chism in Austin at the Warren McDonald campaign event and the second encounter in El Paso at the Andrew Smith fundraiser.

Volkov looked out at the Kremlin. "It sounds as if Miss Spencer has a high degree of curiosity. Apparently she does not recall the old adage, curiosity killed the cat." He dropped the butt of his half-smoked cigarette to the icy gravel walkway and stomped it with the heel of his heavy military boot.

"Pass orders to Yazkov to scare the hell out of Jennifer Spencer. He must make certain she stops asking questions if she wants to stay alive. Tell him to keep her under constant surveillance."

"Knowing Sergei, he will frighten her to death." Kiriyenkov smiled. "But what if she continues?"

"He is to kill her and get out of the country."

Volkov turned and headed for his car.

Vladimir hastened to follow. "I will send the orders today. Anything else before I go?"

Volkov pulled the door shut and lowered the window. "Make arrangements to eliminate Sergei Yazkov once he reaches Havana. I will tell you when I am ready to give the final order."

Kiriyenko's mouth involuntarily dropped open in shock. "But, General, I thought ..."

"If you thought you are supposed to follow my orders, you were correct. If you thought I intend to allow the possibility of my connection to yet another murder in Texas be revealed, you are wrong. You will do as I say or I will make other arrangements." Volkov took a long gulp from his flask and coldly stared at the man shivering in the night air.

"*Nyet, nyet,* certainly I will do as you say. You have my word on that."

"Good. Get in your car before you freeze to death." With that he raised the window and watched Kiriyenko hurry away.

Night had fallen and illumination from the dim street lights created a stark contrast between the black sky and the whiteness of the ground. Volkov slapped the privacy window, an indication to proceed, then leaned back in comfortable seclusion. "Maybe I should insure my distance from Sergei Yazkov even more," he muttered to himself. "Once Vlad has served his purpose, he too shall be terminated."

CHAPTER 27

▼

AUSTIN
FEBRUARY 19

The moment Juan stepped into the DPS conference room, he was certain he had misunderstood the directions received from Captain Woods. Anticipating a one-on-one meeting with his superior, he was surprised to see more than a dozen Department of Pubic Safety officers and fellow Texas Rangers standing in clusters around the room, engaged in muted conversations. Captain Woods's unmistakable voice resonated across the large room. "Lt. Falcone, over here."

Jordan Woods made his way around the burnished mahogany conference table and shook the younger man's hand. "Good to see ya, Juan. As soon as the colonel arrives, we'll get started."

Before Juan could inquire about the others' presence, Colonel David Spearman, Director of the Texas DPS, entered from his private office at the far end of the room. The retired Marine Corps officer wore a dark blue business suit, rather than the Department's tan gabardine uniform. His imposing military bearing made it appear he was still on active duty preparing to address a platoon of leathernecks readying for a beach landing. "Ladies and gentlemen, get a re-fill on the coffee and juice if you like, and we'll get this briefing underway."

After Juan took a seat next to Captain Woods, he surveyed the assembly of state law enforcement officers, about half of whom he knew, either personally or by sight. Seated to the Director's immediate right Juan recognized Major John Stallings, Chief of the Criminal Law Enforcement Division. Next to Stallings was Susan Myers, head of the Public Information Office, then Jacob Manley, Fugitive Apprehension Unit and Gene Thornton with the Crime Analysis section. If it were not for the presence of the seven other Rangers, he would have assumed he interrupted a meeting of the Department's command and general staff.

Spearman waited until all were seated, giving him their undivided attention. "No doubt you're wondering why I called you in from your regular duties. I'm going to let Senior Captain Stewart explain that. At the conclusion, you'll understand why I want each of you to give this assignment your utmost priority." He paused, letting his words sink in, then turned to the man seated to his immediate left. "Captain Stewart, the floor's yours."

Stewart rose. "Thank you, sir. As y'all may be aware, approximately five months ago Captain Woods assigned Lt. Falcone of Company D to investigate two murders in Maverick and Uvalde Counties, after those sheriffs asked for our assistance. As a result of the lieutenant's diligent work, the division has a suspect, a Russian national by the name of Sergei Yazkov. Due to certain information we've learned about Yazkov, we've decided to elevate his apprehension to a higher level."

Falcone leaned forward, elbows on the table, trying to sort out what he'd heard. So, this little get together is about the Crosser after all. Before he could collect his thoughts, the division head continued.

"Per Director Spearman's orders, effective immediately, Captain Woods will command what will be called the Crosser Task Force, to which each of you is hereby temporarily assigned. At this time we have no reason to suspect Yazkov is a terrorist. Even though his background doesn't fit the terrorist's profile, these days one can never be sure. I am confident we will apprehend him and then help with the prosecution of Sergei Yazkov."

Juan slumped back in the over-stuffed leather chair. The meeting's purpose was crystal clear. The good news is you've done a nice job, Lieutenant; the bad news, it's not your case anymore. Move over, Juanito, it's time for the big boys and girls to step in and finish what you've been screwing around with. Why the hell didn't they just tell me to pack my bags and go home?

Stewart turned to the man seated next to him. "Captain Woods, why don't you take it from here?"

Woods walked to a writing board extending the length of the room. "Some of you were assigned to the Texas Seven Task Force when those convicts escaped from the Connally Unit near Kennedy a few years ago." He turned to fix his gaze on each officer as he continued. "Josh, your Fugitive Apprehension Unit did an outstanding job as usual. Susan, I expect almost as much publicity on the Crosser case as we had with Angel Maturino Resendiz, the rail-car killer, several years ago. Each of you will have specific tasks assigned in addition to working your own district."

Juan thought his fellow Rangers sat a little taller when they realized the top officer in their department had hand-picked them for this operation. Success on this assignment could earn recognition and perhaps a pay increase. A little intra-department rivalry might also lead to a successful conclusion, though he disliked the competitive environment it sometimes stimulated.

"Lieutenant Falcone, come on up and give the highlights of your work, from initial involvement to your most recent conversation with the Moscow police."

Juan had anticipated giving Captain Woods a detailed briefing of his work to date and receiving his supervisor's sage advice and direction. What he was now being called upon to do was entirely different, and he didn't relish being put on the hot seat, especially without prior notice. Juan felt as though he were about to make an oral defense of his thesis for a doctorate in criminal justice to a group of professors, most of whom had written the text books.

Glancing at his notes, Juan took a deep breath and proceeded. "I was pleased when Captain Woods requested I assist the Maverick and Uvalde county sheriffs last September. Since then I've worked with San Antonio PD, FBI, Interpol and, most recently, the Moscow Militia. I welcome the creation of this Task Force and look forward to working with all of you as well." With preliminaries out of the way, Juan detailed his initial assignment and progress, through the arrest of Freddie Martinez to the contact with Moscow. Using colored markers, he created a time line on the wall board. When he finished, he looked toward his supervisor for direction. "That about brings us up to date, sir."

"Okay, troops," Woods said. "Let's get with the program. Where do we go from here?" Again, silence. Apparently no one wanted to be first in the spotlight. He decided to jump-start the discussion. "Susan, let's hear it. Surely you've got some bright ideas."

The PIO flushed slightly in embarrassment but spoke without hesitation. "As of now, the public knows nothing about Sergei Yazkov. The first thing I suggest we do is distribute his photo, physical description and other characteristics to local law enforcement agencies using the DPS computer network and also put the information up on our website. Next, I'd issue a press release with the photo. Because of the Russian angle, I think the story would garner page one coverage above the fold. That's how the D.C. area snipers were ultimately apprehended."

Woods returned to the board and made notes of the media suggestions. "Put that at the top of your to-do list, Susan. But what's really going to make people take the risk of looking for this murder suspect?"

Jacob Manley, head of FAU broke the silence. "M-o-n-e-y, and lots of it. We should put Yazkov on the Department's Most Wanted List. Texas Crime Stoppers should be willing to put up at least a five thousand dollar reward for information leading to his apprehension. Also, get the word out to the crime stopper chapters so they can publicize it."

Woods wrote the phrase "reward fund" and drew dollar signs. "That's good, state and local crime stoppers. What else?"

Ranger Tommy Ann Parks of Lubbock looked down the table at Juan. "How 'bout the locals in Eagle Pass and Uvalde? There's a lot of oil and cattle money in the Brush Country. Would they put up a pot to capture someone who killed one of their own?"

Juan had been thinking the same thing. "Yeah, Roberto Salazar was a ranch hand for a Mr. Rex Hardy. I'll go down and talk with him. Maybe some of the bankers, lawyers, docs and businessmen and women would kick in too."

Woods noted the contacts on the list but shook his head. "Sergeant Parks, why don't you follow up on that? Juan, I want to save you for something else. Come on, ladies and gentlemen, we need more, lots more."

The more suggestions and assignments Juan heard, the more dejected he became. Piece by piece the Crosser investigation was being removed from his domain. He couldn't argue with the logic that it was more than one person could handle, even a Texas Ranger. Crossing his arms, he sat in silence, feeling he'd become a fifth wheel.

Ranger Nan Davis raised her hand for recognition while Woods made note of the assignments. "Captain Woods, there are a couple of other aspects of the suspect we haven't discussed, namely appearance and language."

"I'm listening, what's on your mind?" Woods added her contribution to the board.

"Given the fact he's Caucasian, he can easily blend in. If he's fluent in a number of languages, he might use one or more of them as a cover. Speaking Spanish he wouldn't be out of place anywhere, but to use his Russian, German and French, I'd bet he might head for some university campus. Because of his age, he could pose as a foreign student, maybe enroll in a graduate level program, or at least act like he has."

Woods made note of the comments, then turned back to Davis. "What else comes to mind about appearance?" He expected the woman to hit the softball question out of the park and she proved him right.

"Disguise. If he hasn't changed the color of his hair, grown a beard or purchased glasses yet, you know he will once he sees his mug shot in the newspapers and on television."

"You just won yourself an assignment. Check out the University of Texas and Texas A&M campuses. Then go to Houston and canvas the University of Houston, Rice, Texas Southern University and St. Thomas." Woods pointed to two other Rangers. "Daniels, you take TCU and SMU and Haley, you go to San Antonio and cover St. Mary's and Trinity. Once we have flyers made, distribute them in the book stores and other nearby commercial establishments. Coordinate with campus security too."

"Y'all check with me before you leave," Major Stallings said. "My division has a complete list of all costume shops in the state. Since the pickup was found in San Antone, I suggest, Haley, you go there first. Yazkov may have already made a purchase there."

Woods nodded. "Thanks, Major. Sergeant Haley, interview the staffs at each shop in San Antonio and show them the mug shot. The rest of you call the shops in your city and fax the mug shot. Alert them to call you if someone comes in fitting his description." Woods paused and looked about the room. "Anyone care to add anything else before we wrap up?"

After several more suggestions, all sat in silence. "This has been an excellent briefing," Woods said. "I'm delighted with your analysis and suggestions. It appears this Russian is a trained killer who has demonstrated his capability to elude the authorities. He may have come solo, but my hunch is he was sent here to make a hit. We don't have a motive or a target so that makes it difficult to speculate where he might be. If he doesn't have friends or accomplices here, we lose the possibility there's a Judas out there who'll rat him out. We will reconvene in this room at the same hour seven days from now. Until then, do your jobs well and proceed with caution. You're dismissed."

While the officers exchanged small talk and exited the conference room, Juan tossed his notes and file materials in his briefcase and headed for the door.

"Lt. Falcone, may I speak to you a moment?" Captain Stewart called out. "Lieutenant, unless I'm mistaken, I'd say you've got a burr under your saddle. Something botherin' you?"

Juan looked down at the briefcase containing the Crosser files held protectively at his side. "Nothing really, sir."

"Come on, I may be dumb but I ain't stupid. What is it?"

Juan paused before responding. "May I speak freely, sir?"

"Of course. What's on your mind?"

"To tell you the truth, sir, I feel like I've been striped of all responsibility for finding Yazkov. I've done my best, but the agency seems to be saying my best is not good enough."

Stewart shook his head. "That's not true, Lieutenant. After Captain Woods reported his conversation with you, I briefed Colonel Spearman, and we decided this guy deserves as much attention as we can devote to him. Can't you see from your fellow officers' suggestions more needs to be done than you or any other single person can handle?"

"Yes, sir, but once all the assignments were made, I'm left holding an empty briefcase."

"Captain Woods will fill you in later about your role. I want you to be his second in command. I don't want to tie you down with any particular assignment but rather have you free to see the big picture and put it all together for us. The next time something of this magnitude comes along, Lieutenant, I want you to have had some broader experience. It could be you who heads up the next task force."

A slow smile crossed Juan's face. "Thank you, sir. I'll do my best."

Stewart reached out and took Juan's hand. "Now go home and get some rest. Tomorrow I want to meet with you and Captain Woods and look at all the pieces of this puzzle. Your job is to insure Sergei Yazkov is taken down before he completes his mission, whatever it may be."

CHAPTER 28

▼

AUSTIN
FEBRUARY 19

Jennifer Spencer surveyed the handful of hard core supporters at Warren McDonald's campaign headquarters. This was not the visual campaign manager Suzanne Chism expected for the television cameras on
primary election night. The candidate had yet to make an appearance
but was reportedly on his way to go live for the ten o'clock news.

Jennifer studied a printout of the most recent county-by-county
election results. The vote totals coupled with the room's stale cigarette
smell made her nauseated. Warren McDonald's looming defeat was
palpable. The Austin area's raging thunderstorm matched her mood,
total depression. She looked up to see percentages flash on the TV
screens, all showing Warren McDonald in last place, politically dead.

One station's consultant proclaimed, "I think it is clear now that
political novice, Andrew Smith, will easily become his party's nominee
to face Senator Russell Creighton. Mr. Smith, however, will have an
uphill battle against the well-funded incumbent."

Swallowing the bile in her throat, tears welled as she saw Warren
arrive for his concession speech. No reporters were present for the last

place finisher. The candidate smiled, trying to appear upbeat to the small crowd, congratulated Smith on his campaign, then announced his retirement from politics. This is my retirement as well, Jennifer thought. A person works hard for the best candidate, only to see the wrong one elected.

She'd had enough for one night. Walking toward the exit, she passed Suzanne Chism at a table with her companion, Wendy Thompson. The campaign manager puffed on an ever-present cigarette and scrutinized the vote totals. "Well, kid, the good news is Warren has come in first in his hometown of Houston, and second in both Dallas and Fort Worth. The bad news, that's not going to be enough."

"I don't understand why you say that," Jennifer replied in frustration. "Those are the biggest cites in the state."

"Because the vote totals out of Abilene, Midland/Odessa and Lubbock have been trending for Smith all night. He's way ahead in El Paso, the Lower Rio Grande Valley, Galveston and the Upper Gulf Coast area of Beaumont, Port Arthur and Orange."

Jennifer realized she *could* feel lower than she had a few minutes earlier. "It's not fair."

Exhaling smoke over her shoulder, Suzanne lit another off the cigarette butt. "Come on, whoever told you life was fair? Welcome to the real world of politics, girl. Smith had more nutty supporters get out and vote for him than Warren had sane ones. Andy won the primary, and Mr. Good Government McDonald is making his concession speech and ending his political career."

Suzanne reached over and tugged Jennifer's forearm. "Come on over to Warren's suite at the Driskell Hotel with Wendy and me. Have a nightcap and debrief. It will do you good."

Jennifer pulled away. "That's the last place I want to be right now. I'm going back to Houston. No telling how much work has piled up at my office. At least I can find something productive to do there."

"Hey, you did great, kid." Suzanne stood and gave Jennifer a long hug. "You raised a hell of a lot of money for Warren. Get some rest and call me next week. Be careful driving back. This storm looks like a real bastard."

Jennifer forced a smile, then turned and headed out into the wind and rain. Two bolts of lightening flashed across the nighttime sky, illuminating the Capitol dome in an eerie glow. Hurriedly, she unlocked the car door and slid inside.

"Damn, what the hell is this?" Jennifer snatched a small envelope resting on the dash. Using the overhead light, she read the typed message.

Good evening, Jennifer Anne. Your candidate lost. Give up and back off. We have succeeded. Be smart and you might live a long life. If you foolishly continue your little investigation, you will live only long enough to regret it. Be very careful driving home.

Jennifer tossed the note onto the seat next to her, her hand shaking. She questioned how anyone could get in her car. Quickly, she hit the automatic door and window locks. She picked up the envelope and stared at her name and address. The hairs on the back of her neck stood up.

"Someone is stalking me," she said to herself. Streaks of lightning flashed around her, accompanied by a prolonged roll of thunder. As the night sky lit up like day, Jennifer turned and saw an old man staring at her from a late model car parked next to her's. He sat in the passenger's seat less than five yards away. Between his interior lights and the lightning she could see his wrinkled face pressed against the window. White tufts of hair encircled his otherwise balding scalp.

Jennifer slammed the car into gear and shot through an opening in the row of cars in front of hers. In the rearview mirror she saw his car pull out to follow.

Forty-five minutes later, Jennifer entered the Bastrop city limits. A car was trailing her, but she wasn't sure if it was the old man's.

"Damn, I should have thought clearer, gotten a tag number. I don't even remember the color." It was then she noticed a sheriff's patrol car parked at a twenty-four hour diner. She made a U-turn and decided to report what had happened.

Making a frantic dash through the rain for the diner's entrance, she saw another set of headlights pull into the lot and park next to her.

Yanking open the café door, Jennifer exhaled in relief at the noisy crowd and country music. She brushed wet hair out of her eyes and walked a bit unsteadily toward the middle-aged man in uniform seated at the counter. "Pardon me, sir, but I really need your help."

The officer spun around on the barstool. "What's wrong, miss? Car trouble?"

In her haste she had forgotten to bring in the note, but explained everything that had happened. "He's even followed me here. Come over to the window and I'll show you. He's right out there."

The deputy looked out into the rain as she pointed toward the parking lot. The car was no longer there. "He, he was there, honest."

"Miss, have you by any chance been drinking tonight? I don't see the car you described, but I'd swear I detect alcohol on your breath." The deputy moved closer. "Maybe I ought to take you in and run a breathalyzer."

Jennifer rubbed her forehead. "I had one beer several hours ago and coffee after that. I assure you I'm fully capable of driving to Houston. I'm telling you, officer, someone's been following me from Austin. I've got a threatening letter in my car, and he could be parked over by the highway waiting for me to leave."

The deputy stared at her for a long moment. "I tell you what I'll do. How 'bout I follow you for a while? I'll even turn on my overhead flashers, if that will make you feel better."

For the first time all evening, Jennifer felt a sense of relief. "That, that would be great. Could you follow me all the way to I-10?"

"No, ma'am, my jurisdiction doesn't extend that far, but I'll radio the deputy in the next county to meet you at an all-night service station. How 'bout that?"

"Thank you, thank you very much. Here, let me pay for your dinner." Without waiting for a reply, Jennifer tossed a twenty on the counter and headed for her car.

When she saw the patrol car move behind her, flashers on, she sped off. At the county line, the patrol car's headlights flashed, the car slowed and made a U-turn. There were no customers at the all-night station where Jennifer was to meet the next deputy, and initially she saw no patrol car. Then, from behind the station, a white Ford with blue markings slowly pulled forward. She was relieved when the driver lowered his window and indicated for her to proceed. He turned on his overheads and fell in behind her as she got back on the loop around town.

The rain began to let up the closer she got to Interstate 10. Once on the interstate, the deputy dropped off, flashing his headlights as he slowed. Jennifer had seen no other cars get on the highway and felt safe once more.

Not fifteen minutes later, she noticed a car approximately one hundred yards behind her. The driver flashed his high beams off and on. Jennifer could see no other headlights in either direction.

Fear replaced logic. She pushed the accelerator to seventy miles per hour, but the car moved closer. Seventy-five, eight-five, ninety. As Jennifer increased her speed, so did the other driver. Putting all her weight on the gas pedal, she watched the speed indicator climb past one hundred ten. At last the trailing vehicle seemed to be standing still.

She contemplated getting off the highway and hiding out for thirty minutes, hoping the stalker would pass, when she suddenly observed flashing red and blue lights on a car parked on the shoulder. Once she had flown by, the state trooper pulled onto the eastbound lane in hot pursuit, siren blaring. Letting up on the gas, her car came to a gradual stop on the shoulder. At least she had police protection for a while.

The trooper approached the convertible and shined his flashlight into the car. "May I see your driver's license, please ma'am, and proof of insurance?"

Jennifer's emotions were so mixed she didn't know whether to thank the officer for being there or worry about the huge fine she would be paying. She handed over the requested papers then slumped her head onto the steering wheel, exhausted and relieved to no longer be alone on the deserted highway.

The flashlight's beam illuminated the envelope and paper lying on the passenger seat. "Is that the note, Miss Spencer?"

Startled about his knowledge of the note, Jennifer placed a protective hand on the papers. "Yes, but, how did you know?"

The officer smiled. "Oh, you've made quite a bit of news this evening. I heard the deputy on the scanner explain your predicament. He asked if I would be on the lookout for you, to give you some cover. But at the speed you were going ..." He returned her license and insurance card.

Jennifer showed him the note, told him about the old man following her out of Austin, the stop in Bastrop and finally the car behind her again on I-10.

The officer frowned. "How do you know the car behind you on the interstate was driven by that same old man?"

She thought a moment then shook her head. "Well, I don't really. Maybe I'm just being paranoid because of everything that's happening."

"Never mind, Miss Spencer, under the circumstances I'm not going to ticket you. This note substantiates part of your story, and I suppose the rest is possible. If you like, I'll follow you for a while, but I'll have to drop off when we reach the county line. I'll radio ahead and see if I can get another trooper to escort you once we get there."

"That would be wonderful. Thanks so much." Jennifer reached out and shook his hand with both of hers. "Oh, here's my business card. If you ever need a lawyer, please call. I owe you one."

The trooper smiled, putting the card in his pocket. "That's what I'm out here for. I'd like to keep the envelope and note. I'll send it into our criminal analysis division and have it checked for fingerprints. They'll have your driver's license and plate number and will get in touch if there's any need."

As she listened to the officer, Jennifer found her concentration wander, her gaze going past his shoulder to the highway. Approximately five hundred yards away, she saw the headlights of a car sitting on an overpass. Putting her fingers to her lips to interrupt his next comment, she pointed back down the deserted highway.

The trooper turned. "Think that's him?"

"I'll bet my life on it. Who else would be sitting out here at this hour of the morning?" She slapped the palm of her hand against the steering wheel. "Damn! I never had a chance to get the make or model of his car, much less the plate number."

"Don't worry about that. Let's go. I'll also radio Houston Police to dispatch a blue and white to meet you at the city limits and escort you to your apartment. Hey, one more thing. Try to keep it under eighty-five this time."

Forty-five minutes later the HPD officer waited while Jennifer went through the security gate, then honked and drove away. Jennifer took the steps two at a time to her apartment. She felt secure, hearing Lad's welcoming bark, but then saw the message scrawled on her front door. She stared at the door and reflexively covered her mouth to muffle what otherwise would have been a terrified scream.

"Welcome Home, Snoop" was written in what appeared to be blood. Jennifer pulled the cell phone out of her purse and dialed 911.

CHAPTER 29

AUSTIN
FEBRUARY 22

Savannah Spencer walked briskly to the Governor's Public Reception Room, the most lavish space in the immense pink granite State Capitol and stepped into the Victorian parlor with its cherry wood trim and wainscoting. A polite young receptionist seated behind a mahogany desk noted the Spencers' ten o'clock appointment, while an ever-observant DPS security officer smiled and nodded as Savannah surveyed her surroundings.

A side door flung open, and Governor Jeffrey Bates made his entry. His six foot two inch frame appeared to carry no more weight than when they had both served in the state senate years earlier. Savannah noticed distinguishing streaks of gray in the governor's otherwise dark brown hair, as he flashed his trademark photogenic smile. "Savannah, it's great to see you again. Welcome to my humble quarters."

Savannah extended her hand, but as their eyes met, Bates took her in a warm embrace. The staff paid little attention since the gregarious politician was known to greet both men and women in such fashion. "It's been too long, Savannah," he whispered before she could pull her head away. "We could have been a great team, sweetheart, you know that."

She took both his hands and stiffened her arms, politely but firmly pushing him away. Her smile was demure. "I know, Jeff, but that was then, this is now." Before the governor could respond, the exterior hallway door opened.

Blake Spencer was a self-confident physician in his mid-fifties. Usually nothing intimidated the orthopedic surgeon, whether he was dealing with patients, hospital staff or high-ranking politicians, but Savannah could instantly tell he was equally impressed by the surroundings.

Governor Bates immediately took control. "Dr. Spencer, good to see you again. Savannah and I were just reminiscing about old times." He pointed toward the door by the security guard on the east side of the Reception Room. "Come on. Let's go back to my office where we can visit. There's someone I want you to meet."

The security officer opened the door, and they proceeded through the governor's suite. A large antique table at the south end of the large room served as the chief executive's desk. Behind it, between ceiling-high windows, was an historic roll-top desk used by governors since the turn of the century. At the far end of the room was a sitting area with Victorian sofa and four antique occasional chairs. On a cherry table in the middle was a silver coffee service.

The governor then introduced the Spencers to a Ranger awaiting their arrival. "Savannah, Dr. Spencer, I'd like for you to meet Texas Ranger Lt. Juan Falcone." He turned to Juan. "Lieutenant, this is Dr. Blake Spencer and his wife, Savannah."

Juan stepped forward from his position at the far corner of the casual sitting area and extended his hand. "Doctor, Mrs. Spencer, my pleasure."

"Y'all have a seat and let's get down to business. From what little you told me on the phone yesterday, Savannah, I presumed you wanted me to call in the DPS or Rangers. I called Colonel Spearman, and he sent over Lt. Falcone."

Savannah cast a knowing smile, while the governor poured coffee for everyone. "As always, Governor, you were correct in your presumption. I should have expected no less."

"Why don't you take it from the top about why y'all are concerned for your daughter's safety and what she's been up to."

Juan opened his attaché and prepared to take notes. Over the next twenty minutes, in precise chronological fashion, Savannah hit the high points of her and Jennifer's joint review of the FEC files in Wimberley. She recounted their trip to Smith's fundraiser in Galveston, Jennifer's questioning of contributors in the Dallas-Fort Worth area, the note left in her car, the old man who followed her and the bloody message on the apartment door.

When she concluded, Juan looked over his notes. "I presume, Mrs. Spencer, your daughter kept the note she found in her car. I'd like to have it examined."

"You don't have to leave Austin to do that, Lieutenant. Jennifer told me she gave it to the state trooper who stopped her and that he mentioned sending it to another DPS section for fingerprint analysis."

Juan made a note for follow-up. "Do either of you or Jennifer have any idea who the old man might have been?"

Savannah and Blake looked at each other then shook their heads. "We discussed that and have no idea," Blake replied. "Jennifer's an attractive young lady, and while I wouldn't be surprised if some lecherous old man had been eyeing her, the note in the car is a complete mystery."

Juan solemnly looked at Jennifer Spencer's parents. "It appears someone knew of the calls your daughter had made and her examination of the FEC reports. I suggest she immediately stop all such activity."

Bates turned to the investigator. "Lt. Falcone, I don't intend to ignore your chain of command, but I hope you will make arrangements to go to Houston as soon as possible to interview Jennifer and determine what precautionary measures, if any, need to be taken."

"I can assure you, Governor, that will be done."

"Do you have any comments or questions for the Spencers?"

"Yes, sir, a few."

After reviewing his notes, Juan proceeded with a series of inquires as to precise dates, times, locales and persons present at meetings. He was interrupted when an aide to the governor quietly entered and pointed to his watch then looked to his boss.

The governor rose. "I'm sorry to cut this short, but I'm already late for a luncheon at the Mansion." He motioned the Spencers toward a private doorway leading out to the Capitol rotunda. "Lt. Falcone, I'd appreciate it if you'd give Mrs. Spencer your pager and cell phone numbers."

The Ranger nodded and handed a business card to Savannah.

"And Savannah, I want you to feel free to call Ranger Falcone if anything unusual happens, anytime, day or night. We'll do some pokin' around, and if anything surfaces, I can share with you, I will call."

The governor gave Savannah a light kiss on the cheek and shook hands with her husband. He turned to Falcone. "Would you stay just a minute, Lieutenant? There's another matter I want to ask about."

Once the Spencers had departed, Bates escorted the officer into a smaller private study and shut the door. "Okay, Lieutenant. Cut to the chase. What's your take on all this?" He sat on the edge of the desk and awaited a reply.

"It's difficult to evaluate at this point, sir. Obviously, someone wants to stop Ms. Spencer's investigation. I'll call her when I leave and arrange an appointment as soon as she's available. I'll also go back to headquarters and run down the prints the trooper sent in."

"I assume since the Director assigned you to come over that you're not working any other case right now. Is that correct?"

Having to baby-sit some over zealous lawyer playing private political snoop wasn't Juan's idea of a choice assignment, but he knew it would do no good to complain. "As a matter of fact, I have been working a double murder case. A task force has recently been formed, so I have some time to look into this Spencer matter now that others are involved."

"Yes, I've been briefed on the task force. Good luck with it. Working this Spencer case will be a little diversion for you. This shouldn't take too long. I just want to try and help calm the girl's parents if we can."

"I understand, sir, I'll get right on it."

The governor stood when his aide re-entered the room and politely insisted they leave for the Mansion. "I've got to run. Let my secretary know if you need anything."

"Yes, sir, I certainly will."

Juan placed a call to Jennifer's office, only to find she had gone for lunch and would be in depositions the rest of the afternoon. When told she would be in the office the next day, Juan decided to make an unannounced visit so that he wouldn't alarm her. He intended to wrap up this alleged stalker case quickly and get back to searching for Sergei Yazkov.

Chapter 30

▼

Houston
February 23

The fragrance from a vanilla candle and the hushed tones of baroque music combined to create an atmosphere of calmness in Jennifer Spencer's office. Such personal touches distinguished her environment from that of the exterior offices, but today they didn't alleviate Jennifer's difficulty concentrating on her work.

There was a sinking feeling in the pit of her stomach. How would she tackle the mound of briefs and depositions that had accumulated over the past nine months while she volunteered a couple of days each week for McDonald's campaign and played amateur sleuth? Compared to the frenetic pace of the campaign and her incomplete investigation, her trial practice seemed mundane.

Jennifer swiveled her leather chair to gaze out the window at Buffalo Bayou and the green space winding westward from downtown. The quiet solitude of the six-mile running path along the lush, rolling terrain would be a welcome respite.

Turning back to her desk, she absentmindedly drew the outline of a Capitol dome on a yellow legal pad and filled in the tiny windows.

She had dreamed of a three or four year stint in D.C., working in McDonald's senate office. Time in the nation's capital wouldn't hurt her resume if she later chose to dive more deeply into political waters.

Taking a sip of hot decaffeinated chamomile tea to calm her nerves, Jennifer thought back to the events of the previous four days. Perhaps she should call the DPS and inquire about the note and ask if any fingerprints were found. Maybe the stalker episode was only a figment of her over-active imagination, and the message on the door was a prank by a perverted neighbor.

She struggled to convince herself it hadn't been the old man who scrawled the message at her apartment. She had heard nothing further from the police officer who responded to her 911 call. Replacing the mug on its coaster, she turned her attention to the medical records she had been reviewing.

Her spotty concentration was suddenly interrupted by the buzz of the intercom. "Yes Rita, what is it?"

"A Texas Ranger is in the reception area to see you. It doesn't show on my calendar that he has an appointment. I told him you were busy and asked not to be disturbed, but he said it was urgent."

Jennifer smiled. "I know what he wants. Show him in, but tell him I have to leave for the airport in about thirty minutes."

Her secretary hastened to continue before her boss disconnected. "I have Gloria on line two calling from the medical school library. She says she's come across some hot information that will help on your doctor's deposition this afternoon. What should I tell her?"

"Send in the Ranger and I'll talk to Gloria while he's cooling his heels in here."

Jennifer heard the paralegal's voice on the phone but paid little attention when Juan Falcone entered her large private office and stood a discrete distance from her desk. The Ranger's dark brown eyes and black wavy hair easily distracted her from the briefing. His white shirt, heavily starched jeans and highly polished alligator boots demonstrated pride in his appearance. He wore a revolver on his hip and carried a pearl gray Stetson and attaché.

Juan motioned for her to proceed with her telephone conversation, experience having taught him that one could learn a lot about a person by their surroundings. He noticed a photograph of her parents on the credenza, and next to it, one of a young man in navy whites aboard an ocean-going vessel. On the wall behind the sofa were the customary certificates: a diploma from law school, a license from the U.S. Supreme Court and her law review honor.

His focus shifted to an enormous oil painting of blues, yellows, reds and greens that captivated him, bringing forth a flood of pleasant memories.

"Like it?"

"Yes." He turned back toward Jennifer. "If I'm not mistaken, it's Santa Elena Canyon in Big Bend National Park."

"I'm impressed." Jennifer smiled. "Most big city folks have no idea there are vistas like that in Texas. They usually guess Colorado or northern Arizona. You obviously have first-hand knowledge."

"I've been there too many times to count. I grew up in Roma, up the river from McAllen, but went to college at Sul Ross out in Alpine. My buddies and I took many a float trip down the Rio Grande." He nodded toward the painting. "No telling how many times I've laid in a canoe or raft looking up at those canyon walls."

Jennifer came from behind her desk and shook Juan's hand, then stood beside him, admiring the painting. "Yeah, there's nothing like it." She pointed at the photographs of the young man and her parents on the credenza behind her desk. "You've met my parents. That's my brother, Justin, Naval Academy grad, still on active duty in the Persian Gulf. When we were in junior high and high school, our parents took us camping in the Big Bend almost every spring break or summer vacation. I wasn't too keen on it at the time, now I wouldn't trade anything for those memories."

Jennifer glanced down at her boots and denims, topped by a blue button-down shirt. "While I was on the phone, I noticed you did a double take at the way I'm dressed. I guess you expected granny glasses, a blue pin-stripped suit, maybe a rep tie to go along with it?"

Juan chuckled. "As a matter of fact, I did. I understand business casual is the in thing these days, so I shouldn't have been surprised."

"I usually do play lawyer dress-up, but you caught me on the way out of town. I've got a noon flight for Harlingen, then a drive to McAllen for a deposition. Afraid this can't take too long."

"I'm Lieutenant ..."

"Oh, I know who you are, Lt. Juan Falcone. I spoke with my mother last night, and she filled me in. I think it may have been overkill for her to go to Governor Bates and for him to in turn call in the Texas Rangers, but what could I say once the deed was done? I love her to death, even though she thinks I need a full time bodyguard."

Jennifer propped her boots on the coffee table. "When you get back to Austin, you can check with whatever division of DPS dusted for fingerprints on the note left in my car."

"What about the message left on your apartment door that your parents told me about?"

"The HPD investigating officer said he thought it was a type of fake blood product anyone could purchase at a costume shop."

Falcone made note of her comments. "I'll go by HPD and check on that before I head back to Austin." Falcone put his pen down and looked directly at Jennifer. "Your parents are just concerned for your safety, Ms. Spencer."

"I know that and appreciate it, but surely you've got better things to do than sit here and chitchat with a damsel who is no longer in distress."

"As a matter of fact, I am assigned to a task force searching for a suspect in a double murder case, but when the governor calls, the department responds."

"Sounds more exciting than what I have to offer." She glanced at her watch. "I really need to prepare for a deposition. May we get started?"

He nodded. "Why don't you start at the beginning and tell me about the investigation and what ideas you have as to who left the messages."

"Let's see. As my folks probably told you, I started part-time volunteer work in Warren McDonald's Senate campaign about nine months ago."

"Right. Tell me what you've been doing."

For the next thirty minutes Jennifer explained her volunteer fundraising for the McDonald campaign and her suspicions of illegal contributions to his opponents. She went into detail about her private investigation and the man who had followed her from Austin.

When she concluded, Juan sat in silence before responding. "While I don't want to alarm you, Ms. Spencer, I suggest you take the warning messages seriously and cease your detective work."

"You don't have to worry about that, Lieutenant. I've had it with politics and don't plan to be constantly looking over my shoulder for some old man to nab me." She pointed to the files piled up on her desk and beside the sofa. "As you can see, I've plenty of work to keep me busy. Unless the old codger, or whoever it was, has an arrest record, you probably won't find anything on file with the fingerprints, will you?"

"I'm afraid you're correct." Juan nodded. "We'll probably find prints on the paper but it's possible there won't be a match. Same thing with your apartment. I'll be happy to call and let you know what we find." He handed her one of his business cards. "Call me if anything else comes up."

Jennifer placed the card on the coffee table and shook his hand when they stood. "It was nice to finally meet a real Texas Ranger. I've heard so many stories about you guys all my life. You can go back to Austin and tell Governor Bates you did your duty and nothing further needs to be done."

She escorted Juan into the reception area. "You mentioned you grew up near McAllen. Got any recommendations for good Tex-Mex down there? I'm spending the night after I get through grilling my defendant during his depo."

Juan laughed. "La Tapitia is a great little cantina on US Highway 83. Tell the owner former Sheriff Falcone sent you and you'll be treated like royalty. He's my cousin. Have a safe trip, Ms. Spencer, and I'll give you a call when I find out about the fingerprints."

Sergei Yazkov sat patiently in a parking lot across the street from Jennifer Spencer's office building, a *Houston Chronicle* positioned to hide his face. Thanks to the disguises purchased at the San Antonio costume shop, he appeared nothing like the murder suspect whose image appeared on page one alongside an article concerning two brutal murders in the South Texas brush country.

Removing a large pair of sunglasses, he looked in the rearview mirror and checked his shoulder length blonde wig and ruby red lipstick. Mascara and eyeliner glamorizing the aqua blue contact lenses matched his silk blouse. He had applied sweet jasmine perfume and a size 38C bra filled with foam rubber, which he adjusted. He had shaven closely, almost taking off a layer of skin in the process, before applying blush, eye brow pencil and makeup base. Stacked heels, slacks, small silver earrings and a string of plastic pearls completed the ensemble. If someone were to inquire, he was an unemployed clerk scanning the classified ads in search of a secretarial or bookkeeping position.

Yazkov had punched two small holes in the newspaper to keep Spencer's building entrance and underground garage under constant surveillance while shielding his face from curious passersby. Since Spencer's arrival this morning, the only unusual activity was the entry of a cowboy wearing a large revolver strapped to his hip and a law enforcement badge affixed to his shirt. The western style hat and gun made him stand out from the business suits and casual attire of the men and women coming and going from the building.

His recent orders were clear, scare Spencer into ceasing the campaign contribution investigation and, if she persisted, eliminate her. For now he would wait and see if she understood his intentions. So what if she found out the Russians had funneled money into Smith's campaign? McDonald was defeated and that election was only a footnote in political history. Volkov's investments had worked, and Sergei's next action only depended on Spencer's persistence and stupidity in the face of danger.

Absorbed with the article, Yazkov nearly missed Jennifer's early afternoon departure. He glanced over the top of the newspaper in time to see the now familiar red convertible descend the garage's exit ramp.

Following at a safe distance he decided she was headed home. Since he had already rented an apartment across the street from Spencer, his order to increase surveillance was easy. From his apartment window he could easily observe both her parking space and apartment door. There was no security guard on duty at the gate to her apartment complex, and he had easy access with a magnetic card he had stolen from a careless tenant.

Shortly after her arrival, Spencer departed. Seeing the overnight case tossed into the back seat and the dog in the passenger seat, he surmised she was going out of town. Now was his chance.

The Russian proceeded to her apartment where he placed a six-inch plastic ruler between the door and the facing, sliding it downward. As soon as the flimsy lock clicked open, he slipped inside. From a small black nylon carrying case he extracted two telephone listening devices, one for the portable phone in the kitchen/living room, the other for the phone on the night stand. Late one night two weeks earlier, he had entered Spencer's law offices in the same manner and hidden similar transmitters. Regular monitoring had divulged only tedious legalese about pending cases.

"Damn." Jennifer slammed the palm of her hand on the steering wheel. "Lad, it's all your fault. You made me leave my make-up case on the bathroom sink. What kind of guard dog are you anyway?"

The golden retriever leaned over and licked Jennifer's cheek. Checking the time on the dashboard clock, she hurriedly made a U-turn. "It will be close, but I have enough time to go back and get my things. You certainly don't want me looking like some sweat-hog after my run, do you? Never mind, you don't have to answer that."

No sooner had Sergei placed the bug on the bedside phone than he heard a dog's loud barking. Spencer's? Impossible. She should be to the freeway by now. He detected the sound of a key inserted into the lock and the knob being turned.

Yazkov gently eased the bedroom door shut and hastily looked around for a place to hide. Quietly, he pulled a military utility knife from the sheath strapped to his thigh. He slipped behind the sliding doors of the closet and waited.

"Lad! Calm down! What the devil is wrong with you, boy?"

Jennifer's sixty-pound retriever was wildly barking as he stretched the leash, rearing onto his back legs and straining to get to the closed bedroom door.

"Well, it's a good thing we did come back. I must have left the door unlocked. I can't believe that." After locking it behind her she turned toward the bedroom. "I ..."

Lad was furiously growling at the closed bedroom door. Jennifer froze in terror, barely able to breathe. She never closed that door!

Jennifer unlocked the bolt while tugging on the leash to get Lad away from the closed door. Slamming it behind her, she ran down the corridor toward the stairwell in search of the roving security guard.

Sergei stepped out of the closet and entered the living room to greet his victim. He found Spencer had made a hasty escape. Outside in the apartment complex's common hallway, he saw his prey turn the corner and start down the steps, the barking dog securely in tow.

In her haste, Jennifer looked back toward her apartment and saw Sergei Yazkov. Their eyes locked.

"Oh, my God!" Jennifer's face went ashen. Who the hell was this damn woman and what was she doing in her apartment? She took the remaining steps three at a time as she raced to find help.

While Jennifer searched the grounds for the golf cart carrying the retired police officer, Sergei made his exit. As he sat waiting impatiently for the electronically controlled gate to open, in his rearview mirror he saw Spencer and the guard at the rear of the lot. They were engaged in animated conversation, and the departing automobile failed to divert their attention. Sergei, safely out of the gate, headed toward the congested interstate to be engulfed in a river of traffic.

Once they had entered her apartment, the guard patted Jennifer on the back, then turned up the volume on his hearing aide. "Please slow down, Ms. Spencer. Can you tell me what this person you claimed you saw looked like?

"Who do you mean I claimed I saw? I *did* see her when I was outside starting down the stairs to find you. Do you think I run around in a frenzy all the time?"

An expression of skepticism crossed the security guard's face. "So you didn't actually see her *in* your apartment?"

"No, not inside. Maybe whoever wrote that filthy message on my door the other day decided to pay me a second visit."

"Yes, I got the report you called 911, and the police came out to investigate."

"I know someone was in my bedroom because my dog was barking at the closed door. Plus, I never close that door. The woman I saw had to come from somewhere. I'm telling you, she followed me out of the apartment door."

"Give me a description of this woman you saw out in the hallway, please."

Jennifer closed her eyes and tried to recreate the frantic scene. "She had long blonde hair, about shoulder length. It looked like a cheap dye job if you ask me. Enough make-up to appear in a cabaret."

The guard seemed confused. "Appear in a what?"

"Make that a stage show, you know, like on Broadway. I couldn't tell the color of her eyes. She was pretty tall, nearly six-foot I'd guess. I know she had on a blue blouse and dark blue skirt and big ..." Releasing Lad's leash, Jennifer cupped her hands to demonstrate large breasts. "You know what I mean?"

The man turned beet red. "Oh, yes, ma'am, you don't have to say anymore about those. I've got the picture. Can you tell me if it looks like anything was stolen? Take your time, ma'am, I know you're flustered." The guard made notes on a small note pad while they walked through the rooms.

It appeared to Jennifer that everything was in order. Items on her writing desk had not been disturbed. Her dresser drawers were not ransacked, and no furniture had been moved.

The guard looked around with her. "Jewelry, watches, rings? Anything like that appear to be missing?"

Jennifer went to a box in the top of her closet and pulled it down. "No. Everything is here."

Fifteen minutes later she dropped off Lad to board with his pals and raced to catch her flight to the Valley. Going eighty miles an hour, she swerved to miss a motorcycle getting on the freeway. Did she lock up after ushering the guard out the door? Like he said, maybe the woman didn't come out of her apartment. The keys were in her purse all the time, and the purse was never out of her sight. It had to be a break-in, but why?

She was herded onto the plane, last in the first boarding group. After she had thrown her bag and heavy trial briefcase into the overhead bin and fallen into her seat next to a sweaty cowboy, the intruder's image remained fresh in her mind.

Nibbling on the airline's complimentary peanuts, she closed her eyes. Month by month she reconstructed her schedule, court appearances, opposing counsel, witnesses, campaign events, trials and depositions. Maybe the woman is in cahoots with the old man in Austin. Maybe she was the one who'd written the message on her apartment door.

She recalled the other campaign events she had attended across the state. Maybe she was one of the women she called in the Dallas-Fort Worth area. Perhaps that Kathryn Morton. She had seemed surprised at her call. Jennifer finally allowed herself to doze off, unanswered questions left mingling through her mind.

Soon the hard bump of the plane's wheels at touch down jarred Jennifer back to reality. Peering out the window, she saw the fronds of the palm trees planted around the terminal blowing in the Gulf Coast breeze. Only a few hundred miles from Houston, but light years away socio-economically and geographically. She loved the rich Hispanic heritage from Brownsville to Harlingen, McAllen, Rio Grande City and Roma.

Roma, home of Lt. Juan Falcone. Why hadn't she thought of him earlier? Maybe the Ranger could serve some useful purpose after all.

While the other passengers made their way up the aisle to the jetway, she pulled out her wallet to retrieve Juan Falcone's business card. Not there. Then to her shirt and jeans pockets. Still no luck. She could see him handing it to her. Damn. She had left it on the coffee table.

By the time she reached her rental car and left the parking lot, she had decided, after the deposition and a light dinner, to check into a motel and write a detailed summary of what occurred in her apartment. When Falcone called back to report on the note and the message, she would be prepared to tell him of the latest developments.

CHAPTER 31

▼

ZURICH
FEBRUARY 24

A pleasant female voice responded to Jake Hardesty's long distance call. "Good morning, Badrutt's Palace, how may I be of service?"

Jake double-checked the message from Dan Morton before replying to the Saint-Moritz resort operator. "Would you please connect me to the room of your guest, Ms. Francesca Rosario?"

Sitting at the antique writing desk in the lakeside corner suite of the Baur au Lac, Jake waited patiently while the call was connected. The back of the aristocratic hotel faced Zurich's commercial center, while its front doors and windows overlooked Lake Zurichsee. He admired the hotel's manicured lawns, the placid lake and snow-covered Alps. The fragrance of freshly cut roses on the nearby coffee table added to the hotel's attention to detail.

Jake had been surprised when Morton agreed to temporarily close the Triad Investments account. Given the developments Morton had conveyed regarding further snooping by Jennifer Spencer, he was equally relieved. Rebecca Durham had also reported to York that two women had attended an Andrew Smith fundraiser in early December and had questioned one of the men Durham had paid to distribute leaflets publicizing the event. What was of greater concern was the two women then attended the fundraiser. When she learned this disturbing news, Durham told her operative to follow them home. Their destination turned out to be a Houston apartment complex, the same one Morton found on his Internet search for Jennifer Spencer.

Though Morton had agreed to close the account, Jake had a nagging feeling there was something going on behind his back. He felt considerably better when Morton proposed that he make this trip to Zurich and withdraw what cash remained in the Triad account. The remaining amount would be funneled through York to Durham and her operatives, assuring Smith's victory.

Jake's thoughts were interrupted when Antonio Bolardi, special assistant to Francesa Rosario, answered the telephone and introduced himself. "May I help you?"

"Yes, this is Jake Hardesty calling from Zurich for Ms. Rosario. I believe she is expecting my call."

Shortly after arriving at Baur au Lac, Jake had received a fax from Morton instructing him to call Francesca Rosario. No explanation was transmitted, only her telephone number in Saint-Moritz. While it seemed a bit odd, he came to the conclusion that everything connected to *Tejano* was unusual in one way or another. They were, after all, sailing in uncharted waters.

A woman's soft but business-like voice on the other end of the line quickly got the Texan's attention. "Good morning, this is Francesca Rosario. Welcome to Switzerland, Jake. Dan said you should be arriving at Baur au Lac this week."

Jake was taken aback by the informality. "Dan asked that I call you, so here I am. What can I do for you, Ms. Rosario?" he asked, thinking it best to maintain some degree of formality.

"Please, call me Francesca. From what Dan told me when he called before I left Rome, you and I have a lot in common."

Jake was afraid he knew the answer, but asked anyway. "Oh, and what might that be?"

"*Tejano.*" Francesca paused, letting the word sink in. "Need I say more?"

"No ma'am, that will about do it for now. What would you like to discuss?" His suspicions were confirmed. His partner had recruited yet another foreign investor who wished to be briefed concerning her funding.

"I am interested in learning more about the status of our operation. If I like what I hear, I might be prepared to make further investments."

Jake shook his head in disgust. This was definitely not part of the plan Morton and he discussed prior to his leaving. He must have known of Rosario's interest, or he wouldn't have instructed him to call. He thought they were closing the operation not ramping up. "I'm sorry but Saint-Moritz really doesn't fit in my European travel plans."

"That does not present a problem. I have a private jet and can be in Zurich within an hour. Baur au Lac will make accommodations for me and my staff. Our family has a company account. Dinner this evening? I will meet you at eight o'clock in the lobby bar."

"Yes, Ms. Rosario, eight o'clock sharp." Glancing at his watch, Jake calculated he should have time for lunch, make his bank withdrawal, catch a nap, then see what this pushy Italian broad had to offer. "I'll be the long tall Texan at the bar. Probably the only one wearing boots."

"Very good, Jake," she said with a chuckle. "I look forward to spending the evening with you. *Ciao.*"

"Yes, that is correct. We wish to close the Triad account," Jake politely explained to Conrad Kleindeinst, senior vice president of *Schweizersche Bankgellschaft.*

A look of consternation crossed the distinguished banker's face. "I hope there is not a problem with our service, Herr Hardesty. Service and secrecy have been our hallmarks for centuries, and *Schweizersche* certainly does not want important Americans like you and Colonel Morton displeased."

Jake tried to reassure the nervous banker, while he displayed his passport and other papers necessary to make the final *Tejano* withdrawal. "No, not at all. Our business has been completed, and now we must withdraw the balance for partial payment of the company's income taxes." He gave a knowing wink. "We must comply with the law, you know."

Relieved with the explanation and Hardesty's pleasant attitude, Herr Kleindenist handed over two hundred fifty thousand dollars. After accepting the cash, Jake stepped into a private room available for customers to view the contents of their bank boxes. He placed the cash in his money belt, then hid the belt beneath his sweater. He got a receipt and bid Kleindenist farewell. Exiting onto Bahnhofstrasse, he was relieved, knowing the source of funds to operate *Tejano* had finally been depleted.

Seated at the highly polished mahogany bar, Jake perused the latest European edition of the *Wall Street Journal*. Five minutes after eight he glanced up to see a handsome couple enter. The attractive woman was stylishly dressed in a low-cut mauve jersey sheath while the gentleman, in his early thirties, was outfitted in a double-breasted dark blue suit. The woman motioned for her companion to step to the far end of the bar, then strode purposefully toward Jake.

Francesca extended her hand. "You were right, Jake, the boots were a dead give away, especially with the tuxedo, but I must confess, Dan emailed your photo before I left my office in Rome."

Admiring his dinner companion, Jake held Francesca's firm handshake a few seconds longer than was customary. Her ebony hair was up in a swirl, and diamond earrings and a matching necklace complimented her prominent cheek bones. Noticing an empty table, he motioned toward a secluded corner of the lounge.

"As you like it, Signorina, Rosario, martini, chilled and stirred, two olives." Without another word the bartender set down a re-fill of Jake's whiskey.

"Salute." Francesca touched her glass to Jake's.

Jake savored his second double. "It's obvious this is not the first time you have graced this place."

"That would be correct. My family's company does most of our banking business in Zurich, and I have been staying at this hotel at least three times a year for as long as I can remember."

"You mean to tell me there aren't any trustworthy banks in Rome?"

"Yes, but Papa prefers to maintain accounts in Zurich. He likes the privacy of the Swiss laws over those regulating the banks in Naples and Rome where our company's main offices are located."

"And what would be the nature of your family's business that would require such secrecy, if I might ask?"

Francesca stared at him several seconds before replying. "Oh, it is varied, restaurants, bars, import-export and product manufacturing."

His curiosity was aroused. "Manufacturing? Of what?"

Francesca sipped her cocktail and measured her response. "Like your partner, Colonel Morton, handguns, plus machine guns and other semi-automatic weapons. We export around the world."

No wonder they have Zurich bank accounts to keep their customers and the nature of their transactions secret. The word 'family' suddenly took on a different meaning.

"Enough about the Rosarios, let's talk about Jake Hardesty, no doubt a far more interesting subject. How was your trip over, and what do you think of Zurich?"

This is my first trip to Switzerland, and unfortunately, I only have time to see a little of Zurich. I hope I can get back sometime and take in more of the spectacular scenery I saw coming in from the airport. The city is far more impressive than I expected, and the people couldn't be more hospitable."

"I do wish you would stay. I would love to entertain you." After Francesca finished the last sip of her martini, Jake motioned for the waiter to clear their drink tab. She nodded to Antonio, indicating they were ready to leave.

"I reserved a table down the hall at Rive Gauche for nine." Jake glanced at his watch.

Francesca reached across the small cocktail table and lightly placed her hand on his. "Oh, Jake, you need not have done that. I had my assistant, Antonio, take the liberty of doing the same at a wonderful little restaurant not too far away. You will love it. Please, you are a guest on my continent."

Outside, Antonio waited with the Rolls Royce and uniformed driver. A bottle of chilled white wine was already open, two glasses poured. Puccini softly played in the background on the CD, and the interior overhead lights were subdued. For Jake, the evening was getting more interesting by the minute.

When Francesca's chauffeur pulled into the circular drive at Petermann's Kunststuben, owner/chef Horst Petermann was waiting for them at the front door. "Good evening, Signorina Rosario, welcome back."

Francesca smiled and allowed the *maitre d'* to lead them to their table. Jake was impressed with the manner in which this beautiful young woman took charge in all situations.

The wine steward presented a bottle of *Laboure Roi Pouilly Fuisse* for Francesca's approval. She nodded her approval, and the two chatted about Jake's job as a lobbyist and his rearing in Texas.

"I have been to Houston with my father while his brother was a patient at the Texas Medical Center. Perhaps on my next visit you will take me sightseeing in your big state … show me some real cowboys and Indians."

The table was cleared and after dinner liqueurs served. Francesca leaned forward, revealing ample cleavage. "So, Jake, tell me how *Tejano* is progressing. Is everything as you wish?"

Jake looked down to admire the view, no doubt as she intended. "Before I answer, Ms. Rosario, assuming I do, tell me what business is that of yours?" He realized his response bordered on rudeness, but couldn't think of another way to get an answer.

An attitude of mock seriousness came over her. "I refuse to answer that, Jake Hardesty, on the grounds my answer might incriminate me." She paused for effect, then, allowing a coy smile, continued. "Unless that is, you promise to call me Francesca. I told you that earlier. You really don't have to act so prim and proper."

"Yes, Francesca, my love, or whatever beautiful women from the country of love like to be called."

"Be careful, Jake Hardesty. For the time being, let's talk of *Tejano*. Papa and I have been doing business with Dan for several years. I suppose you weren't aware, but he's introduced us to a number of House members and senators, and we've funneled hundreds of thousands of dollars to their campaigns. Senator Russell Creighton is one of them."

"What does that have to do with *Tejano?*"

"I'm saying we've known Dan a long time. We have mutual interests. We think alike. Dan came to Venice to meet with Papa not long ago to discuss your operation, but I went in his place."

"And why did you do that?"

Francesca explained her meetings in Venice and their family's participation in *Tejano*. "Now I want to hear how my money is being used."

"Make that past tense on the utilization of your *Tejano* contribution," Jake said. "We have sworn to keep the operation compartmentalized, though it seems your close, personal friend, Colonel Morton, has blown my cover. Given the fact that you're my silent partner, I will tell you that we made periodic withdrawals from Triad, ran it through several off-shore and US bank accounts and helped Andrew Smith with both direct and indirect contributions."

Francesa pulled a cigarette and lighter from a black brocade evening purse and handed the lighter to Hardesty. The press of her breast against his forearm was no accident, Jake suspected.

"I read yesterday in the *Herald Tribune* that Mr. Smith won the primary."

"Yes, and our operatives are now working behind the scenes to move support from Warren McDonald, who came in second. Where necessary, we are paying the right people to accomplish that."

Francesca nodded. "It sounds like politics is the same all over the world, money buys votes. And since Mr. Smith is his party's nominee against Sen. Creighton, what's next?"

"We dry up the money source. But for *Tejano*, Smith wouldn't have a penny to his name, and there's no way in hell anyone with good sense is going to back him against an incumbent senator who's also running for president."

"So what do we do with the *Tejano* funds then, put them in Creighton's presidential campaign?"

"No. Morton sent me over here to close out the Triad account. We'll use the remaining cash helping Smith try to unseat Creighton and call it a day."

"Call it a day? You mean stop the operation? But why quit now? I always assumed we would move over and get involved in Creighton's presidential campaign against Templeton."

"When you assume something, you make a fool of me. Well, you made a fool of yourself by assuming we would continue. You're not going to make one outta me." The moment the alcohol-induced comment was said, Jake regretted it.

"I tell you one thing, Mr. Hardesty, I never, ever make a fool of myself, especially when it comes to money and politics. You haven't given me even one sufficient reason to pull out. Apparently, you just don't have the balls."

"I didn't mean that, Francesca, I apologize. Too much jet lag and whiskey, I guess."

Francesca calmed somewhat, recognizing Hardesty's change in attitude. "Apology accepted, Jake. I got upset too. I just mean, I don't understand why we should stop now. Papa and I have invested heavily in your account, and the presidential election has not even taken place. We are in it to the end. That is the way Dan told me it would be when he solicited my money, and that is the way I want it."

"Why are you so damn interested in influencing the outcome of an American presidential election?"

Francesca sat in silence, gazing into the fire, before she finally answered. "In one word, I suppose it would be power. I want to have immediate and direct access to the President of the United States in order to accomplish certain goals for Rosario Enterprises and for Italy."

Jake couldn't hide his amazement at the simplicity of her reply. "And that's it, a power trip? Sounds pretty straightforward, not too different from all the other high rollers in the states willing to dole out big bucks for candidates." He extinguished his cigarette and pushed away from the table. "You do get to the point, lady."

Jake suddenly felt sober as a judge. "Listen, why don't we call it a night? I'm not used to this international travel. Tell you what, I'll sleep on what you've said and let you know what I think in the morning."

"That will be fine, Jake. Enough of this political business for one evening." She feigned a lack of interest as they departed the posh restaurant and returned to Baur au Lac.

CHAPTER 32

▼

AUSTIN
FEBRUARY 24

Juan pushed his swivel chair away from the desk at the task force command post in the basement of DPS headquarters, stood and examined a large Texas map covering one wall. Colored pins indicated sightings of Sergei Yazkov. On the wall above his monitor was an enlarged photo of the Russian. He conducted what had become a ritual of checking email, sending and receiving calls and faxes, checking in with DPS officers and the other Rangers assigned to the Crosser task force. Despite their tireless efforts, Yazkov was still on the loose, and right now Juan wasn't certain the ex-KBG agent was even in the United States.

Mid-morning Susan Myers sat down across the desk from him. "Good morning, Lieutenant. Any new developments today?"

Juan shook his head. "*Nada.* If Yazkov's out there, he's lying low. I'm beginning to think he's high-tailed it back across the border or at least fled to another state. We have no reason to believe Texas was his final destination."

The public information officer clasped her hands and looked at him in a frank, business-like fashion. "Sorry to say I don't have any leads for us, but I did get a call from *USA's Most Wanted*."

"What do the TV moguls in New York think about our foreign visitor?" Juan acted mildly interested.

"John Walker has agreed to put together a segment for one of their upcoming shows. They've got millions of die-hard followers, and the air time would get the word out about Yazkov."

"Great. What do they need from us?"

"What they need is *you*, Lieutenant. You were the first Ranger on the case, so they want you to come to New York City for an interview as soon as possible."

"No can do." Juan turned his attention back to the computer terminal. "I need to stay in Texas."

Susan sat silent a few seconds, fingers drumming on the metal desk. "How 'bout if Walker does a split screen interview with you via satellite? We could set that up in our studio upstairs or at the Capitol."

Juan was not into publicity. The lower his profile, the less of a target he would be for Sergei Yazkov. But if it would help, he would do it, despite the friendly ragging he would undoubtedly receive from his fellow Rangers.

"I guess that will work. If it will help bag Yazkov." Juan looked at his desk calendar. "I'll be here on the phone again all day tomorrow. Set up something, then brief me on how you want me to handle it."

"Will do." Myers made a note. "By the way, we received fifty responses at the phone bank yesterday. None panned out, but we're still entering them in the Quick Alert software tracking program." She handed him a printout. "As you can see, the operators log the location of the sighting, the time of day, suspect's physical description, and what activity he was seen engaged in."

"Damn, look at this." Falcone's index finger zigzagged across the pages. "He's been spotted in Clovis, New Mexico; Lafayette, Louisiana; Tulsa, Oklahoma and Hot Springs, Arkansas. If those reports are accurate, this guy's been cloned."

"I told you we'd get a ton of calls. We take them all seriously and arrange for someone locally to interview the tipster and check out the scene."

"Looks like we have a larger number logged in from San Antonio, Austin, El Paso, and Houston." Juan studied the report more closely. "What do you make of that?"

"What it means is those are cities with tens of thousands of eyes and ears. On the other hand, maybe the guy really was in one or more of those places."

Juan handed the list back to Myers. "What do you hear from Texas Crime Stoppers?"

"Good news." Myers returned the report to her attaché. "They've increased the reward to $75,000. I'm going to get Yazkov's mug shot up on our Texas Most Wanted list and work up another press release." Myers stood to leave. "I want to keep this story on page one, or at least in the state section of as many Texas newspapers as possible. I'll call New York and make arrangements for your interview and provide them with photographs and pertinent information. I'll check back with you later this afternoon."

"Sounds good." Juan punched a button on the phone to take another incoming call and turned to his computer to take notes.

By 4:30 Juan had talked again to all but one of the Rangers, and the updates were anything but encouraging. He rubbed his bloodshot eyes, weary from staring at the flickering computer screen. The chirping of his cell phone interrupted his concentration.

"Lt. Falcone, this is Sgt. Jerry Haley."

Static on the line made it difficult to hear. "Hey, I was beginning to wonder about you, Haley. Anything new to report from San Antonio?"

"Can't really say about San Antonio. I'm in a little Tex-Mex cafe in beautiful San Diego."

Juan leaned back in his chair and smiled. "So what are you doing down in the South Texas brush country? You're supposed to be checking out college campuses and costume shops in San Antonio, if I remember correctly."

"I came to see Consuella."

Great, just when he was looking to catch a break on finding Yazkov, Jerry Haley was out chasing skirts in South Texas. "This better be good, Haley. I don't want to be putting anything in today's report to the captain that will embarrass either of us."

"Oh, I think it might be *real* good, sir. So good, in fact, I need you down here to gather some very important information."

Puzzled, Juan rifled through the sighting reports, sorted by town and county, but saw no mention of San Diego. "Don't tell me you got a fix on the Crosser in Duval County."

"Not quite, but it could be better than that. I struck out on the college campuses and all the costume shops I surveyed in San Antonio, but I think we might have hit a home run with a call I received this morning."

"You have my attention, tell me what you've got down there." Juan quickly typed the highlights of Haley's remarks.

"The phone bank called about a response they received to the photo of Yazkov we've been running in the newspapers. A call from one Mr. Rudolfo Gonzalez who lives in Benavides. He reported his daughter, Consuella, noticed Yazkov's mug shot in the *Corpus Christi Caller Times* and told her father she thought she'd seen him before."

"That sounds pretty far-fetched." Juan removed his hands from the keyboard. "Why would Yazkov be down in the South Texas brush country?"

"He wasn't. That was the encouraging part. The reason the phone bank supervisor called me was Consuella claims she saw the man in San Antonio where she used to work at a costume shop."

"But I thought you interviewed the folks in all the shops in San Antone. How could you have missed her?" Juan's interest piqued.

"I wondered the same thing. Mr. Gonzalez told me his daughter had worked at Alamo Theatrical Supplies in San Antonio. I called Mr. Harry Sachnowitz, the owner, to verify her employment. Consuella had been employed there, but quit by the time I interviewed his people. That's why I missed her."

"When did she work there?"

"That's the good part. She started September first and remained through December thirty-first."

Juan looked at the notes on the computer screen. "The two murders down on the border were in September, and that's also the month Salazar's pickup was parked at the San Antonio airport."

"I know, that's why I thought this might be worth exploring."

"Did the owner say why she quit?"

"Yes, sir. Her mother was diagnosed with breast cancer in December, and Consuella moved home to help her parents."

"I'm getting the picture. You had no luck with any other employees, so you drove down to Benavides where her parents live."

"You hit the nail on the head. I didn't have anything to lose but time and a tank of gas. This could be your lucky day, Lieutenant. You might break open the Crosser case before this day's over."

"I'm sorry, Haley, I don't quite follow you. Why do you need me?" Juan pushed back from the computer terminal and rubbed his forehead.

"I met with Consuella and her father this afternoon at their home. The problem is, she clammed up and wouldn't talk to me."

"Why not?"

"I think when she realized she'd seen a man wanted for murder, it frightened her. When I told her and her father about you, I could tell they would rather deal with a Hispanic officer. I'm thinking if you could converse in Spanish with them and win their trust, we might get somewhere. How 'bout it, Lieutenant?"

It was almost five o'clock and nothing else looked more promising for the day. "Why not? I'll call the State Aircraft Pooling Board and line up a plane. There's a landing strip in Alice where you can pick me up. I'll call later and give you a heads up on ETA. Tell the Gonzalez family what's going down and that I should be to their home between seven and eight o'clock this evening."

Lt. Falcone was riding shotgun with Sgt. Jerry Haley as the two sped toward Benavides. In the fast approaching darkness, Juan leaned his head back and tried to rest. He concentrated on what he might do to gain the family's confidence and persuade Consuella to come forth with some useful information.

Juan reached over and patted the Ranger on the shoulder when they reached the Gonzalez residence. "Thanks, Sgt. Haley. I'll go solo from here, since you've briefed them on who I am and what I'm doing down here. That way I might have a better chance of getting Consuella to open up."

Haley nodded. "That's probably the best approach. Holler if you need anything. I'll be right here." He tilted his hat down over his eyes and commenced a brief siesta.

The stillness of the remote location was shattered by the barking of a large dog, straining on a heavy chain in the front yard. When it bared its teeth, Juan concluded the animal was part wolf or coyote and lengthened his stride to reach the safety of the screen front porch.

In response to the knock on the screen door, an old gentleman quietly appeared out of the darkness. He flipped a switch and a yellow bulb illuminated the porch and front yard. The dog stopped barking at the sight of his master.

Juan smiled and tipped the brim of his hat. "*Buenos noches.*" He continued in Spanish. "I'm Lt. Juan Falcone with the Texas Rangers. I understand Sgt. Haley explained that I would be coming to visit for a few minutes with your daughter. I believe you called DPS and reported that Consuella saw the photograph in the newspaper of a man the Texas Rangers are looking for."

The man still had not opened the door. "*Sí.*"

"I believe my partner, Sgt. Haley, told you I would like to ask her a few questions about the man in the photograph. That's all there is to it, and then I'll be out of here." He smiled again, hoping to gain the older man's trust.

Rudolpho Gonzalez slowly opened the screen door and permitted Juan to enter the tiny living room. "My wife, Lucinda, is resting. Consuella is in the bedroom with her. I will go see if my daughter will speak to you." He pointed to a chair. "*Siéntese, por favor.*"

Taking a seat in a creaking rocking chair, Falcone discreetly looked about and was able to survey the entire home, two bedrooms, bathroom, and kitchen. The television was muted, but he could see an evening Spanish language soap opera in progress. On top of the set were a small statue of the Virgin Mary and a picture of the Sacred Heart. Among numerous family photographs on the wall, he noted a faded picture of President John F. Kennedy.

A petite young woman entered the room, followed by her father. Rudolfo grasped her hand and spoke in Spanish. Consuella extended her hand to the investigator without uttering a sound. Rudolpho and Consuella seated themselves on the threadbare couch and waited in silence. The father nodded for Falcone to proceed.

Juan politely introduced himself in Spanish and stated the purpose of his visit. "Mr. Sachnowitz was very complimentary about your work, Señorita Gonzalez, and told Sgt. Haley he was very disappointed when you left his employment, but he understood you needed to return home to care for your mother. I hope she is all right." He stopped, waiting for a response, but when none came, continued. "He said you gave your address to the bookkeeper and told her to send your check here." Consuella remained silent.

The Ranger reached in his attaché and removed an eight by ten photograph of Sergei Yazkov. A glimmer of recognition immediately crossed Consuella Gonzalez's youthful face. "Do you recognize this man, Señorita Gonzalez?"

"*Si, señor.* I have seen him before."

Though Consuella tried to sound and appear confident, Juan could detect a tremor in her voice, no doubt overwhelmed by what was unexpectedly taking place in her modest home.

Juan spoke with an authoritative but respectful tone of voice. "Señor Gonzales, Señorita Gonzales, I want to thank you for allowing me into your home today. Please tell your wife the same. I know you were not expecting any of this. It is most kind of all of you."

Rudolfo nodded. "You are quite welcome, Lt. Falcone. We want to cooperate with the authorities."

Sensing the young woman slowly letting down her guard, Juan cautiously proceeded. "How old are you, Consuella?"

"Nineteen, but I will be twenty next month," she hastened to add.

"My youngest sister is twenty."

"I have two older brothers, one in the army, and one in college in Corpus. I want to go to college too some day."

"And I am sure you will. If you can help me, there is a possibility of money available, *mucho dinero*." With that seed planted, it was time to plunge further. "I need your help, Consuella. The people of Texas need your help. *Comprende?* I would like to ask you a few questions about the man you recognized in the photo."

"What is it you want to know?"

"The man in the photograph, did you see him in the store where you worked or somewhere else?"

Her head bowed, Consuella sat in silence for a few moments before answering. "He came in the store and looked around for a while."

"Do you remember when this was?"

"Um, let's see, probably around the second week of September. I remember because I knew it was time to get my paycheck. He told me he was buying the disguise material for a community theater group. I thought nothing more about it until I saw his picture in the Corpus newspaper yesterday, and it jogged my memory."

"Do you remember what he bought from you, Consuella?"

"Many things, wigs, both men's and women's, of all colors, balding cap, face mask, mustaches, goatees, fake teeth, sideburns, beards, skin coloring, everything. He also wanted lots of hair color, one of each shade we had in stock. "

Juan quickly noted all of the items in his report. "Balding cap? What is that?"

Consuella's tone brightened as she talked about her work. "It is like a swim cap only it is flesh color and has little white tuffs of hair around the edges. With the latex face mask, it would make him look like an old man."

Juan jotted down the phrase. "And how did he pay for all of this, cash, check or credit card?"

"The man definitely paid in cash. He insisted on not giving me his name. I specifically asked for it because Mr. Sachnowitz likes to have that information for a mailing list he keeps of all his customers."

"Do you recall how much his bill was?"

"I don't exactly remember, somewhere between four and five hundred dollars. I remember he pulled out a big wad of bills, some of it Mexican pesos, and gave me far more than enough to cover his purchases. He told me to keep the change."

Juan continued taking notes. "And did you keep the change?"

"*Si*, I saw no reason not to. Mr. Sachnowitz told us we could keep what few tips we got. The amount above the purchase price I kept and brought home in December. I put it in a coffee can and buried the can in the backyard. I thought one of these days I might exchange the pesos for dollars and use it to help my parents."

"When we are through, would you mind showing me where the can is buried? I want to dig it up and take it back to Austin. This man's fingerprints are probably on the money. We'll give you American dollars in exchange."

"But of course." Consuella gave a meek smile.

"Is there anything else you can think of that happened, or that this man said to you?"

Consuella thought a moment. "I do remember when he first came in he spoke in English, but later in Spanish."

"Anything else about the way he talked?"

"Yes." Consuella continued. "I remember he got very mad when I said I wasn't sure we had any women's wigs. He started talking to himself very fast in some language I did not understand. He stopped when he realized what he was doing and switched back to Spanish."

Russian, no doubt, Juan speculated, making a notation. He remained quiet, allowing Consuella time to think. "Anything else before I go?"

"No, I think that is everything."

When Juan stood up, Consuella and her father did likewise. "Thank you so much, Consuella. You have been very helpful." Without hesitation he leaned forward and gave her an *embrazo*. Putting his arm around Mr. Gonzalez's shoulder, he guided him out to Haley's patrol car.

"Thank you very much for your cooperation, Señor Gonzales. This has been more helpful than you could imagine. Once your daughter shows us where the money is buried and we dig that up, we'll be on our way. *Hasta luego.*"

As the two Texas Rangers drove toward the small landing strip in Alice, Juan looked at the plastic evidence bag containing the tin can and the money Sergei Yazkov had given Consuella Gonzalez. "I'll take this to the lab tonight and have it checked for prints and any other signs of identification."

Haley nodded. "What do you want me to do?"

"Nothing right now. I'm also going to download Yazkov's photograph to the agency's computers, colorize it and print it out in various sizes. Since he's well disguised by now, the sketch artists can reproduce variations using a combination of the items he bought. They can photograph or make drawings with the disguises superimposed. We might come up with the right combination to ID Yazkov in his latest makeover."

With the plane wheels up and headed north toward Austin, Juan looked out at the midnight sky and the twinkling lights of the remote farms and ranches below. In the distance, he saw the lights of San Antonio and further north on the horizon those of Austin. He rested his boots on the empty seat across from him and processed the information he'd obtained from Consuella Gonzalez.

CHAPTER 33

▼

HOUSTON
FEBRUARY 25

One, exhale; two, exhale; three ... Beads of perspiration formed on Jennifer Spencer's forehead and upper lip as she counted the reps of the curls. Her early morning workout provided a much needed respite from the world of politics and litigation.

"Jennifer Spencer, please come to the front desk for a phone call." The sound of her name over the athletic club's public address system came as a surprise.

Picking up a towel, she wiped perspiration from her forehead. "Hi, I'm Spencer. You have a call for me?" She smiled at the young man seated at the desk.

"Yes, ma'am. I'll be more than happy to transfer it into the women's locker room where you can have a bit more privacy."

Once in the locker room, Jennifer pulled off her lifting gloves, and picked up the receiver. "Hello, this is Jennifer Spencer."

"Good morning, Jennifer, it's Rita at the office. I hate to bother you, but that Texas Ranger who came to see you the other day has called several times this morning."

Jennifer glanced at the clock on the dressing room wall. "It's only 8:15. Tell him I'll be back at the office in an hour or so, and I'll call him then."

"I put him off the first couple of times by saying you were in a meeting. Now he's holding on another line, says he needs to talk with you now."

"Okay, patch him through," she replied, rubbing her neck to relieve the tension.

There was a pause and Jennifer detected a faint clicking sound on the phone then the sound of Rita's voice. "Lt. Falcone, are you still there?"

"Yes, ma'am. I was beginning to think you'd forgotten me."

Despite herself, Jennifer felt a degree of comfort when she heard Falcone's deep voice. She slid down the wall and took a seat on the carpeting in a corner of the lounge area. "I can hear both of you. Rita, you can go ahead and hang up, I'll take it from here."

"Ms. Spencer, I'm sorry to interrupt your meeting but I wanted to catch you first thing this morning."

"No problem." Jennifer stretched her legs. "Did your people come up with a match on the fingerprints?"

"You beat me to the punch. That's exactly why I'm calling. I'm sorry to say we didn't."

"Well, no match is probably good news. Look on the bright side, at least we know the note wasn't left by a convicted felon."

"I'm afraid it's not quite that simple. The crime lab found no prints whatsoever on the note or the envelope."

Jennifer sat up straight. Falcone had gotten her attention. "That seems impossible."

"The techs think we're dealing with a real professional. They said he or she was probably wearing latex gloves to prevent prints from being lifted. I'm sorry that's all I have to report. Please call me if anything else unusual happens."

There was a long pause as Jennifer contemplated the apartment break-in and yet another intruder in her life.

"Ms. Spencer? Is anything wrong?"

"Don't worry, it's probably nothing."

"Don't worry about what? Is everything all right?"

"No, everything is not all right!" Several other women in the lounge glanced her way when Jennifer sprang to her feet, raising her voice in mild frustration. She began pacing the room, tethered by the telephone cord. "First, it was the note in the car, then it was the 'hello dolly' message left in fake blood on my apartment door. Then I come home to find some woman in my bedroom."

"A woman in your bedroom? Take three deep breaths and start at the beginning and go a little slower so I can get this all down."

Jennifer dropped into one of the club chairs, inhaled deeply and felt her nerves settle slightly. She briefly covered the highlights of what had occurred since she and Falcone had met.

"It seems your life is growing more complicated by the day. Have you seen the woman before?"

"Not that I can recall. As a matter of fact, the more I've thought about her, the more I realize something didn't look quite right, like she had on a wig or was in disguise or something. I know this sounds bizarre but I've even wondered if possibly it was the old man I saw, dressed in drag. Having one person stalking me is enough, I don't need two."

"Maybe the woman you saw hadn't been in your apartment. Maybe no one had."

Jennifer tried to conceal her resentment at Falcone's assertion. "Okay, Lieutenant, you're right, I'm wrong. It sounds so weird even I have a hard time believing it. Why don't you go back to looking for the cop killer who swam the Rio Grande and I'll get back to my client." With that she stood and walked toward the wall to replace the receiver and head for the sauna.

Juan Falcone's admonition rang from the dangling receiver, catching Jennifer's attention before she could end the call. "Stop right now, Jennifer Spencer, and listen to me!"

Jennifer moved the receiver back to her ear. "Wow, you've got a nice set of lungs there, Lieutenant. I'm here and listening." She sat down again. "Now it's your turn to take three deep breaths and everything will be fine."

"I do believe you, Ms. Spencer. And because I believe you, I would like for you to come to DPS headquarters later today."

"I would if I could, but I have a federal court hearing at 10 this morning and two depositions scheduled for this afternoon. They are commitments I can't get out of. Can you give me even one good reason why I should skip court, get held in contempt and drive to Austin to see you?"

Now it was Falcone who was silent.

"I'm listening and I don't hear that one good reason."

"I really don't want to get into it right now. I will only say that I'd like for you to take a look at some photographs we have assembled at the task force command post."

Jennifer was so startled she nearly dropped the telephone receiver. "You mean photographs of that killer you're chasing?"

"I know it sounds farfetched, but when you mentioned the possibility that the woman you saw might have been the old man in disguise, I thought of Yazkov. There have been some recent developments. That's all I will say on the telephone."

Yazkov? So that's his name. "Listen, Lieutenant, maybe I *was* mistaken. I have no reason to believe there's any connection between the break-in, the woman, and the old man I saw who left the note in my car or the message on the door. And I sure can't imagine why some cop killer would be stalking me."

"I know it's a stretch. I'd just like to rule out any connection between you and Yazkov. If you can't ID the guy from the photos we have, we can go our separate ways and at least have that assurance. Ms. Spencer? Are you still there?"

"Yes, I'm here."

"Listen, Ms. Spencer, I'm not doing this just for your well being. I've got a double murder to solve. The department photographer and computer graphics technicians can apply a variety of disguises to the photo we have of Yazkov. If by some wild chance you were able to identify him, it would help my case tremendously. Right now I don't have a clue why this Russian came to Texas, much less where he is. I hope there's no connection between Yazkov and what you've been experiencing. I'd just like to make sure."

When Jennifer did not respond, Juan continued. "In light of your schedule, I'll agree to put it off for a couple of days. I'll send a DPS plane to pick you up at seven at a fixed base operation near Hobby Airport; have you in this office by eight, eyeball some computer enhanced drawings, have you out of here by 9; on the ground in Houston by 10 and in your office by 11. Can't beat that for public service can you?"

Then Jennifer remembered a docket call hearing on Friday morning. "Okay, Lieutenant, you win, sort of. I can't miss a court hearing Friday morning, but I'll agree to come in late Friday afternoon. While I was in Brownsville I called my parents, and mom suggested I meet them at their weekend retreat in Wimberley on Friday afternoon. I can take care of it on that trip."

After Juan gave a few basic directions and his phone numbers, Jennifer was more than ready to move on. "You owe me big time for this little outing, Lt. Falcone. On a scale of one to ten, I figure the possibility your man, Yazkov, is stalking me is somewhere between minus one and zero, or at least I hope that's the case. I guess I'd just like to have the peace of mind there's no connection with the guy."

"Frankly, Ms. Spencer, I feel the same way. I'll see you Friday afternoon at four. And hey, be careful."

CHAPTER 34

▼

SOMEWHERE OVER THE ATLANTIC FEBRUARY 25

"Good morning, Mr. Hardesty. May I offer you orange juice or a mimosa prior to departure?"

"Why not. Make it a Bloody Mary." He looked at the name tag on her uniform pocket. "Jo Beth. Haven't we met before?"

The young woman smiled. "Not that I recall, and I'm sure I would. I'm sorry, but what I offered is all we have for now. I'll be happy to fill your order when we open the liquor cabinet after takeoff."

The Washington lobbyist winked and opted for the mimosa. Since the luxury section was only half-full, he would be assured of better service than usual.

A few minutes later Jo Beth made a second service run through the first class cabin. "Newspaper? Magazine? We have *Time, Newsweek, The Wall Street Journal,* plus a number of other selections."

After choosing *The London Times* and *Forbes,* Jake casually thumbed through the business magazine but was unable to concentrate. His thoughts returned to events of the last 24 hours. Tossing the magazine into the vacant seat next to him, he closed his eyes.

"Re-fill?"

Jake looked up to see Jo Beth standing over him once more. She had removed her dark blue uniform jacket, and Jake appreciated the fit of the silk blouse as she leaned over to re-fill his glass.

"Let me know if there is anything else I can do for you," she said coyly.

Jake flashed her his winning smile. "Don't worry, I'm making a wish list even as we speak."

Once the plane reached cruising altitude, a large video screen lowered and Jo Beth dutifully brought Jake his Bloody Mary. The image of a small plane made its way across a computerized map of Europe and the Atlantic Ocean. In the corner of the screen a digital clock showed the estimated time of arrival at Washington's Ronald Reagan National Airport. Jake put on a headset and closed his eyes again.

"Oh, beautiful for spacious skies, for amber waves of grain ..." A melodious chorus joined the symphony filling his brain, pushing aside thoughts of *Tejano*. Jake opened his eyes and, seeing the cabin lights had dimmed, switched off his individual reading light and gazed ahead. The screen filled with a pastoral setting of wheat fields, streams and rivers. As if on cue, the "purple mountains' majesty" of the Rockies towered before him. Suddenly his eyes glistened as the beauty brought tears to his eyes.

As the music segued to strains of Arron Copland, Jo Beth brought a linen-covered lunch tray carrying china and stemware. The plastic utensils seemed out of place but that was common security nowadays. Jake watched buffaloes stampede across open prairies followed by scenes of cattle and mustangs.

When Jake selected a German red wine to accompany his chateaubriand, he was reminded of the *Tejano* financial partners. Those selfish bastards want to illegally influence the US government and achieve goals he never dreamed of when he devised this project. They were no better than the goddamn terrorists who flew the planes into the World Trade Center and the Pentagon. They too tried to destroy his country, but they were just more overt about doing so. Somehow he'd managed to let everything get real fucked up on the road to the White House.

In addition to all that, Morton dropped the bomb on him, the call Kathryn received from that Jennifer Spencer. He wondered what Morton told his wife about *Tejano* and what she revealed of her husband's world travels and international connections to Spencer?

Noticing Jo Beth serving someone else two rows in front of him, Jake raised his voice. "Hey, Jo baby, I'm getting thirsty back here. How 'bout another round?"

The flight attendant returned to Jake's seat and looked down at Jake, but he didn't notice as his eyes were closed and his head was bobbing from side to side as he tried to remain awake. His tie was loosened, dark brown hair slightly mussed, brow furrowed. It appeared he'd been deeply engrossed in thought. Jo Beth leaned over, pulled out a sleep mask and gently slipped it over his eyes. In less than thirty seconds he was in a fitful sleep.

Jake felt he was fighting to pull himself out of a nightmare. "No, I didn't want it to be this way," he mumbled loudly. "No, this can't happen."

Jo Beth placed a moist warm towel over the lobbyist's eyes and forehead. "Hey, big guy, wake up. You were off in never-never land. I hope *I* wasn't the one causing the nightmares. Care to tell me what that was all about?"

"No, but I would appreciate some water and aspirins." Jake took the towel and inhaled its steam.

Minutes later Jo Beth returned with the aspirins and mineral water. "Can I help you?"

At the sound of her lilting voice, a light went on.

"Yep. In fact, I think you just did." Jake tossed down the aspirins, chased by the water and closed his eyes again. Now he was wide awake, and his rested mind reeled with a new strategy.

Jake's mental processes went into overdrive. Jennifer Spencer could close this shit down if she knew even half of what he'd done. He could make a deal with the Feds in return for some valuable information. Hell, for all he knew, Spencer might have alerted the FEC, FBI, one of the campaigns or even the press. If she found Kathryn Morton, it wouldn't take much more investigative work to connect the dots to him and Dan.

Jake set his water on the tray, pulled out his wallet and searched for a sheet of paper. He pulled the Airfone from its receptacle in the back of the seat in front of him and glanced around. His row was empty and the few other first class passengers he could see were asleep. Satisfied no one was listening, he swiped his credit card through the slot, got a dial tone and punched in the digits.

CHAPTER 35

▼

HOUSTON
FEBRUARY 25

At first, Jennifer Spencer believed the telephone's incessant ring was part of a dream. She envisioned sitting on the porch of her parents' weekend retreat in Wimberley, throwing a stick for Lad to fetch, but then remembered her father refused to install a phone so the family could enjoy uninterrupted peace and quiet. Then reality struck. She was asleep in the comfort and security of her own apartment.

Pulling the clock closer to read the luminous dial, she saw it was almost midnight. A late night call never brought good news. Half-awake, she reached across the bed and warily picked up the receiver. "Hello?"

"Good evening, Ms. Spencer, I wasn't sure of the time in Houston. I hope I didn't wake you."

"Who is this?"

"No one you know. I understand you are interested in campaign contributions in the U.S. Senate race in Texas." The reception was weak, and the male voice on the other end of the line sounded as if it were in a wind tunnel.

Now fully alert, Jennifer switched on the lamp and began taking notes on a pad of paper she kept on the bedside table. "Maybe so, maybe not. What's it to you?"

"Not much to me, Jennifer, but what I know would be of some interest to you."

"I'll ask one more time, who the hell is this?"

"Let's just say I'm someone who would like to meet and exchange information about why your candidate, Warren McDonald, got his ass beat by Andrew Smith."

Jennifer hurriedly jotted down every word. "Right, like when you tried to meet me in Austin in the capitol parking lot, or when you dressed up like the blonde floozy and broke into my apartment. Thanks, but no thanks."

There was silence on the other end of the line, and at first she thought the caller had disconnected. When he finally spoke, Jennifer detected confusion in his voice. "Austin? Apartment? I'm afraid I don't know what you're talking about."

In the confines of her apartment behind a double-locked door, Jennifer felt secure. "Right, and I guess you don't know anything about the note left in my car or the greeting scrawled on my door. You're just Mr. Clueless."

"I realize you might find this hard to believe, Ms. Spencer, but I honestly don't know what you're talking about."

"Then where did you get my name? Who do you think I'm investigating anything? If you're not working with them, how do I know you? Give me one good reason why I should trust some stranger who calls and wakes me in the middle of the night."

"Excellent questions, Ms. Spencer, but I would expect no less from an honor graduate of the University of Virginia and University of Texas Law School."

Portable telephone in hand, Jennifer wrapped up in a robe and paced the room. "So you know a little something about me. You could get that information out of Martindale-Hubbell. You're avoiding my questions."

"How I got your name is not important. I also know you've been making calls to Andrew Smith's contributors in the Dallas/Fort Worth area and probably elsewhere. Now you tell me what the note in your car and the message on your door said, and maybe I'll tell you more about the operation."

Operation? Damn, there must be something to her speculation after all. If this guy really knew nothing about the messages, then matters were more complicated than she thought. She had yet another stranger in her life. "I might be game, if I have assurances you know what you're talking about."

"How 'bout this for openers? Who would have thought little ol' Andy Smith of Lufkin, Texas, would get all that support and become his party's nominee for the U.S. Senate? *I* would have thought so because *I* know why he did. And Russell Creighton? He gets to spend more time on the road to the White House and ignore that lightweight rookie. I know all about that, too."

So that was the connection, Creighton versus Mr. Nobody. It made sense. But who was behind it? She continued taking notes.

"Okay, you got my attention. Since you're the one who called suggesting a meeting, let's do it. Be in my office at 10 a.m., and we can continue to share information at a more respectable hour."

"Hold your horses, missy, these things take time and patience. Let's take one step at a time and let me think about it. I'll call you back at your apartment in the morning at 8 your time."

She made a note. My time? That meant the guy was not calling from Texas. "You got it, I'll be standing by. Oh, you forgot one thing. What's your name?"

There was no reply, only a dial tone.

Jennifer studied the pad filled with words and incomplete sentences, when it hit her. 'Lightweight.' Creighton will spend more time on the road to the White House. She slammed her fist on the table. That was it!

"I couldn't understand why anyone in their right mind would support that lightweight Andy Smith, and I was right! Andrew Smith is a strawman. He could be on the senator's campaign staff or close to the political players and know what Creighton has been doing to assure victory in his Senate election. There is some kind of Creighton political shenanigans, and this guy knows all about it. He might even be a part of it! But if he is, why does he want to exchange information?"

She wrote down a name: Juan Falcone.

In his apartment across the street, Sergei Yazkov removed the listening device from his ear, contemplating the conversation he had overheard. Someone with inside information wanted to meet with his prey, someone who may be a part of the very operation Boris Volkov hoped to keep secret.

Yazkov let the newspaper he had been reading slide to the floor and admired himself in the mirror. His hair was now its natural dark brown, cut short, making it easier to use various wigs and the balding cap. He picked up the blonde wig from the counter, put it on and applied a small amount of lip gloss.

He moved into the kitchen, took a bottle of vodka from the freezer and poured a tumbler half full. Taking the bottle and glass with him, Yazkov walked into the small living room and sat in a lounge chair in semi-darkness, the room illuminated by lights in the kitchen and bathroom. Stalking Spencer had provided pleasure, but he also relished the kill.

From the end table, he picked up the hunting knife he had used on the deputy at the Rio Grande. With the razor-sharp instrument, Yazkov slowly shaved several inches of hair from his forearm. He intentionally cut himself and sat mesmerized, watching the thin line of blood rise to the surface. A perverse thought entered his mind, a grin spread across his face.

Taking the bottle and knife into the bedroom, he stretched out across the bed and picked up the packet of Rohypnol he'd purchased on a street corner in Mexico City. He recalled the dope dealer had called the chemical compound 'love drug', so inexpensive yet so powerful. Yazkov had also been told the 'roofies' were a potent tranquilizer, similar to Valium but ten times stronger.

The Russian would give sweet Jennifer two or three roofies and tell her it was aspirin to help ease the pain of dying. Then he'd tie her up and slit her wrists, maybe carve a drawing on her chest. He would wipe blood all over her body, then tear off her blouse and bra. He grew excited the more he thought of the killing scene. His palms grew moist thinking of it.

Sergei's fantasy was interrupted with a thought of the stranger who had called with information about the operation. His unexpected presence posed a complication. Now it was possible Volkov's project might be uncovered because of a turncoat. This was so typical of the fucking Americans. The woman alone would be easy, but the man would present an additional challenge. His pulse quickened, thinking about pulling off another double murder, energized at the prospect. He took another slug from the bottle and looked across the room to his backpack.

Crossing the room, he rummaged through the bag until he found the Morton 9 mm. he had purchased at a gun show in Austin. Foolish Americans. Without the necessity of background checks or identification, anyone could walk up and purchase an arsenal, a terrorist's delight. Placing the silencer on the muzzle, he took aim at the door, using the adjustable rear sight. He snapped in the 12-cartridge magazine and fondled the ergonomic hand grip. He tossed the gun aside and relieved his pent-up tension before drifting off to sleep, dreaming of being with Jennifer Spencer and the late night caller in her bedroom.

CHAPTER 36

▼

HOUSTON
FEBRUARY 26

Jennifer took several deep breaths as she walked across the parking lot to her apartment. With Lad obediently at her side, she relished her ritual morning jog along the nearby running trail. Gliding past fern-laden oaks and lush vegetation along the bayou, she had been transported to another world. Like a breakaway tailback, she had darted the final half mile through bumper to bumper traffic. Tires squealed on asphalt, wet from an overnight rain that had moved through the Bayou City.

She entered the apartment and double-locked the door. Thankfully, Lad was not barking at closed bedroom doors again. After filling his bowl with fresh water, she went to the bedroom, stripped off her sweatshirt, running shorts and shoes and headed for a relaxing hot shower. As she reflected on last night's call, her mood was upbeat, excited she finally had information confirming suspicions of questionable campaign financing.

The ringing of the phone and the recognizable voice of last night's caller interrupted her scan of the morning newspaper. "Good morning, Jennifer. I hope I didn't wake you."

"Are you kidding? I've already gotten in a five-mile run and am ready to leave for the office."

"Have you given any thought as to when and where we should meet to discuss Mr. Smith's campaign funding?"

"Yeah, as a matter of fact I have. How 'bout my law office this afternoon at three o'clock?"

"I'm sorry, but there is no way I can get to Texas that soon. Another day, another time, and most definitely another place. Our meeting will not take place in any office building. It must be held outdoors so I can be assured no one else is around. No cops, no listening devices. If I get the slightest hint of a double-cross, you'll never see me much less get anything out of me."

The only reason she suggested the office was because there'd be plenty of people around in case something happened. If he thought he was meeting her alone, he was sadly mistaken. At this point she was taking zero chances.

When she talked to her mom the other night Savannah said she and her dad should get to S-4 by noon tomorrow. That would give her time to brief them on what was going on, find a place for them to hide and keep an eye on her. After the rendezvous with Mr. Deepthroat, she'd still have time to drive to Austin and brief Lt. Falcone on these developments.

"Okay, if those are the ground rules, I can play your game. My parents have a weekend home in Wimberley between Austin and San Antonio. It's remote and we have a big yard that runs down to the Blanco River. We can meet outside, and you'll be able to check out the area to your satisfaction. How 'bout meeting there tomorrow afternoon, say two o'clock?"

"The place and time sound fine. How do I know you'll be alone?"

"Well, you'll have to trust me, just like I have to trust you. I'm telling you I'll be alone, and I presume you will also. If we're going to work together, there's got to be a level of trust on both sides."

There was a long silence on the other end of the line. "Point well taken. I'm telling you I better not find out that you've lied to me. The consequences will not be pleasant for anyone concerned."

"You have my word on it."

"All right, two o'clock Friday afternoon it is. I know San Marcos is half-way between Austin and San Antonio, so give me directions on how you get to your parents' place from both cities. I'm not sure of my final destination."

"One last thing, whatever information you have better be revealing, or you'll learn nothing from me in return."

Jake Hardesty hung up the receiver and smiled to himself. He went to the window of his townhouse and gazed out at the nearby Potomac River. It would be nice to leave cold and gray Washington, D.C. and head home to Texas. He found a travel website for flight and rental car availability and quickly made his reservations.

Hardesty went downstairs to the storage area in the garage and rummaged through his camping and hiking gear until he found a four-foot length of white nylon rope. Back upstairs, he collected his briefcase and car keys before heading to Capitol Hill for his daily round of lobbying activity. He couldn't imagine what had made him think of revealing any details of his project to that nosy bitch in the first place. Had he not called her, though, he wouldn't be flying to Texas. If all went as planned, he would be back in the District before her body was discovered.

Once Jennifer had completed her call, Sergei Yazkov took the listening device from his ear and methodically stowed the receiver. When he had tired of the constancy of the monotonous listening post, he had attached a Russian-made device to a sophisticated voice-activated recorder. The results of this maneuver had paid off. While the late night call from the stranger had come as a surprise, this follow-up posed further challenges. But that was what made his job interesting.

Yazkov packed a few personal belongings. The end of his assignment was near and he would need to travel unencumbered. The rendezvous in the country called for a completely different execution than the apartment scenario. He would need to make one stop to purchase the equipment necessary to complete his assignment. Then he'd leave this shit-hole of a country and head home, mission accomplished.

CHAPTER 37

▼

TEXAS
FEBRUARY 27

Sergei Yazkov arrived in Wimberley two hours early. Cautiously, he waded across the shallow river and searched for the most unobstructed view. The limestone riverbed would make crossing easy, should he need to stalk Spencer and her visitor. He estimated a distance of fifty yards from the river to the weekend retreat.

He soon located the perfect spot, hidden, yet providing a clear field of fire. From it he could see the cabin and surrounding acreage. The caliche ground was too impenetrable to dig a foxhole, so the Russian gathered twigs and branches to provide additional camouflage. A light mist began to fall.

From his vantage point, Yazkov looked over an abundance of cedar trees which provided perfect concealment. Even the bald cypress down by the river were assets. The tall bluestem and buffalo grasses growing in the rocky land also proved beneficial for hiding. Cattle bawled in the distance and the gobbling of a wild turkey added to the pastoral setting. The burlap tarp, camo shirt, pants and gloves he bought blended perfectly with the grasses and dense trees covering the field. Five black Angus grazed twenty-five yards away, unperturbed by his presence.

Sergei observed the killing zone through binoculars. He rolled onto his side and surveyed the equipment he had purchased at a San Antonio gun show. The young man making the sale had paid more attention to the faces on the wad of bills Sergei had shoved at him than that of the purchaser dressed in faded jeans and a tattered work shirt.

As if it were a pet, Sergei lovingly stroked the synthetic stock of the 7 mm. Remington sniper rifle. Though the weapon was outdated, he knew he was well within the 1,500 yard firing range to make the hit. He wiped the fine mist from the 3 x 9 Leopold Mark IV mounted scope with a soft cloth. Satisfied with its sturdiness, he adjusted the spring-loaded bipod stand attached to the muzzle. Resting against the hard plastic rifle case, he squinted through the high-powered scope at the details of the wood grain on the front door, then at the picnic table in the yard.

He laid the rifle aside and admired his weapon for close-range work, the Morton 9 mm. resting beside its waterproof carrying case. Sergei watched and waited for Jennifer Spencer and her visitor.

Jake Hardesty encountered little difficulty booking a flight Friday morning to Austin. Though he was accustomed to flying first class on his constant travels for Dan Morton, he thought it best to pass it up this time. As he adjusted his seatbelt for takeoff, his emotions were mixed, something he hadn't anticipated and did not like. Excluding his service in Vietnam, he had never killed anyone. He had tried to forget how many he killed or maimed in the jungles and rice paddies of Southeast Asia, but that had proven impossible. On numerous occasions, he awoke in a cold sweat to the ear-piercing thunder of the long-range cannons. This afternoon, however, would be entirely different. He would kill a young American woman.

When the time came, would he be able to look the woman in the eye and slip a noose around her throat? He inhaled a deep controlling breath. Why should he kill her? What had she done to him? She might not have a clue about *Tejano.*

When the pilot announced the plane had crossed the Mississippi River and was approximately one hour from touchdown, Jake peered out the window and saw nothing but thick clouds. What a fucking nightmare, he thought. Should he shut her up or spill his guts? If he talked, his career would be ruined, his reputation destroyed. He would have double-crossed Morton, York and Durham. He reached to his waist and felt for the nylon rope tightly knotted beneath his belt. He wondered briefly about national security and the ease of getting the rope through the airport check point.

Leaning back in the seat, he closed his eyes and allowed his mind to drift. His instincts would carry the day, no matter his rationalization.

Traffic leaving Houston had been heavy, typical for a Friday afternoon. After listening to the traffic and weather reports, Jennifer popped a CD into the player. She pushed the speed up to seventy. Lad, in the seat beside her, was whining at the cattle in pastures along the highway. She glanced at the dashboard clock, 12:45. The court hearing had caused her to leave later than intended.

The cell phone resting in the console released its annoying ring. She pushed the talk button and shouted into the unit, trying to be heard above the sound of passing traffic. "Jennifer Spencer."

"Sweetheart, I was afraid you might not have your cell phone turned on."

Jennifer shifted the phone to her left hand and turned down the CD player. "It's a little hard to hear over the road noise, Mother. I'll pull over first chance I get."

"Where are you?"

"Let's see, I'm about ten minutes east of San Marcos. What time did you and dad get to S-4?" Seeing a convenience store ahead, Jennifer pulled in.

"That's what I'm calling about. Unfortunately, we're still in Waco and I don't know when we'll be able to leave. There was a major traffic accident on the interstate. Your father's been called to the emergency room and literally has his hands full of broken bones."

Once she had stopped, Jennifer slouched back in the seat. Damn, the timing of this news couldn't be worse. Why hadn't she thought of a contingency plan?

Savannah continued. "The good news is you'll have some time alone. Take a nap or take Lad for a walk along the river this afternoon. You should probably stop in San Marcos and get something to eat."

"Sorry about the accident," Jennifer replied. "I know Dad is needed there, but something has come up, and I was planning on the two of you being with me this afternoon."

"What is it, Jen? Is everything all right?"

Jennifer hushed Lad when he began barking at a car entering the small parking lot. "To be perfectly honest, I'm not sure." With that, she launched into the story of the late night caller and the meeting she had arranged.

"My God, Jennifer, you can't meet that man out there alone. What on earth were you thinking?"

"I know that, Mom. I only agreed to meet him because I thought you and Dad would be there. I just need to find out who the caller is and what he has to tell me. I'll be all right."

"Absolutely not." Her mother's voice carried a note of finality. "This stranger might very well be the one who left the note in your car or that old man you saw following you back to Austin."

Jennifer grimaced. "Any suggestions as to what I should do?"

"Why don't you call the Hays County Sheriff's Office, or better yet, stop by there when you get to San Marcos and ask them to send someone out?"

Rain now steadily beating on the roof, combined with this recent development, depressed Jennifer's mood. "I don't think that would do any good. I doubt if they would detail a deputy to Wimberley to serve as an escort service for a meeting I've arranged. Next suggestion?"

"When your dad and I met with Governor Bates, he introduced us to that Texas Ranger, Lt. Falcone. You told me the other night he'd come to Houston to see you. Why don't you call and ask him to come to S-4 while you meet this stranger?"

Now was definitely not the time to tell her he wanted her to look at photos of some killer. That would really get her worked up. "Great idea. I've got his business card in my wallet. I'll call him as soon as we hang up."

"Promise me you will. Don't do something crazy like meeting that man alone."

"I promise."

"Good. I'll call you as soon as your dad can leave the hospital. And I want you to call me once your meeting is concluded."

"Don't worry. I'm sure the Ranger will take care of me. I'll talk to you soon. Love ya and be careful driving down."

With that, Jennifer hit the disconnect button and pulled out her wallet for Juan Falcone's telephone numbers.

Balancing himself with one leg on the fender of his sedan, Juan Falcone completed his stretching regimen prior to his mid-day run around Lake Lady Bird. He would have plenty of time to grab a sandwich, shower, change clothes and get back to DPS headquarters for his four o'clock meeting with Jennifer Spencer. He punched a button on the digital dial, switching it to stopwatch mode, then walked across Caesar Chavez Street to the nearby running path.

Encouraged by the match of the fingerprints on the money Yazkov had given Consuella Gonzalez with those on Roberto Salazar's pickup, it came as no surprise to learn Yazkov had purchased disguise materials in San Antonio. That explained why he had not been sighted since DPS had disseminated his photograph.

The unexpected vibration of the cell phone from the pack around his waist startled him. Slowing to a walk, he took several deep breaths, trying to slow his breathing. "Lt. Falcone here."

"Hey there, Lieutenant. Sounds like I caught you chasing down one of the bad guys."

The voice was familiar, but he couldn't place it. "Excuse me, but who is this?"

"Thanks a lot. My feelings are hurt. I guess the visit in my office and our conversation the other morning didn't make much of an impression on you."

"Ms. Spencer, of course. There's a lot of noise in the background on your end of the line. Are you already in Wimberley?"

"No, I'm about forty-five minutes away."

Having regained normal breathing, Juan walked briskly along the path, occasionally stepping aside for other mid-day runners. "Please don't tell me you're calling to cancel our meeting."

"To the contrary, the sooner I can see you the better."

"That's certainly a change in attitude." Juan stopped and covered his ear so he could hear better. "Mind telling me what brought this about?" Juan came to a halt.

"I'll be glad to." Jennifer told of her late-night caller, her plans to meet him, and the call she had just received from her mother.

Juan began moving again, anticipating her next words. "So I hope you're calling to ask if I'll come to your parents' place. If so, the answer is yes. If that's not the reason, I'm coming anyway. I agree with your mother, you don't need to be meeting this guy out in the country by yourself."

"As you can tell, I'm kind of an independent gal who likes doing things on her own. Under the present circumstances, however, the sooner I see you, Lieutenant, the safer I'll feel."

Juan began to jog. "Forget trying to win an award for Miss Independence. Tell me the location of your folk's property. Given the time constraints, I'm going to requisition a helicopter. DPS has one standing by for emergencies like this."

Juan did his best to concentrate, while Jennifer told him how to get to S-4 from Wimberley's town square. His breathing came harder as he ran back to his vehicle. "Okay, I think I've got it. I should be there by two o'clock. In the meantime, Jennifer, don't do anything foolish. Your investigation isn't worth it, plus I really would like to see you again. I was serious about taking you to dinner."

"We'll worry about dinner later. Right now I'd appreciate it if you'd get yourself down here ASAP. *Adios.*"

Juan descended the ramp on the Lamar Street bridge and covered the final yards to his car where he hurriedly striped off his T-shirt and put on his uniform. Opening the trunk, he pulled out his holster and Sig Sauer 357 magnum, removed his bulletproof vest, Winchester Model 94 30-30 rifle and a box of ammunition. He carefully laid them in the passenger's seat.

CHAPTER 38

▼

AUSTIN
FEBRUARY 27

Lt. Falcone gathered his weapons and ran to the waiting Bell 407. Prior to departure, DPS Sgt. Jessie Washington was scrutinizing a clipboard, making his final check of the turbine-powered aircraft. "Good afternoon, Lieutenant. Glad I got your call. I've been sitting here waiting for some flight time and action."

Juan stood back and absorbed the scene, the pungent odor of high-octane fuel and oil filling his nostrils. "Not sure how much action there'll be. Short flight and a drop off. Pretty routine stuff." He briefly explained their mission.

Washington opened the access panels to check fluid levels, wiring and others items on his pre-flight checklist. "What time do you need to get to S-4?"

"I'd like to be there by two o'clock at the latest."

"Then we better haul ass." Washington climbed down. "Hop in and buckle up, I'm through here." He stepped into the spacious wide-body cabin, got in his seat and began a last minute check of the collective, cyclic and anti-torque pedals. "Be my guest," he patted the empty seat beside him.

Juan got in and watched while Washington rolled the throttle and raised the rpms. The pilot flipped switches, tested caution lights and keyed the radio. Once he received take-off clearance and the blades were cranking at the desired level, he lifted off. Turning into the stiff wind, he moved forward with gathering speed until the helicopter seemed to soar on its own.

Juan glanced at the digital control panel and noticed they were cruising at close to one hundred ten knots. "What's our Wimberley ETA?"

Washington's voice crackled through the headset intercom. "Given the strong wind out of the south, I'd say a little after 2, maybe 2:15."

Juan shook his head. "Not good enough, Sergeant. You're going to have to push the envelope."

Juan found himself growing more anxious as they neared their destination. Even though a cool wind was blowing through the cockpit, he felt perspiration forming beneath the armored vest. "Head for the town square and from there I'll give you directions on how to get to the Spencer property."

"Roger that. It's pretty uneven terrain as we get closer to the river. I'm not sure we'll be able to find a safe LZ, especially with this head wind."

Juan pulled out a slip of paper with the directions to S-4. "I understand. Just get me there ASAP. I'll worry about a bumpy landing later."

Making a high reconnaissance over the small community, Washington headed toward the river and S-4. Once there he made slow circles at five hundred feet, the blades loudly churning. As expected, the rocky field was filled with thick clumps of cedar, sumac and willows.

"No way I can make a soft landing here, Lieutenant. The blades would be sheared off by those trees. How 'bout I follow the Blanco River till we come to an open field? I can radio a trooper or deputy sheriff and have him pick you up."

When Juan looked below, he knew that would not be good enough. He saw a car pull up in front of the Spencer cabin. Jennifer Spencer's visitor had arrived.

Whack! The paring knife sliced easily through the crisp green apple and struck the carving board. After spreading peanut butter on the apple quarters, Jennifer put them on a paper plate along with some carrot sticks, and took her lunch out to the porch. Lad barked as she sat down on the steps. "I know. You're as happy to be here as I am," she lovingly said, pampering the dog with attention. "How 'bout a run? Want to see if you can scare up any rabbits before it rains?" Jennifer put down her plate and threw a small tree branch into the yard, watching the golden retriever bound toward the river.

Across the river, Sergei Yazkov wiped condensation from binocular lenses and watched a car enter the narrow driveway. He raised the sniper rifle to the firing position and took a bead on the man getting out of the car.

Jennifer heard the crunch of tires on the gravel as a vehicle slowly made its way down the private road toward the cabin. She stepped back under the covered porch out of the mist and anxiously waited. Her attention was suddenly diverted when the golden retriever splashed across the shallow river, headed for an open field. "Lad, get back over here!" She let out a shrill whistle, but the dog ignored her as if preoccupied with chasing some varmint.

Before she had time to think further about her pet, the visitor greeted her. "Good afternoon, Jennifer. Sorry I'm a few minutes late. Traffic was heavy coming out of Austin."

Although Jennifer didn't know exactly what she expected, the night caller's handsome features surprised her. In his casual work clothes, he could have passed for one of the cedar choppers who frequented Wimberley's general delivery store five miles away.

"Hi." She forced a smile and extended her hand. "Come on in."

Jake Hardesty reached out to take her hand. "No, I told you I wanted to meet outside. No listening devices or recorders." He released

Jennifer's hand and stepped into the yard. "Let's talk out here in the open, down toward the river. This won't take long." With one hand behind him, he twisted the length of nylon rope in his back pocket.

Jennifer tried to think of what she could do to delay the discussion. She was nervous as hell having to proceed without Falcone.

Sergei Yazkov couldn't ask for easier targets. Spencer and the stranger were actually walking toward him. The only question was who to take out first. He took aim at the man's heart, released the safety and gently eased his finger onto the trigger.

Just as he was ready to pull, he was distracted by a large dog racing toward him. Quickly Yazkov refocused on his target but the growling animal pounced on his back, sinking his canines into the softness of his neck. Unintentionally Yazkov squeezed off a round, striking Jake in the left shoulder, five inches above the heart.

Yazkov rolled over and with one swift blow swung the rifle solidly into the dog's head. Lad let out a bone-chilling yelp before being knocked from his feet, landing unconscious several feet away. Blood oozed from the animal's mouth. Yazkov pivoted back into firing position, regained his concentration and took aim again.

Jake had heard the crack of the rifle's report at the same instant he felt searing pain and saw blood seeping through his work shirt. "Goddamn it. I've, I've been shot!"

Chest heaving, eyes blinking against pain and shock, Jake shook his head trying to release the roaring in his ears. Instantly, he was back on patrol in Southeast Asia. He looked up and saw an Army medic Huey hovering over the landing zone to pick up his artillery squad. Across the rice paddy he could make out approaching Viet Cong.

Sgt. Hardesty glanced over at an Army nurse hunkered down next to him. "Stay down, ma'am," he shouted to Jennifer. "I'll try to divert their attention." He turned away to taunt the approaching vision. "Hey, you motherfucker, over here! Come and get me!"

Jennifer had been equally startled by Lad's barking in the field across the river. Now there was a bleeding man in the yard, screaming like a mad man. She wasn't sure whether the bullet in the stranger had been intended for her, but she knew to seek safety. She ran to the picnic table and threw it onto its side, the top facing the river. As she did, she felt white-hot heat in her right thigh. Looking down, she saw the faded blue denim turning dark red.

Oh, my God. As she lurched behind the table, Jennifer heard another round splinter the heavy wooden top. Temporarily shielded, she clutched her leg to stop the flow of blood.

"Set this mother down, now!" Juan had seen the stranger go down, then saw Jennifer take a round in the leg. He surveyed the entire area, looking for the shooter. It was the golden coat of the big dog lying in the field that first caught his attention. It was only when the attacker stood and started toward the river that Juan identified Sergei Yazkov. By then, it was too late.

Juan saw the flash of a rifle being fired from across the river, simultaneously with the shattering of the chopper's windshield. Another shot hit one of the rotating blades.

Yazkov took aim through the scope, gently squeezed the trigger and put the next round through the pilot's shoulder. "There's a rope ladder behind your seat," Washington yelled. "If you want down there you'd better use it 'cause I'm losing control. Get the fuck away from here, Lieutenant!"

Smiling, Yazkov took aim once more at the man with Spencer. Suddenly he heard a shot from overhead and felt a bullet hit his left leg. He looked up to see a man descending a rope ladder, rifle in hand. Shifting weight to his right leg, the Russian decided to speed the shooter's decent. He took aim and fired.

The round struck Juan's left arm, causing him to drop and roll on the rain-soaked ground. It was all he could do to keep from passing out.

Struggling to maintain consciousness, Jessie Washington heard more shooting. He looked down and saw Falcone fall to the ground. He pulled back on the throttle and the chopper lifted and veered toward the river.

Jake looked up to see his fellow GI fall from the sky and land thirty feet away. "Damn you bastards!" Gritting his teeth, he shifted direction and began crawling toward the wounded soldier. He pushed the trooper's rifle out of the way, rolled the wounded man over, but saw no Army insignia, only the name plate: "Lieutenant Juan Falcone".

Jake laughed. "Well, at least they sent an officer out to the boonies for this little rescue operation." He pulled the imposing Sig Sauer from its holster and reached for the rifle. A second bullet slammed into Hardesty's body, this time in his left hip. Jake fell onto the Texas Ranger, firing three quick bursts in the direction from which he had heard the last shot.

Yazkov gasped for air as one round pierced his left side, entering just below the rib cage. A flicker of movement to his right caught his attention while he was aiming at Jake's chest. His main target was getting away!

Yazkov threw down the sniper rifle and checked the ammo supply in his handgun. More than enough to take care of Spencer and return to put the final touches on the two men lying in front of him. Holding his side, he limped toward Spencer, pistol at the ready.

Seeing the shooter crossing the Blanco, Jennifer gathered all her strength and crawled toward the cabin. Once inside she pulled herself to the gun cabinet. She took out a thirty ought six deer rifle and furiously rummaged through the cabinet in search of ammunition. "Damn it, Dad, where'd you hide the ammo?" She tried to ignore the shakiness in her voice as it echoed about the cabin.

No sooner had she hobbled to a standing position and taken the rifle by its barrel than Yazkov flung the door open and stepped inside. Jennifer swung the rifle stock with all her strength, striking the intruder squarely in the midsection. When he fell to the floor she hit him again, this time with such force the weapon flew from her grasp. "Who the hell are you? Why are you trying to kill me! Answer me, damn you!"

When Yazkov struggled to his knees and yelled something in Russian, she hobbled to the kitchen in search of anything else that might provide protection.

Suddenly, Jake Hardesty staggered through the front door, a rifle held waist high. He fired, striking the Russian in the right shoulder. Sergei collapsed to the floor, blood covering his shirt.

"Son of a bitch!" Jennifer cried out. Seeing her attacker down and unarmed, she rushed to her rescuer's side as Jake crumpled to the floor.

"Damn it, you can't die on me!" she cried, cradling his head in her lap. Jake's clothes were drenched in so much blood Jennifer didn't know where to begin stanching the wounds. "I'll call 911."

"Not enough time," Jake whispered. "I can't hold on." He gasped for air, his words barely audible. "Listen to me, Spencer. *Tejano* got fucked up big time. I never intended for it to get so out of hand."

"*Tejano?* What the hell are you talking about?" Jennifer cried. "Who are you, and who is that bastard over there?" She put her face closer to Jake's to hear his weakening voice.

Yazkov blinked several times to bring Spencer and the stranger into focus. The woman's back was to him. Using a coffee table for support, he hoisted himself to a standing position and approached.

Hearing movement behind her, Jennifer turned and saw Yazkov limping toward her. She lowered Jake's head to the floor and tried pulling the rifle from beneath him. It wouldn't budge. She began backpedaling across the floor, knocking over chairs and tables to block her attacker's pathway. Yazkov kicked them aside and kept coming, his bloody hands outstretched.

Reaching the kitchen cabinet, Jennifer pulled open the drawers and began furiously flinging pots and pans at him. One struck him hard on the forehead. He stopped when warm blood streamed from his temple.

Jennifer opened another drawer only to find food items. She grabbed a bottle of cooking oil and splashed it on the tile floor between them. When Yazkov took his next step his feet slipped out from under him and he fell face first not ten feet from her, cracking his nose and cheekbones.

Frantically looking about, Jennifer spotted the knife holder beside the butcher block where she had cut the apple. Pulling out a butcher knife and picking up a can of bug repellant, she sprayed the chemical in his face. When Yazkov rose to his feet, he let out a horrifying scream, trying in vain to rub the poison from his burning eyes.

Hearing a scraping sound coming from the porch, Jennifer turned to see Falcone limping through the open door. Juan leveled his revolver and fired at the killer he had been tracking for six months.

Yazkov collapsed onto Jennifer, wrapping his bloody fingers around her throat. His death grip immediately released when he fell on the knife. Jennifer felt the razor-sharp blade slice through skin, muscle and organs.

CHAPTER 39

▼

SAN MARCOS
FEBRUARY 28

Slowly he pulled the knife from his stomach and wiped the blood on his trousers. He lifted the weapon above his head and started a swift downward motion.

"No! No! Please, God, no!" Jennifer yelled, watching the knife's decent toward her face.

Savannah Spencer was startled out of a fitful sleep at the sound of her daughter's piercing scream. She pushed herself off the recliner chair and rushed to Jennifer's bedside. She clutched her daughter's hand, her tone comforting. "Wake up, you're safe. It's okay, baby. Mother is right here. It's just a bad dream."

Jennifer was at the bottom of the ocean, straining to reach the surface while unseen forces kept pulling her down. She saw a man's red and white face in the greenish blue water above, but then it disappeared. In the distance, above the surface, she heard a familiar voice. Wiping her tired eyes, she looked around the room. "Where am I? What's going on? What happened?"

"You're in a hospital in San Marcos. You're being treated for your injuries." She smoothed her daughter's hair back. "As to what happened, I'm afraid only you know that. The Highway Patrol officer told your father and me a few things, but he was reluctant to go into detail. There'll be plenty of time to talk."

Jennifer surveyed her surroundings. A pulley elevated her right leg at a 45 degree angle. Both of her arms sported IVs.

Still in the grip of the anesthesia from surgery, her tongue felt thick, and she couldn't form her thoughts. As much as she wanted to stay awake to ask more questions, she involuntarily drifted to sleep, getting what she needed most, rest.

Early the next morning, Jennifer awakened to the reality of her circumstances. Still groggy, she asked her mom, "What's wrong with my leg? Am I going to be able to walk again?"

"Of course you will. Your father was very impressed yesterday with the orthopedic surgeon who performed your operation."

"Daddy? Is he here?" She looked past her mother.

"Yes, yes, he's out in the hallway, on the phone as usual. He will give you the medical details."

"Oh, Mother, it, it was like watching a horror movie, but I couldn't get up and leave because I was a part of it," Jennifer cried.

"It's over, darling." Savannah gently soothed her tear-stained cheeks with a cool cloth. "You're alive and well. Don't talk about it now. Try to relax."

"But it's all I can think about, all I've been dreaming about. I feel like I've been here for weeks. Lt. Falcone? Is he …?"

"He'll be fine. Your father can fill you in on that too. I believe he talked to the lieutenant's doctor."

Jennifer asked for a sip of juice from a glass on the bedside tray. "There were two other men...." She grimaced at the thought of them. "Who were they? Are they...."

Sitting on the side of the bed, Savannah pressed her fingers to Jennifer's lips. Her mother started to speak but could only shake her head.

"They're dead, aren't they? Mother, I killed one of them! I stabbed a man to death!" In her mother's embrace, she cried uncontrollably.

Savannah pushed the call button. When the nurse's station responded, she asked them to bring a sedative and to call Dr. Spencer to the room.

Moments later Blake Spencer and a nurse entered. After Jennifer had taken the medication and the nurse departed, Blake attempted to lift his daughter's spirits. "How's my baby girl? No crying, young lady. That's against doctor's orders."

"Okay, Doc, whatever you say." Jennifer brushed away a tear and forced a smile. She tapped the splint. "What did your colleagues do to me?"

"X-rays showed you had a comminuted fracture of the right femur, the long bone in the upper part of your leg. Dr. Jones performed what's called an open reduction, internal fixation."

"Dad, plain English, please."

Blake smiled. "That means he inserted a rod along the femur. It will be permanent, but you won't be able to feel it's there. You'll be on crutches and using a wheelchair and walker for a while, but he doesn't anticipate any permanent disability."

"Will, will I be able to run again? Will I have a limp?"

"One question at a time. Yes, you will be able to run but it will be a while. Walking for a few months in a cast, building up to the jogging. You'll need some physical therapy, and you shouldn't have a limp."

Jennifer momentarily recalled the scene in the cabin with the shooter, the late night caller and Juan Falcone. "I suppose it could be a lot worse. I'm lucky to be alive."

Her father nodded. "From what little the DPS officer told your mother and me, I couldn't agree with you more."

"I remember seeing Lt. Falcone." Jennifer closed her eyes again and rubbed her forehead. "He was in the cabin with me and those two other men. Is Juan all right?"

"Yes, he'll be fine. After he was stabilized in the emergency room, the Department of Public Safety life-flighted him to an Austin hospital where he's being treated. He had a simple fracture of the humerus, the main bone in the left upper arm, from the bullet he took before he fell. He'll probably be in a cast for six to eight weeks."

"Did he have any injuries from the fall?"

"Luckily, nothing serious, a few bumps, bruises, pulled muscles and a twisted ankle."

Jennifer collapsed back on the bed, trying to absorb the nature and extent of injuries she and Falcone had sustained. So much had happened in so little time. It was almost impossible to comprehend it all. "The helicopter, I saw it leave. Was the pilot able to make a safe landing?"

Blake took his daughter's hand and shook his head. "I'm afraid not. The pilot performed heroically. He made a crash landing in a ravine about a mile down river. He had enough control to avoid hitting any houses. Unfortunately he did not survive.

"Before he ditched, the pilot radioed a DPS trooper who was patrolling the area. The pilot told him there had been a firefight and to call for back-up and emergency medical services. EMS arrived on the scene and brought you and Lt. Falcone to the hospital. The trooper called your mother, and we left Waco immediately."

Jennifer shook her head in disbelief. "That part I don't remember at all."

"That's understandable. EMS said you were unconscious when they arrived. You'd lost quite a bit of blood from the leg wound. You awoke in the ambulance, went into shock and had to be sedated. As soon as you reached the ER, the physician on duty prescribed a strong pain medication, and you were out like a light until after the surgery."

Trying to put the thoughts of human carnage out of her mind, Jennifer looked around the room again. She tried to ignore the depressing sight of an aluminum walker and crutches in the corner of the room. "Where did all those flowers come from?"

Savannah stepped over to an arrangement on top of the television. "These are from your office staff. That large bouquet by the door is from Lt. Falcone. He called a couple of times while you were asleep."

Looking past the flowers toward the open door, Jennifer noticed a man in a blue uniform, a gun on his hip. "What's that police officer doing in the hall?"

Blake glanced at Savannah. "We were going to explain, but given your condition, wanted to wait until you were a little stronger. He's a private security guard we hired to be with you for a while."

Jennifer looked at her father in bewilderment. "What on earth for?"

"One of the Austin radio stations was monitoring the police scanner and picked up the transmission by the helicopter pilot to the DPS officer. By the time EMS got to S-4, the station had dispatched a reporter to Wimberley."

"But what does that have to do with a security officer?"

"Once you and Lt. Falcone reached the hospital, the Associated Press had put out a wire story about the confrontation, and there were three television news crews waiting at the emergency room wanting more information. The Rangers had already informed the press they were searching for Sergei Yazkov as a double murder suspect, so when the word leaked that he was one of the men killed, that really created a media feeding frenzy."

"To make matters worse," Savannah added, "the press recognized our names as the owners of the place where the shootout occurred. Being the daughter of a former state senator gave them another angle to deal with. It seems our photographs have been prominently displayed both on television and in a number of newspapers over the last twenty-four hours."

"My gosh. The last thing I wanted to do was drag y'all into this."

"That's of no consequence," Blake reassured her. "The reporters have been like a pack of rabid dogs trying to establish your connection to Yazkov and Jake Hardesty."

"Jake Hardesty? I don't know anyone by that name."

"Apparently he knew you," her father replied. "He was the other man who was killed. The Texas Rangers who arrived on the scene got the name from his driver's license. When that information also leaked, it got the attention of the *Washington Post* and other national media outlets. Yazkov had been profiled on the USA's *Most Wanted* program, and they sent a reporter. The *Post* also sent down a reporter who wants to interview you as soon as possible. We felt it was too much to ask of the hospital staff to keep all of those reporters at bay. That is why we hired the security guard."

"But why the *Washington Post?* Why would they be interested in Jake Hardesty?"

"I found that out from the *Post* reporter, a very nice young woman about your age," Savannah said. "She told me Hardesty was a very successful lobbyist on Capitol Hill. The *Post* has another investigative reporter back in D.C. digging to find out more about him and who'd registered as his clients."

Blake took his daughter's hand. "Jake Hardesty leads to another situation we may as well tell you about while we're on that subject. The Rangers had been working with the FBI in their efforts to apprehend Yazkov. When the FBI learned of the deaths of Yazkov and a well-connected Washington lobbyist, they took an increased interest in finding out why this Russian was meeting with you and Jake Hardesty."

"But you don't understand, Dad. I wasn't meeting with Yazkov. I didn't even know he was there until he started shooting at us."

"That's why the FBI sent an agent down to interview you as soon as you're up to it. They want to sort out exactly what happened and what connection Hardesty may have had with the Russian. This now has national and perhaps even international implications. Based upon what they learned from the Rangers, they also thought it was best you have some personal protection for the time being. I don't want to alarm you, but the FBI agent said Yazkov may not have been acting alone."

Jennifer squeezed her eyes shut, holding back the tears. "I don't want to hear any more about the FBI and the news media and killers right now. There's a throbbing pain in my leg and all of this has given me a terrible headache."

"I'm sorry, honey. That's to be expected with all you're going through." Blake picked up a plastic tube running from a bag on a pole into her arm. "This I-V carries a morphine solution for pain control." He picked up a small device at the end of the line. "Push this button as often as every ten minutes for an injection for relief. The drip is programmed, so you can't overmedicate."

As visions of the confrontation temporarily vanished, the complications and discomfort of her present and future circumstances were beginning to sink in. "By the way, when do I get out of here?"

"The doctor said you'd probably remain here for at least three more days. The bed rest will do you good. You've been through a lot, both physically and emotionally. From the description I received, it was a pretty traumatic scene. I just wish to hell we'd been there for you."

"Forget about that. If you had, both of you might be in beds down the hall or worse. Will you and Mom drive me back to Houston?"

"Yes, but no time soon. After discharge we're going to take you to S-4 for some well deserved R&R. No more investigation and no work for a while."

Jennifer shook her head. "I don't care if I ever go back to that place after what I saw, what I did. Plus, I've got to get back to my law practice. I've got trials and depositions scheduled."

"You have a lifetime ahead of you for that. I talked to your assistant, and she's in the process of rescheduling everything." Blake leaned over and gave her a kiss on the forehead. "You really should rest now. Here's your call button for the nurse's station in case you need anything."

Savannah gave her daughter a hug. "We love you, darling, and are so thankful you're alive and well. We'll be back after while. Try to get some rest, and don't think about anything."

Don't think about what she'd been through? Easier said than done. One man wounded and three dead. One she killed. And here she was with a broken leg, a morphine drip and looking at future physical therapy. Yeah, don't think about it! Right.

The sedative was having its effect and Jennifer began feeling groggy. She pushed a button, dimming the overhead lights. Periodic calls for doctors and nurses over the PA system grew distant.

It all seemed surreal. If Falcone hadn't dropped out of the sky. If he hadn't managed to crawl to the cabin, she would have been killed by one of those men. Why had Jake Hardesty called? Why was Sergei Yazkov there? So many questions.

An hour into her deep sleep the nightmare recurred. Seeing the killer's face covered in blood, Jennifer screamed at the top of her lungs and bolted upright.

CHAPTER 40

▼

SANTA FE
FEBRUARY 28

Dan Morton stood in the circular drive and watched the car slowly proceed up the hill. He waved a greeting when it neared. "Welcome to Casa Encantada," he said when Bill York lowered the window. He pointed to a small parking area. "Anywhere over there will be fine."

Although Dan had met him a few times over the past several years, it wasn't until he had returned York's urgent telephone call two days earlier that Morton became aware of York's involvement in *Tejano*. Although Dan and Jake Hardesty agreed not to disclose the involvement of others, Jake had obviously apprised York of Dan's role.

Dan extended his hand. "Welcome to our humble abode. Come on in."

As the two made their way up the gravel path, York surveyed the Morton's second home. He could only guess at the square footage of the two-story adobe structure. Probably ten thousand at a minimum. "Quite a place you got here, Colonel."

Dan patted him on the shoulder while they walked through the entryway. "Yeah, we love it. And please, cut the formality, we're partners. It's Dan to you."

York surveyed the expansive living area, Southwestern oil paintings and sculptures on display. "How long have you been coming to Santa Fe?"

"About ten years. My wife, Kathryn, was an art history major and loves the Southwest." He waved his arm about the room. "This town is full of outstanding galleries she likes to frequent. When you come to our home in Fort Worth, you'll really see where my money goes."

Bill glanced down a hallway toward the kitchen. "Is Mrs. Morton around?"

"Naw, she's gone up to the ski basin with some girlfriends to tackle the double black diamond runs, so we'll have some privacy. Have a seat over by the fireplace while I fix us a drink. Name your poison, I'm having a whiskey on the rocks."

York walked over to a leather club chair near the kiva and sat while his host tended bar. "Sounds perfect. I'll have the same."

Returning with the cocktails and a bowel of mixed nuts, Dan took a seat on the sofa across from York. He reached over and held up his glass for a toast. "Here's to Jake Hardesty. God bless our dearly departed friend and partner. May he rest in peace." They touched glasses and sat in silence a moment.

"Before we discuss anything else, Bill, I want to tell you how pleased I was you called. I'm not sure where we go from here, but we're in this together to the end." He extended his hand as though sealing the partnership.

Bill shook hands, then settled back in his chair and absorbed the warmth of his drink and the rich leather. "I don't know about you, but I was absolutely shocked when I heard of Jake's death. I called as soon as I could."

"Yeah, I couldn't believe it either. He was chief lobbyist for my company and a long time friend. I can't help but wonder what this means to our political project."

"That's part of what I wanted to talk with you about. What do we do now with *Tejano*? With all due respect to the recently departed, why in the world was Jake with Jennifer Spencer and some damn Russian? Based upon what I've seen in the news, I've got to tell you I'm worried as hell our operation has been compromised. If you asked for my vote right now, I'm ready to shut down the son of a bitch."

Dan lifted his hand as though directing traffic. "Wait a minute, let's take it one step at a time. The Santa Fe and Albuquerque newspapers didn't have much coverage of what happened back in Texas, so I went on line to the *Dallas Morning News* and some other news websites. The coverage was mainly about that fellow, Sergei Yazkov, the Texas Rangers had been searching for. Why don't you start at the top and bring me up to speed on what you know."

Hoping it would relieve his nervous energy, York got up and began pacing the room. "I'll be happy to. The story was plastered all over the news in Washington. The *Washington Post* had the story above the fold on page one with photographs of Jake, Yazkov and Jennifer Spencer. On the Internet I read everything I could find in the major Texas newspapers. From what I pieced together, Jake was at the country home of a Doctor and Mrs. Blake Spencer from Waco. They weren't there, but their daughter, Jennifer, was."

"Unfortunately, I know that name." Morton briefly told of Jennifer's call to his wife concerning Kathryn's name on Smith's FEC reports, and his Internet search on Jennifer. The key question now is, what does Spencer know about our activities?"

"That's what has been troubling me the most." York stopped his pacing and faced Dan. "I have a hard time believing he went there with the intention of blowing the cover on the very project he conceived."

"I agree, but the way I analyze it, he had only two options: Expose the project or eliminate Spencer. I hope it was the latter."

"Well, if he intended to take her out, he failed. The newspapers reported she was shot and is hospitalized in San Marcos. The Texas Ranger who was there, a Lt. Juan Falcone, was also wounded and is in an Austin hospital. Both will be getting out in the next few days."

"That's another concern I have. What the hell was a Texas Ranger doing there? Was there anything in the news explaining that?" Morton threw another log on the fire.

"Only that the Texas Rangers had been tracking this Russian. I guess Falcone had some reason to believe Yazkov was at the Spencers' and came to arrest him. That doesn't explain why Yazkov was there in the first place. What connection did he have to Jake or Spencer?"

"Keeping with our new full disclosure policy, I need to fill you in on where the money has been coming from to fuel our little conspiracy." Morton then explained his role in soliciting funds from around the world.

"Damn, I always assumed you had overseas funding sources, but I never knew the specifics or the extent of your efforts. That still doesn't explain the connection to Yazkov."

"Let me take it a step further. Once Kathryn told me about Spencer's call, I mentioned it to my moneyman in Moscow, Boris Volkov. Knowing the way the Russian Mafia works, I think he may have sent Yazkov over here to protect his investment. It's possible he was there to put a hit on Spencer."

"Holy shit! Why don't you call this guy, Volkov, and ask him about Yazkov? That seems pretty easy to confirm."

Dan shook his head. "I don't want to contact Boris until we have some idea whether Spencer and the Rangers learned anything from Jake about the *Tejano* project."

York covered his face. "Damn, I can't believe this is happening! What in God's name are we going to do now?"

"To tell you the truth, Bill, I'm not sure. I've never had a contingency plan for such a development. I know that we've got to keep our mouths shut."

"I'll sure as hell keep my mouth shut, and I'll meet with Rebecca Durham as soon as possible and tell her to do likewise. Any other suggestions?" York finished his drink and went to the bar to help himself.

"Yes. We should hire the best damn criminal defense lawyers in the country. I'll loan you and Durham the money if you need it. If O.J. Simpson could get off two murder raps, we sure as hell can do the same for some political conspiracy charges, if that's what's in store for us. If and when the time comes, we can always cut a deal for a few years' probation or go to some country club-like federal penitentiary."

"I suppose you're right. Come to think of it, what have we done wrong? It's not the end of the world just because some money came in from other countries to a political primary campaign. For all we know, Smith might have won the nomination without our money. I say we pull the plug on *Tejano* and call it a day."

Dan shook his head. "I'm afraid it's not quite that simple. I haven't been collecting the big bucks from a convention of Sunday school teachers. It won't be long before this story reaches the international news, if it hasn't already. Once that happens our financial partners will start calling me asking all kinds of questions. If, for some reason, Jake told Spencer about them, there's no doubt she will tell that Texas Ranger and they'll report it to the feds."

"Surely Jake wouldn't have done that."

"I hope you're right," Morton replied. "While Jake's motives were not as pure as the new driven snow, I know he didn't approve of those I selected to become involved."

"Yeah, now that you mention it, I got the same impression."

Morton continued. "I'm willing to hold off for a while and see if Spencer and the Rangers know about *Tejano*. From what you've said, there's been nothing in the news about it. Maybe Jake didn't tell her anything before he died."

"But what about Creighton's presidential campaign? Given what has happened, surely you don't propose we get involved there, do you?"

"I sure as hell do. Up until now we've been thinking of what's good for Russell Creighton and how we stand to gain financially. Now we're talking about prison and staying alive."

"I'm sorry, I don't follow you."

Dan continued. "If we shut down *Tejano* because of this incident, I'll be a walking dead man. People like Boris Volkov won't quietly fade away. Even if the US authorities can't reach them, their names would be in the news and their reputations ruined. President Templeton might be able to get one or more of his allies to take action against them, or agree to extradite them, to the United States on criminal charges."

"Damn, I never thought of that."

"Look at it this way, Bill, I'd rather deal with an Attorney General appointed by a President Russell Creighton than Templeton's hatchet man. More importantly, I'd rather take my chances with the FBI and a bunch of bumbling bureaucratic prosecutors in the Justice Department than with foreign mafia types and drug dealers who've invested in the project. We've gotten in bed with the devil, and we'd better make the most out of it."

It was all Bill York could do to maintain his composure. "Son of a bitch!" He gulped down the rest of his drink.

The ringing of a telephone startled both Morton and York. "I'll be right back." Dan walked to the phone in the kitchen. A few minutes later he returned. "That was an FBI agent. He's on his way over to arrest us." York jumped to his feet, almost knocking over his glass. Dan laughed. "Calm down, I was just kidding. Don't be so jumpy. It was only Kathryn. She and the gals have been relaxing at a spa up the road. She should be here in about ten minutes. I think it best you're not here when she returns. The less she knows about all of this, the better."

York got up. "I'm glad you invited me out here, Dan, even though I can't say I like most of what we've discussed."

Morton opened the front door and the two walked outside. "Some good can come of what happened. I hate it that Jake was killed, but it means you've become that much more important to the success of *Tejano* and to my own business. I'm going to need a lobbyist and I can't think of anyone better than Bill York." He stopped and extended his hand. "I want you to be the lobbyist for my handgun business. Jake would want it that way. Will you do it for me?"

"You know I will," he said without hesitation.

"Outstanding. That's the only good news I've heard lately. Where are you staying?"

"At the Inn of the Anasazi on the plaza."

"I'll meet you in the lobby at eight in the morning for breakfast, and we can nail down the details about the lobby work."

"Sounds great." With the prospects of employment with Dan Morton and his company, York was willing to take his chances with Morton's plans for *Tejano*. "I think we're in agreement. Cool it for a while and see what Spencer and the Ranger know, then gear up *Tejano* all the way to the White House. See you at eight."

Dan turned and walked back into the warmth of the hacienda. He'd be damned if he was going to let Jennifer Spencer ruin his career and his plans of what's best for this country.

CHAPTER 41

▼

S-4, WIMBERLEY
MARCH 3

Idly plucking wood splinters from a bullet hole in the picnic table, Jennifer flicked them toward Lad who sat motionless a few feet away from her wheelchair. She watched the golden retriever staring intently at the field across the Blanco River. Lad must have bad memories too, she thought. He seemed to instinctively watch for movement across the shallow river. The vet said the animal had suffered a mild concussion but would be as good as new in a few weeks.

Jennifer had reluctantly acquiesced to her parents' urging that she convalesce at S-4 for a week. With the use of her cell phone and e-mail, she kept in constant contact with the office. The sounds of the rippling water and the first signs of wild flowers, however, caused her thoughts to drift from work to recent painful memories.

"You sure seem engrossed in thought." Savannah had walked up behind her and set a glass of mint iced tea on the table. "See, I knew you could practice law up here if you wanted to."

"Oh, actually I was wondering why Jake Hardesty and Sergei Yazkov came here. Was Yazkov here to kill me or Hardesty or both of us?"

Savannah glanced at her watch. "It's ten twenty-five. Lt. Falcone will be along shortly for the de-briefing. Maybe he'll have some answers for you."

Jennifer looked toward the cabin. "Is that TV truck still out by the front gate?"

"Yes, it is. I'm glad we decided to keep that private security guard a while longer. He'll keep them from trespassing. But if you'd give the press a short interview, maybe they would be satisfied and leave you alone."

"I doubt that. The more I said, the more they'd want to know. I saw in this morning's Austin newspaper that someone said I had done fundraising for Warren's campaign. The next thing you know, some enterprising reporter will try to put him in the story too."

"The reporters just have a job to do, honey. You have to admit, this kind of thing is not an everyday occurrence around here. And with the Russian connection, this is probably an international news item." Savannah turned when she heard the sound of an approaching car. "That's probably Lieutenant Falcone now. I'll go around front to meet him."

"Here, let me help you, sir." A DPS trooper reached in the sliding door of the Highway Patrol mini-van to assist Juan out of the vehicle.

"No thanks, Sergeant. I can make it on my own." Juan ignored the pain in his bandaged ankle and slowly hobbled down the rocky pathway.

"Well, if we don't look like a couple of crippled birds." Jennifer extended her hand. "Please, excuse me for not getting up. How're you doing?"

"The doctor says I'll be limping for a few weeks, and the shoulder's sore, but I'm getting used to it." Falcone settled on the picnic table bench and opened the attaché the driver had placed on the table. He noticed Jennifer reposition herself in the wheelchair. Her shoulder-length hair was down, and she wore a sweatshirt and jeans with one leg cut off for the cast. He discreetly admired her well-proportioned features and angular face.

"How 'bout yourself?"

"Physically I'm okay. It's just a broken leg. Mom insisted I use the wheelchair for a while. I plan on discarding it in a few days and using the crutches. Mentally and emotionally, it's a different story. I'm a wreck." She closed her battery-powered lap top and pushed a stack of legal pads out of the way. "I can't seem to concentrate on my cases." Jennifer looked past him toward the river. "Have you ever killed anyone, Lieutenant?"

Juan remained silent for a moment. "Yeah, a couple of times. It comes with the badge. Why do you ask?"

"Until the other day I never had, and I hope I never have to again. The memories are far worse than the act itself. I keep seeing that monster coming toward me. He just wouldn't stop." Jennifer brushed away a tear.

Reaching over, Juan's hand settled lightly on hers. "You acted in self-defense, Ms. Spencer. It's the only thing you could have done. I'm the one who should feel bad about what went down, not you."

"Why do you say that?"

"If I'd gotten to the cabin sooner, he never would have reached you."

"That wasn't your fault." Jennifer was surprised by Falcone's perception of the events. "We're both lucky that guy didn't kill you too."

"You don't have to carry his death on your conscience for the rest of your life," Juan said. "According to the autopsy, the shot I fired entered his chest, right below the heart. That bullet is what caused Yazkov to fall on your knife."

Jennifer's eyes widened. "Yazkov? You mean the guy from Russia you've been searching for?"

"Yep, the one and only. We got a positive ID on his fingerprints and a photo from the Moscow police. Considering the fact Yazkov was here waiting for you, I have a hunch it may also have been him you saw dressed as a woman outside your apartment and as the old man who followed you home from Austin. When you feel up to it, I still want you to come to headquarters and look at photographs of him with disguises applied."

"But why do you think Yazkov would have been in disguise and following me? And another thing, why did Jake Hardesty try to save my life?"

"What do you mean, save your life?" Juan's attention intensified.

Jennifer explained Jake's action in the cabin and his comments about *Tejano*.

"That's very interesting." Juan hastily made some notes. "He may have tried to save you, but there's also evidence Hardesty may have come here to kill you. The DPS trooper who first arrived at the scene found in Hardesty's back pocket a length of nylon rope typically used as a garrote. Something must have happened to change his mind, maybe Yazkov's actions. Unfortunately, we will never know."

Jennifer lifted herself out of the wheelchair and onto the bench across the table from Falcone. "One good thing about being in the hospital for a few days, it gave me time to think. For some reason this Hardesty character wanted to meet and exchange information about possible illegal campaign contributions. Maybe Yazkov was here to prevent that from happening."

"That could be. What I *do* know is that if you can identify Yazkov from the photos I show you, I can complete my second assignment of securing your safety."

"I'd still like to know why Yazkov and Hardesty were here? I wonder if Yazkov was connected to this *Tejano* thing Hardesty mentioned?"

"I'm sorry to say, Ms. Spencer, I don't have answers to those questions either. Sergei Yazkov killed two men in South Texas, plus Jake Hardesty and a damn good DPS chopper pilot. I would like to help you, but unless I'm given further orders, I don't have the authority to go probing into those matters. I believe you could be on to something and suggest you contact the FBI or the federal prosecutor in Houston about your concerns."

Savannah Spencer had quietly approached the couple from the cabin, bearing a tray of sandwiches and a pitcher of iced tea. "You two needn't starve yourselves." She threw a bone out for Lad. "Time for a little break."

Juan hoisted himself to a standing position of sorts. "Thank you, Mrs. Spencer. I'm just about through." He closed the attaché and motioned for his driver to take it to the van.

"I better get going. It was very nice to see you again, Ms. Spencer."

"Please, let's drop the formalities, at least as far as I'm concerned. I'd feel a lot more comfortable if you'd call me Jennifer."

"Okay, Ms. Spencer, I mean Jennifer. What I was going to say is," Juan was interrupted by the ringing of his cell phone. He quickly pulled it from his belt. "Falcone here."

"Lieutenant, this is Henry Cable. I'm Special Assistant to Governor Bates. Hold one second, please. The switchboard is placing a call to Jennifer Spencer."

No sooner had the sentence been completed than the cell phone lying next to the lap-top computer rang. After Jennifer answered, Henry Cable introduced himself and explained that Lieutenant Falcone was patched into the call. "News travels fast in politics. The governor would like to commend both of you for your valor and courage under fire."

Jennifer and Juan looked at each other in amazement. Jennifer managed to respond first. "Please, tell the governor I'm flattered and honored by the call and thank him very much."

"You both can do that, in person. Governor Bates would like to invite you to a private luncheon here at the Governor's Mansion. Does this coming Friday at eleven fit your schedules?"

Juan knew a gubernatorial request was actually a command, no matter how politely the aide tried to sugarcoat it. "Certainly, sir, I'll be there," he promptly replied.

"Excellent. Ms. Spencer? You too, I presume? The governor also wants to hear first hand about your investigation and learn more about the men who were killed."

"Certainly, Mr. Cable. Tell Governor Bates that Lt. Falcone and I will be at the mansion at 11 sharp."

"Great," Cable replied. "My office will work out the logistics with your superiors, Lieutenant Falcone. I look forward to meeting you both in a few days."

CHAPTER 42

▼

AUSTIN
MARCH 7

While Juan Falcone posed for photographs with Governor Jeffrey Bates, Jennifer scanned the historic surroundings of the Governor's Mansion. Her parents were seated on one of the sofas perpendicular to the fireplace in the formal living room. Henry Cable stood a respectful distance from the guests, speaking in a lowered tone with a distinguished-looking African-American man dressed in a conservative chalk-stripe suit. The men had their backs to her and as Cable departed Jennifer was surprised to recognize the state attorney general, Charles Braniff.

"All right, **Ed,**" the governor said to the photographer, moving away from his **massive** fireplace, "let's get a couple of shots over by the Russell." **He motioned** the White House photographer toward a bronze bust of *The Bronco Twister* across the room.

Governor **Bates** turned to Jennifer's parents. "I've asked the mansion curator to give y'all a special tour while I'm having lunch with Jennifer and Lt. Falcone. When you're through, your lunch will be served. We should be through by one o'clock. Is that acceptable?"

"Certainly, Governor," Blake replied. "Savannah and I are just along for the ride. Needless to say, take all the time you want."

After the Spencers departed the governor turned to Jennifer and Juan and clapped his hands. "Okay, troops, let's get down to business. I'd like to introduce Attorney General Braniff," who stepped forward and shook their hands. "Although this meeting will be off the record, I asked Charlie to sit in. I find two sets of eyes and ears are better than one."

Braniff's imposing six-foot six frame, flecked gray hair and stern features exuded authority. Jennifer had met the former Texas Supreme Court justice when he'd spoken to a law school convocation. Rumors in legal circles were that he was destined for higher office.

Jennifer hadn't noticed a door in the wall paneling until a steward in a white serving jacket quietly entered and announced lunch was served. He led them into a small study where a table was set for four.

Bates pulled out Jennifer's chair and passed her crutches to the steward. "Dig in. I hope you like it," he said, taking a seat next to her. "I'm hooked on these King Ranch enchiladas."

After sorbet and coffee were served, Governor Bates eased into the subject at hand. "Given the fact that a well known Washington lobbyist and a Russian national were involved in the fiasco in Wimberley, I was thoroughly briefed on all of the events soon after they occurred. Like you, we didn't understand why these two men were there, and I'm interested in some first-hand knowledge. Jennifer, I understand you have concerns about possible illegal contributions to Andrew Smith's senate campaign. Tell me about your investigation."

"Certainly, sir."

Bates turned to Juan. "I also want to hear about your search for Sergei Yazkov. I'm particularly interested as to when your stories began to overlap. Jennifer, why don't you begin?"

The lawyer described in detail her suspicions of illegal funding of Smith's primary campaign and her investigation. At the appropriate time, Juan interjected information about the killings in Maverick and Uvalde Counties and his search for Sergei Yazkov. Soon the two were jointly telling one story of the manhunt and Jennifer's pursuit of the money trail. Jennifer explained that she had gone to DPS headquarters the day following the call from Henry Cable and identified photographs of Yazkov in disguise as the old man at the state capitol and the woman outside her apartment.

With the saga completed, Governor Bates was the first to speak. "Both of you acted courageously. I read the task force reports that Lt. Falcone provided his superiors, but after hearing your personal accounts, I'm astounded by your bravery.

"Mr. Hardesty represented some very influential and wealthy clients in Washington. In addition to lobbying for them, I suspect a portion of the money he was paid found its way into the campaign coffers of congressional candidates. That isn't uncommon in this business."

"While I was recovering in the hospital, I tried to make sense of what happened," Jennifer said. "What I still don't understand is why Hardesty wanted to exchange information with me."

"We don't have an answer, but intend to find that out and much more." Bates turned to the attorney general. "Charlie, why don't you capsulize our proposal?"

"Frankly, the two of you have learned a great deal in your independent investigations and I commend you both," Braniff said. "Even though Hardesty and Yazkov were killed, there are a number of questions that need answers. Cutting to the bottom line, the governor would like for both of you continue your investigations.

"Lt. Falcone, you would remain in your position, but I will arrange for you to work in conjunction with the Department of Homeland Security, FBI and CIA. We need to determine if Yazkov was acting as an agent for someone in Russia or elsewhere, and if so, why they wanted Ms. Spencer's investigation stopped."

"Damn," Falcone muttered under his breath. The remark could be heard by all in the room. "Excuse me, sir, I apologize. It's just that, well, I don't know what to say."

"Don't say anything right now. We didn't expect an instant acceptance."

The attorney general turned his attention to Jennifer. "Your role would be different but equally important. The governor has proposed, and I concur, that you be granted temporary status as an assistant state attorney general, reporting directly to me. Your assignment would be to organize the information Ranger Falcone gathers. You would dialogue with the Federal Elections Commission and continue your investigation of this operation Jake Hardesty referred to as *Tejano*. If evidence surfaces that shows anyone made contributions to a federal campaign, including the presidential election, you would assist the U.S. Attorney's Office in prosecution of any criminal or civil cases. In addition, if cases can be made in other countries, you would coordinate with the FBI, CIA and prosecutors in the appropriate foreign jurisdictions to see that the criminals are brought to justice."

Jennifer could hardly believe what she was hearing.

"Both of you know too much for us to pursue this matter without benefit of your investigations," Bates added. "You are bright and energetic. I need you to continue on this case, Lieutenant. Jennifer, you wanted political involvement, well, here it is."

"Governor," Jennifer was finally able to say, "I probably speak for Lt. Falcone when I say that we're honored by this private luncheon and now these requests. But I must admit, I'm overwhelmed."

The governor nodded sympathetically. "Don't worry, you won't be flying solo. If your investigation concludes that Senator Creighton, Andrew Smith or anyone else is involved in illegal campaign financing, I don't intend to drop the hammer on them just because the two of you say so. Your recommendations would be thoroughly analyzed by many others before any action was taken."

"And one final thing," he added. "This will not be a witch hunt. I don't want the public to think I'm abusing the power of this office. Your work will be done under top secret classification until time comes to lift the cover."

As Jennifer tried to assimilate all she'd heard, the governor's young assistant entered the study. "Excuse me, Governor Bates. It's 12:25, time for your next appointment." He nodded toward the room behind him.

"Thank you." Bates turned back to Jennifer and Juan. "As much as it irritates me at times, this fellow does a damn good job keeping me on schedule. Greg, would you please see that Ms. Spencer and Lt. Falcone get the abbreviated private tour before they meet Dr. and Mrs. Spencer?"

When the governor stood, everyone followed suit. Bates escorted them to the door. "All I'm asking you to do right now is think about it. Talk it over. Juan, talk with your superiors. They know I intended to make this request, they've given the green light. Jennifer, see what your parents advise. I don't expect an answer until ten o'clock Monday morning so that gives you the weekend. Time's a wasting. You two have got to get back to work on the *Tejano* case. A lot more needs to be done."

Once they'd departed, Attorney General Braniff returned to the room to find the governor reviewing notes for his next appointment. "Do you think we've got 'em, Governor?"

Wayne Bates put down the notes and smirked. "Are you kidding? You don't think those two are going to say no to something like this do you?"

"I must admit, sir, your plan is masterful. No one will be able to accuse you of misusing your office for personal gains to destroy Russell Creighton. These outsiders will be more aggressive than anyone who would work the case."

"Yeah, I think they bought it, hook, line and sinker. Hell, Charlie, you know the old adage, use it or lose it. That applies to political power too. I don't think Falcone or Spencer suspected a thing unusual about my request. They may end up doing some good for the country, but in the meantime those two super sleuths will do a damn fine job for my re-election campaign without even knowing it."

Twenty minutes later Jennifer and Juan stood on the front steps of the Governor's Mansion with Savannah and Blake. "What a great day," Savannah exclaimed, putting her arm around her daughter's waist. "You won't believe what all we learned."

Jennifer reached over and squeezed Juan's hand. She was pleased when he responded likewise. "Oh, I don't know about that. Let's go over to the Driskell for afternoon coffee while Juan and I fill you in. I think you'll find our meeting tops anything you have to tell."

CHAPTER 43

▼

AUSTIN
MARCH 7

Following the debriefing at the Driskell with Jennifer's parents, Juan accepted Jennifer's offer to linger at Lake Lady Bird, located only a few blocks away. "Are you sure you're up to this?" Juan asked, as he opened the car door for her.

Jennifer shifted weight from her walking cast. "Absolutely. I might have a bum leg but I can certainly handle sitting for a spell, especially on a beautiful spring day like this."

Minutes later they rested on a park bench watching a hoard of walkers and joggers pass them on the nearby pathway. "God, I love this place," Jennifer said. "When I was in law school I used to come here all the time on study breaks to relieve the tension and take my mind off the books."

Juan gently placed his hand on her elbow to assist with her balance as she repositioned herself. "So, were you surprised by your parents' reaction to Governor Bates' proposal?"

"No, not really," Jennifer replied. "Mom and Dad tend to be very analytical. You heard the way they went about it, hitting the pros and cons of whether I should continue the investigation or forget it and stick with my law practice. When it's all said and done, I know they will say the ultimate decision is mine, and they will stand by me, whichever choice I make. I'm the one who has to live with it, not them."

"So, have you decided what you're going to do?"

"No, not completely." Jennifer glanced down at her cast. "I have mixed feelings. How 'bout you, are you ready to step it up a notch, work with the FBI, CIA and all that good stuff?"

"No decision on my part either. I'm like you, I can see a number of reasons to continue or tell the governor thanks but no thanks."

"If you asked my advice," Jennifer said, "I think you should take this gig."

"Oh, and why is that?"

"A lot of reasons. First, criminal investigation is what you do for a living and you're good at it. Surely you're as curious as I am to find out why Sergei Yazkov came all the way from Russia to hunt me down. I doubt he just woke up one morning and decided to come looking for me in Texas."

"You're probably right about all of that." Juan shook his head. "I don't know. I'm afraid I'd be way out of my league."

"Come on now, you mean to tell me you've never worked a case involving a contract killer or had any training in that area?"

"Now that you mention it, yes I have. That was covered extensively in Ranger school, and I've missed on three or four murder-for-hire cases over the past several years."

"Well, there you have it. Forget that as an excuse. You could handle it. Plus, you would have access to the brightest minds in the FBI and CIA. Any other reservations?"

"I never intended to get enmeshed in national, much less international politics. I'm comfortable in what I do. Were it not for the governor's request, I'm sure my department would consider the Yazkov file closed. Maybe I should do the same and move on to my next assignment."

Jennifer paused. "But don't you see, this was meant to be your next assignment. When the governor personally requests you continue to work on a file, your destiny is determined. You didn't seek this out, he sought you."

"I suppose you're right. I must admit, it would present a significant challenge. But let's talk about you for a change. Since you're so convinced as to what I should be doing, I presume you're ready to accept the governor's request."

"I never said that. It's different for me, Juan. You do this type of thing for a living. I'm trained to try lawsuits."

Juan didn't intend to take no for an answer. "And that's exactly what Governor Bates said he wanted you to do, try lawsuits, civil and criminal cases against anyone we find who's been making illegal campaign contributions. What you said to me applies equally to you. You try lawsuits for a living, and by the looks of your office and how busy you are, I suspect you're pretty damn good at it."

"You're right. But what Bates proposed would wreak havoc on my trial practice. I just can't prance off and leave my clients sitting high and dry."

"You're a partner in a law firm. Your partners and associates could take over your cases, right?"

"I suppose so."

"You could also tell the governor your professional situation and that you'd have to work out of your law office while overseeing reassignment of your cases."

She grew excited thinking about the possibilities. "The A.G.'s regional office in Houston is only five blocks from my office. I could probably work out of there if I needed to. And since we'd be working together as a team, you could help me by coming to Houston," Jennifer quickly added.

"Always negotiating a better deal, aren't you? Yes, ma'am, if that would help you, I'd be glad to. You already admitted you want to find out who Yazkov was working for. And if you think it would help my career, just think what it would do for yours—reporting to the governor and state attorney general. You would be a hot commodity when this is over. It sounds to me like it's a done deal. Why don't we call the governor and sign up right now?" He reached in his jacket, pulled out a cell phone and began punching in the numbers.

She reached over and placed her hand on his to protest. "No, wait. I'm not ready. There are some other issues that aren't so easy to deal with. Ever since that afternoon, I've had nightmares. I always see Yazkov coming for me." She lowered her head to hide the tears. "I wake up screaming and crying."

"But Yazkov is dead. He will never hurt you again."

"I know, but if someone could dispatch one monster, Juan, they could do it again. If I work on this case, I'm afraid the nightmares would never go away. I'm afraid I would always be looking over my shoulder for another hit man."

He looked her in the eye, trying to imagine the fear with which she was crippled. He stood and took her by the hand. "Let me tell you a story before I take you back to meet your parents." They slowly headed in the direction of his car.

"When I was a kid, my father taught me how to swim," he said. "He took me to a stock tank near our home and got in with me. I'll never forget how he held me at first. I felt so secure in his arms as I paddled my arms and kicked. But then he got out and I was all alone. I was afraid I was going to drown, and I began crying like a baby. I was so ashamed."

Jennifer had a hard time believing that this Texas Ranger was afraid of anything, much less that he would share her vulnerabilities. "And then what happened?" Jennifer could barely hear his reply. Juan's voice was so soft.

"Papa told me the only way I could ever overcome any fear was to tackle it head on. He assured me I wouldn't drown, that he was there for me, that I had to get out there on my own and try. He said that once I realized I could do it, I would never again be afraid to swim."

"What did you do?"

"I trusted him. I let loose of the bank and swam with all my might. And do you know what? I didn't drown. More than 20 years later I'm alive and well in Austin, Texas, having a conversation with a beautiful and intelligent woman." Juan reached over and placed his hand on Jennifer's shoulder and pushed back her hair.

"What I'm trying to say, Jennifer, is you have to trust that I will be there for you. This time you will have the protection of the Texas

Rangers and maybe even the FBI. What more could you ask for?" He smiled and withdrew his hand. "Now are you ready to call the governor?"

"Okay, I trust you, but don't call yet. There's something else that you'll probably think is silly."

"Silly? Are you kidding? Silly is not a word I would ever use to describe Jennifer Spencer. What is it?"

"I now know you and I have a lot in common, but we're also different. You started your search for Sergei Yazkov because it was your assignment. I got involved in Warren McDonald's campaign because I felt he was the best person for the job. Now I've seen it's not necessarily the best candidate who wins, it's the one who's receives the most money, either legally or illegally. Those who profit from access to the officeholder have as much or more influence on government policy than the officeholder. I suppose I've been an idealist and naive to boot."

"It's not exactly a character flaw to be an idealist." Juan smiled at her. "Frankly the world could use more idealism. As far as being naive, it's not your fault. You didn't have experience in the real world of hardball politics."

"I watched my mother campaign for state senate, but I wasn't personally involved in politics back then. I started my investigation because I felt someone was tampering with the political process. Apparently, that was the case."

"With all due respect, that's no reason to say no. So you've grown in the process of your investigation. You still haven't given me a good reason to quit. Where's all that idealism that got you here in the first place?"

She didn't have an answer for him but was still hesitant to say yes. "There's one last thing. I'd like to find out who's been screwing with the electoral process and see they are punished. But now I feel the governor might be using us to accomplish his own purposes, to win re-election. Where's the idealism in that, may I ask?"

"Your point is well taken. However, you've got to mix in some pragmatism with that idealism I admire in you. The bottom line is would you rather sit on the sidelines and let those involved in *Tejano* accomplish their objectives or finish what you started? It strikes me that Jennifer Spencer is not a quitter. If you ask for my vote, I say it's time for you to move to round two. Plus, I can't think of anyone I'd rather work with. What do you say?"

Jennifer took his hand and smiled. "I'd say you'd make a pretty good lawyer yourself, Lt. Juan Falcone." She leaned over and gave him a tender kiss on the cheek. "I also think you just might have yourself a new partner."